DRAKE FOREVER

BOOK SEVEN IN THE UNRESTRAINED SERIES

S. E. LUND

ACADIAN PUBLISHING LIMITED

S. E. Lund Newsletter

Sign up for S. E. Lund's newsletter and gain access to updates on upcoming releases, sales and freebies! She hates spam and so will never share your email!

S. E. LUND NEWSLETTER SIGN UP

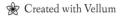 Created with Vellum

KATE

THE FIRST TIME I went to the Russian Tea Room with Drake, I didn't know what to expect.

It was our first date and he was completely new to me. I didn't quite know how his mind worked, but I was about to find out. Despite my fears about being alone with him, that night had been amazing, and now when I entered the Russian Tea Room, wearing a slinky black dress that Drake picked out, my hair done up, with my special black velvet submissive collar with the diamond tear drop pendant, I knew exactly what to expect.

I was still almost giddy with excitement despite the intervening years and despite knowing Drake so well that I could anticipate his words and deeds.

We entered the elevator that would take us up to the third floor, which Drake had reserved for the evening. When the doors closed, he pulled me against his body, grinding his hips into mine.

"Excited are you, Mrs. Morgan?"

"You know it, Dr. Morgan," I replied and leaned against him, sighing in delight when his arms went around me. He was wearing a very expensive suit with a crisp white shirt and royal blue silk tie that brought out the blue in his very blue eyes. He gazed down at me, his eyes half-lidded, his black eyelashes long enough to make a girl envious.

He was -- *gorgeous*. And he was all mine.

Although, in truth, I was all his. He had me wrapped around his fingers, but that was exactly the way I liked it.

"We have a few moments to wait before they arrive," he said, a gleam in his eye. "I wonder what we could do in that time..."

"I'm sure you'll think of something."

He bent down a bit more to kiss me, a smile quirking his lips, but before we could, the elevator doors opened behind us and reality set in once more. We left the elevator and entered the opulent space, the tables dressed in white linen and silverware, crystal glasses and candles everywhere. It was our anniversary and instead of having everyone over to our place, which was crowded, or to my parent's place, which was smaller than their previous apartment on Park Avenue, we decided to rent out the entire third floor of the Russian Tea Room and have our anniversary dinner catered.

Heath and his wife and children would be arriving, but Sophie stayed home with Karen Mills. Sophie was too young still to be staying up so late, and so we decided to leave her at home. Karen was a great sitter and Sophie always looked happy to see her each time she stayed with Sophie so Drake and I could go out on a date night.

Drake took my hand and led me to a set of plush sofas off to the side of the space. He sat and then pulled me down so that I straddled him, one thigh on each side of his lap.

"Dr. Morgan, what if the wait staff come up and find us?" I asked, leaning down to him, my forehead pressed against his.

"I imagine they'll get an eyeful," he replied, one hand sliding up my thigh and then around to my buttock. "Right now, I want a kiss. And my wish is to grope my beautiful wife a bit before everyone else arrives."

"Your wish is my command," I said with a smile. I kissed him, our mouths pressed together, warm and firm before opening to each other. The touch of his tongue on mine sent a thrill through my body. His hand moved up from my hip and around to my breast, which he squeezed while he kissed me more deeply, his tongue exploring me. My heart raced when he pulled down the strap of my dress and exposed the top of my breast. Then, he ran his tongue along the top, over the swell of my breast before pulling the fabric down even farther to bare one nipple, which tightened when exposed to the cool air.

When he took my nipple into his mouth and ran his tongue around the areola, I gasped with pleasure, a sweet sensation jolting through my body right to my clit.

"Oh, *God*," I murmured, trying to keep my voice down. "If you keep that up, I'll be wet all evening."

"That's my goal," he said and looked at me, his eyes

narrowed. "I want you wet and aching and thinking of how I'm going to tie you up and fuck you senseless when we get back home later tonight. I want you in sweet agony thinking about it, imagining it so that you'll come from the slightest touch of my tongue on your clit and then my cock inside of you."

I closed my eyes and imagined it. We had started to include a bit of bondage back into our sex life, and it made me feel like I did when we were first together. Breathless. Under his total and expert control, my body his to command. Anticipating what he would do and when he would do it.

I left our sex life up to Drake and luckily, our libidos and our desires matched perfectly so I was never worried if he was happy or satisfied. I knew he was.

I was as well.

Of course, it was at that moment that Drake's cell chimed, ending the moment. He reached into his jacket and pulled out his cell, reading a text.

"They're here," he said and showed me his phone. "We better straighten up. Not that I don't want Ethan and Elaine to know we're madly in love and lust with each other but still..."

I smiled and kissed him quickly, then he gave my nipple one last hard suck, before pulling up my strap. I slid off his lap and stood up, smoothing my dress and making sure my hair was still neat. Drake stood up beside me and adjusted himself, straightened his tie. He went to the table where a bottle of champagne was chilling in an ice bucket. When the elevator doors opened to admit my parents, he held up the bottle just as my father rolled into the room in his motorized wheelchair.

"Dad, Elaine, welcome," Drake said, smiling.

I went right over and gave my dad a kiss, then kissed Elaine.

"Come in," I said. "Drake has some champagne so we can celebrate."

I led Elaine inside while my father wheeled himself over to where Drake stood.

"Is it the good stuff?" my father asked, spying the bottle in Drake's hand.

"It is. You sent it over so I decided to open it tonight."

"It's a special occasion and I didn't want it to go to waste. Who knows how much time we have left? Better that I don't let it sit in the cellar and gather dust."

"Daddy," I said and frowned, going to his side and taking a glass that Drake handed me. "Don't think like that. We're lucky to all be together and have each other."

"We are, sweetheart," he replied and squeezed my hand with his good one. "I don't mean to be gloomy, but I have so much wine and champagne that I could never drink it all in the time I have left. I want us to enjoy it while we can."

"We will enjoy it and each other while we can." I leaned down and kissed him, then adjusted his tie which had come askew. "That's what tonight is about."

He nodded and smiled up at me. Then he glanced around. "Where's Heath and family? Are they late again?"

I laughed. "He has two children. I imagine it's a lot more effort to get everyone ready and in the car on time, unlike us."

"I wish Sophie was here, too," my father said, pouting.

"Maybe next year. She goes down at seven or seven thirty, and is a grouch if she doesn't get her twelve hours of sleep."

"I know," he said and patted my hand. "I'm just greedy. I want to see all my grand babies together."

"On Thanksgiving. We'll eat earlier and spend the afternoon together. How does that sound?"

"Sounds perfect."

That settled, Drake finished pouring champagne and then we went to the seating area and talked about our activities over the past week.

We had only been back in Manhattan for a short while and were still getting back into our respective routines so everything still felt new and uncertain.

There wasn't much to update them on my part. My life was taken up with Sophie and Drake. When I had time and when Sophie went down for her afternoon nap, I might work in the studio on my paintings.

As for Drake, he wasn't working. He and his former supervisor at NYP thought it was best that he didn't start working again until after the murder trial of Lisa Monroe was finished and the publicity around it had died down. That meant he'd have to wait until the following September to continue in his practice.

His fellowship was also up in the air because of the drama,

so Drake had nothing to look forward to except the trial and seeing Lisa finally put away for good. He hoped to finish his Fellowship and then start working as a pediatric neurosurgeon in a year if his supervisor agreed and the department approved. That was his goal.

It would likely take longer than we both hoped for it to come to fruition, but I knew it would -- eventually. Until then, Drake was at loose ends.

About ten minutes later, Drake's cell dinged again announcing that Heath and his family had arrived and were on their way up. The elevator doors opened to admit the four of them -- Heath looking like a younger version of my father, his pretty wife, Christie, and two much more grown up children. We welcomed them in, Drake poured them champagne and provided some sodas for the children. We spent the next fifteen minutes catching up on all their news.

At about quarter to eight, the wait staff began bringing up the meal, and so we all sat at the table with my father at the head, Elaine at the other end and the rest of us on either side. Music played in the background -- my favorites, including Debussy and some Tchaikovsky, given the Russian setting. Everyone was busy talking, laughing and enjoying themselves as we feasted on wonderful Russian food. Drake explained each dish while the wait staff served us, giving a bit of background on where the dish came from and what it contained. He'd been responsible for ordering the dishes and enjoyed the chance to introduce some traditional Russian food to my family.

I sat beside him and watched as he entertained the kids, telling them stories about Russian history -- leaving out the Communist revolution, of course. Drake seemed so happy to be in that role of a man surrounded by his close family, regaling them with stories while the wine flowed and the food was served.

He seemed so content, despite everything that was going on behind the scenes.

We had the looming murder trial, which would result in countless headlines and news stories about Drake's past relationship with Lisa and Derek Richardson, and of course, bringing everything up again from the more recent trial of Lisa for attempted murder in my case. Then, Lisa would be tried for her role in encouraging Jones to kill himself. The drama wouldn't end as soon as I would have wished, but it was our new reality.

I knew that while Drake was happy in the moment, with our family, and the fact we were all together again, he was concerned about how the trial and revelations about his past would affect his career. He couldn't even be involved in his foundation because of the adverse publicity his name might cause.

It was so unfair. One mistake on Drake's part – agreeing to be the third man in Derek's and Lisa's little voyeuristic fantasy – meant years of pain for Drake, for me and for everyone involved.

Once the dinner plates had been cleared and we were done with dessert, my father clicked his glass with his spoon and caught all our attention, our talk dying down.

He held up his wine glass. "Tonight, we're gathered to celebrate the anniversary of Drake and Kate's marriage. It's been only three years but life has been full in that time. So much has happened to us all. Much that makes us realize how fragile life is, and how much we mean to each other."

We all toasted each other and then Drake stood up and spoke.

"I want to thank everyone for coming tonight to help us celebrate our wedding anniversary. It means so much to the both of us to be able to spend time with our families. To me especially. You all know my history and the fact that when I was young, my mother left my father and me, and I didn't see her again for many years. I never had a big family, and I never got to enjoy holidays with them, never knew my cousins or grandparents. Now, I feel like I have the family I always wanted as a child. The family I always dreamed of. And it's all because of two people. First, it's due to Ethan, my surrogate father who helped me through some tough times after my father died. Thank you, Ethan, for being the father I wish I always had. And thank you for conspiring with me to get us together the first time at the concert on Veteran's Day, the same night Kate and I first came here to the Russian Tea Room. That was a key weekend, very close to five years ago, that changed my life in ways I could only have dreamed."

We all toasted my father, who smiled and laughed, raising his glass to Drake.

"My pleasure. I couldn't have been happier that you two found each other."

Then, Drake turned to face me, still standing, his glass still in his hand.

"And second, to my beautiful wife, Katherine. Kate, you own my heart and are my soulmate. You've given me everything I could ever want or need from a partner, wife, friend and the mother of my child. Thank you for giving me a chance back then. It changed my life for the better and I only hope I let you know every day that I love you more than anything."

He bent down and kissed me, his hand on my cheek.

Everyone clapped, and when our kiss ended, I turned to face them. Drake sat down in his chair beside me and I stood, wanting to say my own words of thanks to my family and express my love for Drake.

"Five years ago, I was confused and lonely, knowing I wanted to be happy, but not really understanding what I needed. Then I met Drake, and everything seemed clearer to me. My life was fulfilled with him, and when he asked me to marry him, there was no hesitation because I couldn't imagine life without him. I've never regretted that decision and despite the hardships we have both faced since then, our love has never wavered." I bent down and kissed Drake and everyone clapped. Then I stood back up and continued, because I had more to say. "Now, Drake and I have our beautiful Sophia, who we love even more every day, and we have Liam, who we hope to have live with us soon. We have all of you. Life is so good. Thank you -- all of you -- for everything."

I held up my glass and we all took a drink.

Then I sat down and we continued our celebration, surrounded by those we loved and filled with happiness for how lucky we all were.

About nine thirty, the kids started to yawn and I knew it was time for the evening to end. My father looked a bit tired, and was leaning to his weak side more than usual, which meant he, too, was at the end of his energy reserve.

We all got up from the table and hugged and kissed each other, promising not to wait too long before we spoke or got together again.

"Thanksgiving's coming up and I want all of you at our place," my father said, as he wheeled himself to the elevator. "Our place is smaller than the apartment, but the dining room can hold us all. I want you to come by early in the afternoon and spend time with us before dinner." He turned to me. "You bring that baby with you and Liam too if he's available."

"We will," Drake said and leaned down to kiss my father on the cheek. "I know how much you like to have her around."

We said goodbye and then Drake and I stood and looked at each other as the last of our family left on the elevator.

"Well, Mrs. Morgan," he said and took me into his arms. "It's just you and me. Shall we get our coats and go? It's a nice night and I'd love to walk a bit. I'll let John know so he can follow us."

"That sounds perfect," I said and sighed. "I wish we didn't need bodyguards. It spoils the effect that we're happy and carefree."

"We are happy," he said. "Just not totally carefree. Not for a while, anyway. Besides, John is discrete."

John, Drake's bodyguard, was discrete but I couldn't help notice him waiting on the street whenever Drake went out.

It made what would be a wonderful evening a little less wonderful, reminding me once again that there was danger out there that we had to be protected against.

I would be so happy once Lisa was in prison for good and the publicity around the trial was over and long forgotten.

We took the elevator down to get our coats from the coat check and walked outside along the sidewalk, arm in arm, the city noise all around us, the cars honking in the distance. I glanced back and sure enough, about a quarter block behind us was John, dressed in his black overcoat, looking like one of those Secret Service agents you'd see with the President. I turned back and tried to forget he was there, wanting to enjoy the walk as much as possible.

We passed pedestrians going to and from restaurants and clubs along the street. The weather was cool and the air crisp. It had rained earlier and the raindrops glistened on the streetlights, making them appear like so many diamonds.

We stopped on the street corner, waiting for the light.

"We're so lucky to be here," I said, pulling him closer, my arm around his. "I love Manhattan. I enjoyed San Francisco, but it isn't home."

"No, it isn't."

We kissed, and the kiss was warm and full of affection.

"Oh, I have something special for you," he said and reached into his pocket to pull out a small box. "Here, my love. To the happiest five years of my life. May we have sixty-five more years together. Or more."

I took the box from his hand and covered my mouth. "Drake," I said. "You didn't have to. I thought we agreed that we'd hold off on gifts until we go away to Nassau for our weekend."

I gave him a playful frown, although I was happy to receive a gift from him. I untied the bow and opened the box, to find inside a green gemstone ring, Marquise cut with two large white diamonds on either side. It was magnificent.

"Is it an emerald?"

"No," Drake said and slipped the ring on my finger. "A green diamond."

"Green?" I asked and admired the ring on my finger. It fit perfectly, of course.

"Yes," Drake said and took my hand, kissing my knuckles. "The rarest of rarities for the rarest of women. My perfect match."

I looked deep into his eyes and felt my chest tighten with emotion.

"I love you," I whispered and we embraced.

"I love you," he replied. "So much."

We kissed again and then we were bumped by the passing pedestrians as they made their way down 7th Avenue.

Drake smiled at me and we started walking again, hand in hand.

"The green tint isn't caused by inclusions, like other colored diamonds, but by radiation. I saw it and it made me think of your green eyes, so I had to buy it."

"You are a hopeless romantic," I said with a smile, swinging his arm as we walked.

"I am." He raised my hand to his lips once more to kiss my knuckles.

Of course, it was then that the sky opened up again and the rain began to fall, our brief reprieve over.

"Let's go back and get in the car," Drake said and pulled me back in the direction of the Russian Tea Room, where our car was parked. "I wanted to walk for a while, but Mother Nature apparently has different plans."

"She does," I said and laughed as we ran back to the car, me doing my best to run in my three-inch heels. I saw John wait while we passed, a smile on his face.

We finally arrived at the car and by then, my hair and face was covered in raindrops and Drake's hair was hanging in his eyes in this very sexy way. He opened the door for me and I slipped inside. He went around to the other side and got in, then John got in the driver's side and turned on the car.

"Thanks, John, for letting us indulge ourselves for a little walk," Drake said when the car pulled out of its spot.

"Don't mention it, Dr. Morgan. It's too bad it had to start raining again."

We drove through the busy street and Drake turned to me, leaning in closer so that his mouth was by my ear.

"It's just as well," Drake murmured and took my hand. "I have plans for you when we get home, *Katherine*," he said, squeezing my hand suggestively.

"You do?" I whispered, smiling. My body warmed immediately.

"Oh, yes," Drake said, his voice low and sexy. "I have very special plans for you tonight. I hope you're not too tired, but even if you are, I promise I'll wake you up."

"I know you will. Just the thought of finding out what you have planned will be sure to keep me awake."

As John drove the rest of the way to the apartment on 8th Avenue, I had no idea what Drake planned but whatever it was, my body ready for him.

DRAKE

KAREN MILLS WAS SITTING on the sofa when we arrived home. I took Kate's coat and hung it up while Kate went in to check on Sophie.

"Hey, Drake. You guys are home early."

"We thought we'd be later than this, but Ethan was tired and the kids were getting antsy. Then, we were going to go for a walk, but the rain started, so..."

"Too bad," she said. "But I'm glad you were able to go out and celebrate your anniversary. Let me know when you want to go out again. I'm pretty flexible so even last minute is fine."

"Thanks, Karen," I said, happy we had been able to find such a trustworthy sitter for Sophie. It really made the difference for Kate. "We appreciate your flexibility."

"No problem," she said and stood up, stretching. "I told you that you could stay out late if you wanted. I have tomorrow off, so I could sleep in."

"Maybe next time," I said and helped her with her coat. Kate popped in just before Karen left and thanked her as well.

"How did she do?" Kate asked. "She didn't sleep very long this afternoon."

"She went down no problem. She had a bath and we read some stories. I gave her a bottle and down she went."

"She was tired," Kate said, nodding. "Thanks again."

Then Karen left and Kate and I were alone. I removed my jacket, hanging it on the back of a chair in the entry, and loosened my tie.

"Care for a shot of Anisovaya, Katherine?" I asked, barely able to keep from smiling.

"Yes, Sir," Kate said, this gleam in her eyes.

I knew what that gleam meant. It meant she was more than excited to do a scene. We'd only recently begun including a bit of B&D into our sex life again after a long drought due to the accident and Kate's recovery. Both of us were eager to find our way back to some sense of a new normalcy.

I poured us both a shot and handed her one. She held it up to my shot glass and together, we threw back the vodka. I enjoyed the slight taste of anise and the burn as the alcohol went down my throat, warming my blood once it hit my stomach. I merely had to glance at Kate to know she felt the same excitement that the taste of the vodka elicited. We were Pavlov's dogs, the two of us.

Of course, it was at that precise moment that my cell rang, interrupting my plans for the rest of the night.

I reached into my pocket with reluctance. Who could be calling this late at night on a Friday?

I checked the call display and saw the name. Lara...

Why would she be calling me during my anniversary celebration? It could only mean one thing. Something had come up in discovery at Lisa's trial that she felt she had to tell me about.

"I have to get this," I said to Kate, whose expression changed the moment she saw the call display and Lara's name.

"The trial?"

I nodded. "I expect so."

I slid my finger across the screen and put the call on speakerphone so Kate could hear.

"Hey, Lara. What's up that's got you calling me at almost ten o'clock on a Friday night -- the night of my wedding anniversary?"

"I'm so sorry, Drake, but I had to call and at least let you know that one of my contacts in the DA's office told me, in total confidence, there is a video of someone the defense claims is you abusing Lisa at Richardson's mansion. I haven't seen it, but he has and he says it's pretty damning. I guess Lisa's defense thinks it may lead to a reduced sentence because it seems to support the defense's allegation that you and Richardson systematically abused Lisa over the course of several years and that Jones was acting in self-defense when he killed Richardson."

"What?" I said, rubbing my forehead. "I never laid a hand on her in any abusive way. I never did more than give her a thorough fucking. They claimed they were into voyeurism and a bit of bondage. Not S&M or I would never have become involved and you know it."

"Of course, I know it. She's claiming that Jones killed Richardson when he found Derek attacking her. So, he killed Richardson to stop him from hurting her."

"That's not at all plausible, if they knew Richardson. He was a voyeur, not a sadist."

"These kinds of nuances are lost on most people in the public. They don't know the difference between sadism and dominance or how one can be a Dominant without being a sadist."

"When is the video going to be shown? Do we get the chance to see it and deny that it's me?"

"You're not involved in this, Drake, except as the defense's theory of the case in contrast to the DA's. You and the tape are just evidence to create reasonable doubt in the minds of the jury. If they believe that you and Derek abused Lisa on a regular basis--"

"I was only with her on three occasions!"

"I know that and you know that, but the defense will claim it was many other occasions and as long as there are several real occasions that you were her sexual partner with Derek, that will be enough to support the theory that she was an abused woman whose new boyfriend tried to protect her from Derek when he became violent. The jury will be more inclined to give her the benefit of the doubt."

"But it's not true. Derek was not a sadist. He didn't abuse

her. He watched her have sex with other men and then he had sex with her afterward."

"She claims he punished her afterward and that the sex with other men wasn't about voyeurism at all. It was about hurting her for being a whore -- which he forced her into being with other men."

"She signed contracts."

"You know those contracts are not enforceable. She claims she was threatened into signing."

I sat on the sofa and Kate sat beside me, realizing that the phone call was going to take longer than we imagined. Not to mention that the news killed any arousal either of us felt earlier.

I was silent for a moment, wondering for the first time if I had misjudged Richardson, but I never heard a whisper about him being a sadist. Some men enjoyed watching their lovers have sex with other men. It made them aroused to see their partner enjoying it, acting like a nymphomaniac. Then, they would have sex with the woman and enjoy the fact that their partner was so sexual.

I didn't feel that way. I was possessive and wanted Kate all to myself, although I knew that other men would be lucky to have someone as sexually responsive as her. I'd been a willing partner to the whole voyeurism scene because Derek and I were friends. Both of us were professional men, born into wealth, and having an interest in BDSM, albeit for different kinks.

"Will they show the video in open court?"

"I don't know. There's no reason, other than not wanting it

to get on the news, so the judge may rule it can be shown in open court. If that's the case, it will be shown on every network around the world. I'll have to wait and see if there's any way we can refute that it's you, but that may not be until it's already public. By then, the damage will already have been done."

"Great," I said, a sick sensation in my gut. I turned to Kate and brushed her cheek, needing to reconnect with her at that moment. Her face had fallen, her eyes sad. She shook her head as she listened to Lara.

"Can't you argue that if the video can't be proven to be Drake that it shouldn't be allowed as evidence?" Kate asked, frowning. "It's defamatory to put a video out and claim it's Drake if it isn't. It can't help but hurt his professional and personal reputation. He's already paid such a high price for all of this."

"I know, Kate," Lara replied, sighing heavily on the other line. "You're right, of course, but that doesn't mean that the defense won't release the tape by accident anyway so they can discredit the state's argument that Lisa acted with premeditation and killed Derek so she could take his money and escape with Jones. They apparently had plane tickets and were getting ready to go to Mali. Lisa claims that they were trying to escape Derek and went to the cabin to retrieve some personal effects and that's when Derek attacked her and Jones killed him to protect Lisa."

"That's such bullshit," I said, unable to stop myself.

"It is, to anyone who knew Derek or Lisa in the lifestyle. Lisa was far from a shrinking violet. She was a switch who occasionally liked to top submissive men. She was in it for

Derek's money. She became obsessed with Drake and began stalking him. That's the sole reason that she entered medical school -- to live out her fantasy life of you and her becoming lovers and marrying. Classic erotomania combined with sociopathy. A very scary combination. Anyway," Lara said and we heard papers rustling in the background. "I wanted to let you know because I'm afraid that the defense will leak the tape any time now. If it was me acting as Lisa's defense, I would. Anything to muddy the water and raise reasonable doubt."

"What can Drake do?" Kate asked, rubbing my shoulder. "What can you do to stop it? Don't the police have rules about evidence that you could use to stop its release?"

"I'm afraid I'm somewhat constrained in this, because Drake isn't a defendant and we have no standing in the case. Drake's going to be a witness, and testify for the state, and will have the opportunity to deny Lisa's claims. There isn't enough evidence to charge Drake with anything and so the police and DA aren't going down that road, but Lisa's defense can do a lot of damage to his reputation regardless."

"It's so unfair," Kate said, her voice wavering. "Lisa may be going to jail for the rest of her life, but she's ruining Drake's life in the process."

I sighed and rubbed my eyes, frustration with the whole issue overwhelming me. "Well, thanks for calling, Lara, and keeping me informed about what's happening. Not that I can do anything about it but wait for the fallout."

"I'm sorry to be the bearer of bad news, but it's better to know what's coming instead of being blindsided. You should come to my office tomorrow afternoon and we can talk more about our response."

"Okay. Good night."

"Good night and happy anniversary, I guess."

"Yeah, thanks," I said and ended the call. I turned to Kate who was frowning. "Happy anniversary," I said, sourly.

"She could have waited to call until tomorrow..."

"She did what she thought was best in case we wake up to the news that a video purporting to be me is plastered on the television and all over the internet."

"We could have at least had a nice night without this," Kate insisted.

"Ignorance is bliss?" I replied and pulled her onto my lap, her legs sideways across my body. "I don't think so. For me it's more like, 'Better a cruel truth than a comfortable illusion.'"

She laid her head on my shoulder and played with my tie, which was loose. "So much for our scene. I don't know about you, but I'm in the mood for more vodka."

"Lots more vodka," I replied.

And so, for the next hour, we toasted each other with vodka and discussed the case. Not what I had imagined for my third wedding anniversary... I had hoped that we'd make love and that I would take control of Kate's mind body and my mind.

Before we went to bed, I pulled her onto my lap, and had her straddle me, her arms slipping around his neck. We were both a bit tipsy, having done several shots each, but despite the alcohol, I was still ready at the touch and the proximity of her soft feminine body.

"I want you," I said, my voice throaty.

"I'm yours. Forever."

I took control and immediately, my body responding to the sound of submission in her voice, my cock swelling. I pushed me down onto the sofa and lay on top of her, her body soft beneath mine. I slid my fingers over her cheek, then touched the scar on her bottom lip.

"You're mine, *Katherine*," I said. Our eyes met and her expression was so filled with desire, it made me feel even more aroused. A moment passed between us and that bond we had when in scene took over. I became her Dom and she my sub.

I bent down to kiss her. The kiss was intense and despite being a bit drunk, we both responded like Pavlov's Dog to each other. I ran my hand over the curve of one breast, then down her side until I cupped one buttock, pulling her body against mine. I traced the upper curve of her breasts with my tongue, and she responded with a gasp. I squeezed one breast through the fabric of her dress, my finger and thumb finding her nipple and tweaking it.

She moaned, pressing her breast into my hand, her back arching.

I spread her thighs open with a knee, pulling up her dress around her hips, my hand pressing against her mound, a finger searching beneath her panties for her clit. She groaned when I found it and closed her eyes, enjoying the sensation. Finally, when I'd worked her up enough that she was wet and thrusting against my hand, I pulled it away and instead, ground my erection against her.

"Look at me," I commanded. "Into my eyes."

She opened her eyes and stared into mine, her eyes half-lidded and filled with desire. She was more than ready.

Then, I sat up between her thighs and reached for her panties, grasping the waistband and removing them so that she was bare from the waist down.

I pressed her thighs wide open, exposing her to me and the sight of her body, wet and aroused, made me even harder.

"Nice and *wet*."

I stood and pulled her up as well then turned her around, pulling the shoulders of her dress down from behind. After I pushed her hair out of the way, I began kissing her shoulder, biting it as the dress fell off her body into a puddle on the floor. I slid my hands over her shoulders and around to her breasts, cupping each one briefly, squeezing them through the lacy black fabric of her bra. She leaned back, I pressed my erection hard against her buttocks.

"Spread your thighs."

She did and when my hand moved back to her slit, she couldn't help but press against it.

Finally, I turned her around and unclasped the hook of her bra, freeing her breasts, which spilled out, her nipples instantly hardening in the cool air. I looked at her, my eyes moving over her body.

"You look delicious, I'm going to eat you and lick every inch of you." I knew those words would be enough to make her body clench. "Now, it's your turn to undress me."

She stepped closer, obediently reaching for my shirt, her eyes demure while she removed it and then unbuckled my belt. My erection was pressed against my slacks, straining against the fabric. She unzipped and slid my slacks down until they fell to the floor. Beneath my slacks, I wore a pair of black boxer briefs, which she removed as well, smiling to herself as my erection sprung out, almost striking her face.

"I'm so ready for you," I murmured.

She grasped me, stroking my shaft, then cupping the head. I was so hard it almost hurt and couldn't wait for her to take me into her mouth.

"Lick me," I commanded.

She knelt and grasped me one more, pulling the head to her lips. Very slowly and very deliberately, she licked the head, tasting my salty fluid. I couldn't stop from groaning.

"Suck me."

She ran her tongue around the head, stroking the underside and then took my cock into her mouth, sucking the head in further, moving her wet lips over me deliberately slowly. I reached down and guided her head, grabbing her hair in a fist, increasing the speed, pushing inside her mouth deeper until she gagged. Then I pulled back just a bit, my pace slowing.

She glanced up and met my eyes with my cock in her mouth.

"So *good*..."

I pulled her off my cock and lifted her up, kissing her roughly, one hand on her breast. Then, I took her hand and led her to the bed, where I sat on the edge and pulled her closer, my face nuzzled into her breasts. I tongued each nipple briefly, blowing on them to make them erect, then squeezed them, my mouth moving from one to the other, sucking hard. She groaned, her eyes closing.

"Watch me."

She opened her eyes and watched as I sucked each nipple. Then I pushed her up onto the bed, moving her back and into position.

When I knelt between her thighs, I gripped my erection and rubbed the head against her slit.

"Nice and wet," I said approvingly. "Almost ready."

I entered her, penetrating only an inch then slid the head out and up, over her clit, again and again until she was so close, I knew when I entered her completely, she'd come immediately.

"I'm close..." she said, panting. "I'm going to come."

"Not yet," I said. "I've been waiting all night for this and I'm going to enjoy every inch of you."

"I want every inch of *you*," she said, despite it being impertinent, but I knew how much she needed it – needed me.

"Oh, you'll get every inch, *Katherine*," I said firmly, reminding her to stay in scene. "But not until I decide so don't try to tempt me to give my inches to you any sooner."

She bit her bottom lip and tried to look contrite, but she was smiling at the same time.

"Naughty girl," I whispered and pulled my cock away, stroking it absently while I examined her pussy. "Maybe I should just please myself while looking at you, deny you my inches."

"Please, no, Sir," she said, doing her best to sound submissive. "This one promises to be good the rest of the night."

She fluttered her eyelashes and I had to bite back a grin.

"I have just the thing," I said and went to the closet and returned with a blindfold and some leather straps. I decided to do a bondage scene so Kate would stay focused. After I tied the blindfold around her head, I wrapped her wrists and secured the straps to the headboard and her ankles to the footboard. She tugged at the restraints, needing to feel completely under my control.

"You're mine completely," I murmured as I leaned back over her. "Behave."

Then I began kissing her again, my tongue sliding over her jaw and down over her collarbone to her breasts once more. My cock ached to feel her warm wetness and bring me relief from my lust, but I was going to take my sweet time and she could do nothing about it. When I began moving lower, my mouth trailing around her navel, she gasped, knowing what would happen next.

"Sir, I'm afraid I'll come as soon as you lick me."

I stopped and smiled to myself.

"That aroused, are you, Ms. Bennet? You are a responsive little thing."

She said nothing in reply and I waited, wondering whether to let her come right away.

"That's okay, Katherine. You can come right away if you must. I plan on making you come at least twice anyway."

When I put my mouth on her, and my tongue pressed against her clit, she moaned.

"Oh, God," she cried out, and I could tell she was coming. I pressed my thumb against her clit, and slid my tongue inside of her, wanting to feel as she clenched in her orgasm. When I glanced up, her back had arched and her nipples were hard.

She spasmed again and again, her hips thrusting against my tongue, needing every bit of sensation. "Oh, *God...*"

Before she was finished, I rose and got into position, shoving my cock into her, wanting to catch her spasms before they finished. The pressure of my cock filling her up sent her over again and she came and came...

I relished the sensation of her body clenching around my length, and thrust until my own orgasm, ejaculating as I leaned over her, my cock so hard, my motions slowing as I shuddered, emptying myself inside of her.

When I collapsed on top of her, my mouth by my ear, she smiled.

"I thought you were going to make me come twice," she said with a mock-pout.

"Ha!" I said and kissed her cheek. "You came twice. I know your body like the back of my hand."

"You do," she said with a sigh. "It was one right after the other."

I removed her blindfold and then untied her bindings, kissing her wrists and ankles before going to the bathroom and getting a wet cloth so I could clean her up.

We lay together after and she snuggled against me. I threw my thigh over her possessively and stroked her arm while we lay together.

"Happy Anniversary, my love," I said.

She leaned up and smiled. "Happy Anniversary, my love."

Wrapped up in her embrace, warm from my orgasm, I was so happy despite the threat of the looming trial and video.

I didn't even remember falling asleep.

KATE

I woke up the next morning with a blistering headache.

Sophie's soft babbling over the baby monitor and the image on the tiny screen showed me she'd woken and was happily playing with her toys. I lay back and rubbed my forehead. That would teach me not to drink too much vodka and expect to feel up to being a good mother the next morning. All I wanted to do was turn over and go back to sleep, but that wasn't going to happen. I knew Sophie's rhythms. She woke early, played for a while with her pacifier in her mouth, and then started to squawk once she was bored with her toys. She'd stand up and bounce with her hands on the crib rail and I'd panic that she'd one day manage to bounce right out of the crib.

I had maybe five minutes at best.

I turned over to find myself staring into Drake's blue-blue eyes...

"Good morning, Mrs. Morgan. Regret that last shot of vodka, do you? I know I do."

"That I do." I reached out and brushed hair out of his eyes. "I'm glad we were able to do a scene, despite everything. I wish I didn't have to even think about the video and what's going to happen next. I just know we'll be followed around and people will point and talk. It makes me sick."

Drake rolled over closer to me, pulling me into his arms. "I'm sorry about all this. You didn't sign up for sexual scandal when you met me and agreed to marry me."

I looked deeply into his eyes while he brushed hair off my cheek.

"I signed up to be with you -- *you* Drake. All of you. Every inch. Everything about you, good and bad. So, we're dealing with some of the bad right now. One day, it will all end and we'll go back to some new normal. No one will even care about the trial or remember it. We'll be just two more people on the street with our children."

"I hope so. I hope we're not a couple of old fogies by then."

"Old fogies... You could never be an old fogie. I'll bet your dad was still a rake even when he was in his fifties."

Drake sighed and lay on his back, pulling me beside him. "He didn't get much beyond that, sadly. God, I wish he was still alive. There's so much I'd want to say to him. When I was younger, I resented the hell out of him because he was always so damn busy with his work and with the company. Now, I understand a lot more about him. He was a lonely man who filled his life with work to compensate. He didn't know how to do anything else. He didn't know how to show love. To be with other people in a way that made them feel secure. I hope I never get like that, Kate." He turned to look in my eyes. "Please tell me if I do."

"You could *never* be that way."

He smiled at me but shook his head. "I was exactly like that before I met you. You must remember he was my role model. It's so easy to fall into old patterns and become self-absorbed. It was meeting you and realizing what I'd been missing and why I was missing it that changed me – for the better. I realized the difference between Ethan and my dad and what kind of man I really wanted to be. I wanted to be more like Ethan. Devoted to his family. Involved. Strong for them, but accepting of who they really were."

I lay on my stomach beside him and laid my head on my arms.

"I never really saw him that way until I met you. It's strange but I felt like my father was a controlling old bastard for most of my life. Like, I could never live up to his expectations, and he never approved of me. You showed me that all along, he was just accepting everything I did and said but was helping me figure out what I wanted. I just didn't realize it."

"He questioned you when you challenged his authority, but he allowed you to be rebellious and so rebellion became normal. What it did was make you know yourself by making you justify your decisions. Being a judge probably allowed him to see different points of view and respect them and know how to get to the truth of things."

"I know that now, but back then? It felt like he was always judging me." Then I laughed. "Of course, he was a judge, but all he was doing was making me judge myself and my ideas."

"Exactly. I think it's called the Socratic Method."

I leaned up and kissed him softly on the lips and he smiled.

On the baby monitor, Sophie let out a call, her pacifier still clenched between her teeth. I glanced over at the tiny screen and saw that she was standing up, holding onto the crib railing.

Next, she'd start bouncing.

"We're lucky she wakes up happy," I said and rolled off the bed, pulling on my robe and slippers against the chill of the floor.

"We are."

I turned back and took in Drake as he lay on the bed, his arms folded behind his head, his chest bare, the sheet covering his ample package. He looked so desirable that I would have liked it if we could have a shower together and then a nice leisurely fuck before breakfast. Those days were gone unless we woke up extra early before Sophie did. Given how much work she was and how we enjoyed our evenings together once she fell asleep, that wasn't often an option. Both of us needed our sleep.

"I'll go get her. Do you want to have a shower?" I asked, for it was my day to get up with Sophie and get her ready. Drake and I alternated days.

"I do. I'll be out in about fifteen."

I smiled and left the bedroom, taking the hallway to Sophie's room. When I opened the door, there she was, standing at the side of her crib, her hands on the rails. She smiled widely when she saw me and her pacifier fell out of her mouth to reveal her front teeth.

"Good morning, baby," I said and went over to her. She babbled in response and picked up her pacifier, which was attached to her onesie with a safety pin and popped it back into her mouth. Then, she held her arms out wide, asking for me to pick her up.

Which I did, giving her a big hug and kiss.

I carried her to her change table and changed her diaper, then dressed her in a playsuit for the day. It was bright blue and designed like a worker's overalls. The fabric was soft and stretchy, and she could run around or crawl on the floor without worry. The color of the overalls brought out her blue eyes -- her inheritance from her father. She also got his thick dark eyelashes. I knew one day that the boys would all get weak-kneed when they looked into them the way I did when I looked into Drake's eyes. I hoped I could be a good mother to her and make sure that one day, she would be a strong and happy woman.

When I was finished, I took her downstairs to the kitchen and placed her in her high chair that stood next to the kitchen island. Drake was already finished with his shower and was standing in a pair of faded jeans, white sweater and slippers. He came right over and gave Sophie a big kiss.

"How's my girl?" he asked, brushing her soft brown curls off her forehead. "Did you have a good sleep?"

She smiled up at him and played with the Cheerios I placed on the highchair tray. Finally, she popped her pacifier out of her mouth and began munching on the cereal, picking up each piece with her fingers. I loved watching her feed herself. It was so enlightening to watch a little human master new skills. She'd crawled and walked early despite being a preemie. She was saying two words together now and naming everything. I'd been around Heath's kids only rarely since he and Christie were always traveling to and from various locations in Central and South America doing their charity work, so I'd missed a lot of their development.

Now, I got to watch it all first hand.

I thought that I'd be bored with being a mother, but it was never boring. It was sometimes tiring, but Sophie kept me on my toes, watching her walk around, exploring. Plus, her verbal development was fascinating.

Pointing was her big thing. She seemed to love her pointer and was always poking everything with it, looking up at Drake or me to see if we were as fascinated with whatever it was she was pointing at as she was and naming it.

"What's on the agenda for today?" Drake asked as he poured fresh water into the coffee maker. "I'm going to meet with Lara, but I'll be home all morning. Do you want to go to Central Park and walk for a while? It might clear our heads to get some fresh air and exercise."

"Exercise is the last thing I feel like, but you're right," I replied, mixing up Sophie's dish with some oatmeal, sprinkling some brown sugar on top. I placed it in front of her and she immediately reached for her spoon. She loved trying to feed herself and generally got more of it on her face and bib than in her mouth, but she was learning.

"Go have a shower," Drake said and pushed me out of the way with his hip. "I'll take over here. When you're finished, the bacon and eggs will be cooked and the coffee will be ready."

I kissed him quickly, giving him a smile, and did just that.

OUR WALK through Central Park was pleasant, except for the knowledge I had that my bodyguard Mike was walking about twenty paces behind us, watching the environment for any sign of threat. It changed my day from happy go lucky to suddenly potentially dangerous.

While Lisa was in jail, Drake didn't feel like we knew everything about her and her machinations. She'd orchestrated an attempted murder, an actual murder and had coached her submissive Jones into committing suicide. She had family ties to the NYPD and while I trusted the police to be on our side, given all the evidence, there was no telling what her family might do.

Drake worried that an angry brother or former boyfriend might be convinced that Drake was evil incarnate and try to take him -- or me -- out.

It was unlikely, but after seeing me come in on a stretcher, almost bleeding out in the trauma room, changed Drake's sense of invincibility. We would have bodyguards for the rest of our time in Manhattan.

The rain had stopped and clouds were thinning, bringing us a bit of much-needed sunshine. The air was cool enough that we could see our breaths, but it was invigorating and just what Drake and I needed to recover from our night of alcohol excess. I pushed the baby stroller while Drake walked beside me and together, we enjoyed the trees and views from the park. Drake had put on the baby carrier, which he would put Sophie in once we got into the park. He liked to carry her in it, because he said I got to carry her for almost nine months and now he wanted to do the same while he still could.

We passed by the bridge that we used for our wedding pictures and took Sophie over it so she could look down at the water below. Drake took her out of her stroller and held her up, standing her on the railing. She laughed and bounced and I worried that he'd accidentally lose his grip on her and drop her into the water, but it was just my anxiety. Drake had a firm grip on her and would never let go so I took in a deep breath and tried to relax.

"This is where Mommy and I got married," Drake said to Sophie, kissing her plump cheek. "It was the happiest day of my life up until then. The next happiest," he said and looked over at me, "was the day I found out that you were conceived and then the day I realized that both of you were going to live after all."

Drake's eyes softened and he leaned over and kissed me. I know he was thinking of the horrible day that I was attacked and almost died. He could have lost us both but luckily, the doctors were skilled and we survived.

"I love you, Mrs. Morgan," he said, his voice filled with emotion. "Thank you for the best years of my life."

"I love you, Dr. Morgan," I replied, my throat choking up, my eyes filling with tears. "Thank you for the best years of my life."

We smiled together and then Sophie bounced again and Drake lifted her up and into the baby carrier so they could walk together for a while.

The leaves were all reds and oranges and yellows in Central

Park and we let Sophie down so she could run around in them, laughing as she did. It was my favorite time of the year and for an hour at least, all the cares of the trial and what Drake would face once the video came out and the talk began on television and on the internet were forgotten.

WE ARRIVED BACK HOME and spent the rest of the morning lazing on the sofa, watching a show on a home channel, looking at houses along the coast. Drake and I loved our apartment, but we also loved being close to the ocean when we were in San Francisco and had talked about getting a house on the beach. Maybe on Fire Island. It could be our summer place and we'd divide our time between the apartment on 8th Avenue and the beach house. Drake suggested we build a brand new house exactly to our specifications and so we enjoyed watching home renovation and design shows on cable. I figured it would give Drake something other than the trial to focus on and I encouraged it. I'd love to be able to walk to the beach each morning with Sophie the way I had back in San Francisco.

Drake got a call from Lara a little after noon, and they talked in the office while I fixed Sophie's lunch. I wanted to go into the office and listen, but I was busy with Sophie so I waited for Drake to come out and relay to me what they discussed.

When he finally emerged from the office, his face told me everything.

"The video is live on the internet on some gossip website. They claim it's me, but I watched it and it's not. Not even close. The guy in the video has a pot belly, for God's sake..."

"What?" I said, frowning. "You've never had a pot belly. Not even close."

"I know," Drake said and came up behind me, sliding his arms around me for a hug. "It crushed me to think they'd even suggest it could be me."

I knew he was trying to make light of the situation, but his voice betrayed his true feelings. He was angry and upset.

"When are you going to meet with Lara?"

"Right away," he replied. "We're going to meet at her office. She's asked me to bring her lunch, so I'll eat with her and we can talk about the case while we do. She's meeting with a client at 2:00 so we have to be finished by then. I hope you don't mind..."

I turned around and slipped my arms around his neck. "Of course I don't mind. I know you have to meet with her to figure out how to deal with this. She's busy and you have to work a meeting in around her schedule. I can eat with Sophie. Then, I think the two of us will walk down to the corner store and get some fresh fruit for a fruit salad."

"Make sure you let Mike know," Drake said, reminding me about my bodyguard.

"How could I forget Mike?" I said, only slightly sourly. "My constant companion."

"It's for your protection," Drake chided. "You said yourself that you barely notice him now."

"I know," I said. "I'm being a spoiled brat about it. I just wish we didn't have to worry about it."

"One day soon, maybe we won't," Drake said and squeezed

me. He kissed me on the lips and then let go, moving to where Sophie sat in her highchair and giving her another kiss.

He went to the closet to get his jacket and his boots, and then wrapped a scarf around his neck.

"See you soon," he said and waved at Sophie. "Try to enjoy your walk to the store. Pretend that Mike is just a big bear of a man and happens to live in the same neighborhood as you, is out for a walk and would help you if you needed it."

I smiled at Drake, for that described Mike perfectly -- a big bear of a man. A handsome bear, but still big and burly, his biceps bulging from under his jacket.

AFTER SOPHIE and I finished our lunch, we took the stroller and went out to the street. Before I left, I texted Mike and he said he'd be waiting outside for me when I was ready to go for the walk.

Sure enough, he stood with his hands in his pockets, a pair of dark sunglasses covering his eyes, his blond brush cut and square jaw giving his identity as a former Navy SEAL away. I could almost see the bulge of his concealed weapon at his hip -- or at least, I imagined I could see it.

Strangely, it didn't comfort me the way I thought it would. I was almost killed by a car, not a weapon. I'd read recently about a woman who was stabbed in the gut while she was out walking her dog in the morning. She'd bled out before the ambulance even arrived because the knife blade severed an artery. The culprit walked towards her and at the last minute, slipped the knife out of his pocket, stabbing her and then walking on. When it happened, she was alone on the block in the section of Harlem, close to where I lived before. People had passed by, thinking she was a drunk, but her little dog stayed at her side the entire time. It made my heart squeeze to think of her dying all alone while people walked by. I didn't want that to be my end, but there was no way of knowing. The assailant was unknown to the woman. She was a target of opportunity and nothing more.

A convenient human to kill.

I tried to push the story out of my mind and took a deep cleansing breath, walking along the sidewalk to the grocers down the street. Mike walked behind me about twenty feet and I only noticed him when I stopped at one of the fruit stands outside the store. I glanced sideways and there he was, hands in his pockets, glancing away from me quickly.

I did my shopping and after I was finished, Sophie and I went back to the apartment, Mike in tow. I stopped at the entry and fumbled with my keys. Mike came up a few feet from where I stood.

"Having problems?" he asked softly.

"Just trying to do too much," I said and gave him a smile.

"Will you be going out again this afternoon?"

"No, I'll wait until Drake gets home if we go out again."

Mike nodded and stood with his hands folded in front of him.

"You're not going to stand guard outside the apartment, are you?" I asked.

"No, ma'am. I'm going to sit in the van you can see on the

street. I'll keep watch until my shift's up at seven. If you change your mind about going out, let me know."

"I will," I said and finally managed to get the lock opened. Mike held the door for me and I went inside, checking the mail on my way. There was nothing but a couple of flyers but there was one letter that looked curious. I checked the postmark and it read from Wards Island, New York.

That was where Lisa was staying. She was transferred to the Kirby Forensic Psychiatric Center on Wards Island. She'd attempted suicide and so had been removed to the Center and put on suicide watch.

She'd sent a letter addressed to both of us.

I swallowed hard and went up the stairs, Sophie in my arms, the stroller in the other hand.

Dammit.

The last thing we needed was a letter from her.

DRAKE

I ASKED John to stop at a deli on my way to meet with Lara so I could pick up a couple of corned beef sandwiches and drinks for our lunch. I offered to get him something but he already had a bagged lunch and held it up for me to see.

"No, Sir. I'm doing paleo so I have specific needs. No sandwiches for me. But thanks."

John parked close to the deli and on my way, I passed the spot where I almost lost Kate and had to stop. I remembered back to that day with a sense of dread, despite the fact that she survived and our baby, little Sophia, was delivered and was fine. Sophia thrived, in fact, and had done well, leaving the NICU even earlier than usual.

Still, that day was the result of mistakes on my part. I'd become involved with an unstable woman -- without my knowledge of course -- but she was still unstable. I failed to contact anyone early enough in the whole business to deal with it properly, and Lisa had gone off the deep end and tried to murder Kate to get her out of the way.

I was responsible. No doubt about it. I should have been more thorough in my vetting of Derek's submissive. I usually was, but I trusted that Derek had done his own due diligence. I trusted that Lisa was mature enough and mentally stable enough to know what she wanted when she signed that contract and NDA the nights we were together.

That was in the past, and there was nothing to be done about it except to try to be the very best husband and father that I could be. That was my goal every day of my life with Kate and Sophie -- and hopefully soon, Liam.

I wanted to be the very best father and husband. The best family man -- like Ethan.

I purchased the sandwiches and then John drove me the rest of the way to Lara's office, letting me off half a block from the entrance. My mind was so focused on the case that I almost ran into someone and had to apologize when the older man called out, "Hey! Watch where you're going, buster!"

I walked towards Lara's building and exhaled as I approached the entry. I had to get control over my emotions and not dwell on the case and trial. I was a bit player in it and would have my small role to play, providing testimony for the prosecution as they built their case that Lisa had planned and carried out the murder of Derek Richardson with the help of Jones, her submissive partner.

Then, she coerced him into killing himself -- probably threatening him and making him think that he'd end up in a prison for life, at the mercy of a bunch of prison sadists who wouldn't care about his wishes. From what I had read in the papers, and what Lara and I had discussed, Jones had been suffering with clinical depression for years and when the whole events with Derek transpired. When Jones was arrested, he spiraled back down. Lisa had worked her evil ways with him, and convinced him that he was going to be in hell if he was convicted.

She'd told him he might as well kill himself, according to Lara's contact in the prosecutor's offices.

Lisa was a horrible woman.

I sighed and entered the building, taking the elevator to Lara's floor, bag of food in hand. I greeted Chrystal, the woman who sat at the front desk, and she got up and led me down the hallway to Lara's office. Of course, I knew my way around the office, having visited countless times before, but I gave Chrystal a smile and let her lead me.

"I hope everything goes well for you at the trial, Dr. Morgan," she said as she took hold of Lara's doorknob for me while I balanced the tray of drinks and bag of food. "I think it's horrible what that woman tried to do to your wife and what she did to Derek."

"Thanks," I said. "I'm sure everything will turn out fine." She opened the door. "Did you know Derek?" I asked, stopping to look her in the eye.

"Yes," the young woman said, a blush rising on her cheeks. "We met at a party at his house. This was after Lisa and he ended their relationship. It's very terrible what happened."

"It is. Thank you for the help," I said and went inside. She nodded and closed the door.

Lara was seated behind her desk, on the phone of course. She pointed to the side of the room where a sofa and two chairs were positioned around a small coffee table. I went over and placed the drinks and food down and removed my jacket, throwing it over the back of the chair. I sat and waited while Lara finished the call, trying hard not to listen in. She did most of the listening so I didn't hear much, and besides it was at the end of the discussion.

She hung up and came over.

"There you are," she said and bent down to give me a kiss on the cheek, before sitting across from me. She reached out to take a drink and one of the sandwiches, which I had laid out on the table. "I'm starving. What did you get for us?"

"Corned beef from a little deli around my place. I know you love it."

"I do," she said and placed a napkin on her lap before lifting the sandwich to her mouth, smiling.

We ate our food and talked of nothing serious for a while. I told her about Sophie's latest antics and she told me about her plans to go on a cruise in the Caribbean in January.

Finally, both of us were done with our food and we sat back. She wiped her mouth carefully, giving me the once-over.

"So, tell me how you're really doing," she said and took a final drink from her cup. "I'm sure this must be really stressful."

"I'm fine," I said. "Just feel bad that all this is happening. It shouldn't have if I did my work and vetted Lisa better before I became involved."

"Don't," Lara said and pointed at me. "You can't control someone else's mental illness. She's suffering from erotomania combined with borderline personality disorder and probably, sociopathy. That's a powerful combination. She didn't even have to have sex with you for it to happen. I've read of cases where the person merely met the object of their obsession and built a whole fantasy world completely without even exchanging a word with them. Once you met her and she latched onto you, that was it. It was only a matter of time."

"The thing that gets me is that in the year between when I stopped seeing her and I met Kate, she'd been concocting this whole plan to get involved with me."

"She must have been livid when you met Kate. People like her go way overboard, imaging that the relationship exists despite the fact that nothing happened. Or in your case, nothing more than sex happened."

"We barely said two words to each other outside of scene," I said. "You know what it's like."

"I do. I had no idea she was sick."

A knock came at the door and Lara called out. "Come," she said.

Chrystal entered and came over, handing Lara a small envelope. "Here it is."

"Thanks," Lara said. "You can go now. Don't forget to put in for half a day."

"Thanks," Chrystal said. "I will."

Then she left.

"Give me a moment," Lara said and held up the envelope. "I have to check this out."

"Go ahead," I said and waved at her. I sat for a moment in silence, while Lara went back to her desk, removed something -- a flash drive -- from the envelope, and appeared to plug it into her computer. She clicked on her mouse and watched for a moment and I heard some sounds that sounded muffled.

"Come and take a look," she said and waved me over.

"What is it?" I asked and went to her side. She leaned over her desk, watching a video on a small screen. I glanced at it, standing behind her. From where I stood, it looked like pornography, except the woman was wrapped up in rope. It was a bondage scene. I recognized it immediately.

"Is that what I think it is?"

"It is," she said and stepped out of the way so I could see better. "The full video. I had a friend in the prosecutor's office make a copy and smuggle it out so we could see it and discuss."

"That's supposed to be me?" I said and watched as a man, naked except for a leather jock strap, wrapped ropes roughly around the woman's hands, before hooking them up to a winch on the ceiling. The camera swung around to show the young woman, who was clearly Lisa. While we watched, the man began to strike Lisa, slapping her across the face. Then, he took a riding crop and began to slap her breasts with it, laying a dozen smacks across one and then the other.

"That's clearly not me," I said, and turned to Lara. "I would never do that. Not at that point. I'd already decided several years earlier that I didn't like inflicting pain on my submissives, which was one reason the three of us didn't work out. She's with someone else in this video. That's clearly not me. I don't have that much hair on my chest and back. I never wore a leather jockstrap."

"I know," Lara said. "The problem is that you don't ever see his face. You see some dark hair and a dark beard, but there isn't a single camera angle that reveals the guy's face. It's impossible to prove it's you – or prove it's not you."

"Is there a time stamp on the video?"

We looked more closely, and down at the bottom corner was a time and date. It fit with the time I had met with Derek and Lisa. A year before I met Kate.

"I don't know what we can do to prove that's not you, except check what you were doing that day. I suspect that Lisa already figured out that you'd have no alibi for that date or there's no way they'd release that if we could prove you weren't there."

"Great," I said. "Why are they doing this?"

"To deflect guilt from her onto you and Derek."

The video ended, and so I went back to her small seating area and flopped down, rubbing my forehead.

"What's our strategy?"

"Let's check that day in your Daytimer. I have a record here of yours from the year before you met Kate. We'll see what you were doing and who you were with. Hopefully, you have someone who can corroborate that wasn't you."

Then, Lara opened a file and started to skip through the pages, which I assumed were photocopies of my Daytimer, which I'd given Lara before Kate and I went to California. She flipped through for a few moments and I remembered the images on the video. I hoped that I had something on that night so that we could easily refute the video, but if that night was my normal, I would have come home from work at NYP, had supper, and then gone to bed by ten.

"What day was that?" I asked, wondering if it were a week-night or weekend. On the few occasions I played with Derek and Lisa, it was a Saturday night. During the week, I had either practice with Mersey or a meeting with my submissive.

"You were between submissives at that point," Lara said and stopped at a particular page. "According to your Daytimer, you worked late that night and then came home and went to bed."

She glanced up at me. "I was hoping you had something to show so we could prove you weren't with her when that video was taken, but according to this, you had nothing planned at least. Unless you did something on the fly. Can you remember back to that week?"

I made a face. "What month was it?"

"November. The week before, you had a conference in Southern California on Robotic Neurosurgery. San Diego."

"Oh, yes, I remember that week. I was exhausted that week. I seem to recall coming home every night and just going for a run or watching television so I could catch up on my sleep." I shrugged. "Sorry I don't remember anything on the fly but even if I did, I wouldn't have written it down in my Daytimer."

"Yeah, too bad." She closed the file. "Oh, well. It's not like you're going to be charged with anything even if that was you. She was a consenting adult, and the police already know she's a nutcase. It just makes her appear more sympathetic with the jury, who might think her being used by adult professional men was exculpatory."

"Do you think they'll feel that way?" I asked, a sinking feeling in my gut. "She's locked away in the Kirby Forensic Psychiatric Center. That's got to show that she wasn't of sound mind when she got involved with Derek -- and me. That is probably exculpatory."

"She knew the difference between right and wrong enough to try to cover her tracks and create this huge fiction around you being involved in the attack on Kate."

"It's just noise, Drake. And besides, she just wants to hurt you and thinks this will accomplish that. You have to write this completely out of your mind. Ignore it. We'll find out who that is. There must be some record of who he is. I mean, they'll learn who took the footage and contact them, find out who it was. It wasn't likely Lisa. It was likely the Dominant who took those videos. Hopefully, someone will come forward and either prove it wasn't you or say it was them."

"In the meantime, my reputation will be even further shredded in public," I said wearily.

On her part, Lara nodded and came over to where I sat. "Nothing to be done about it, but at least we have seen the footage and can plan our response. I think we should find one of your former submissives who's willing to come forward and say that wasn't you. Let me see if there's anyone who might be brave enough."

"No," I said, shaking my head adamantly. "I don't want anyone exposing themselves just to bolster my reputation. They might be in danger as a result. You know what Joe Public would do -- they'd go after whoever it was and hound her. I don't want that on my conscience. We'll just put out a flat denial and leave it at that."

"I agree that would be for the best. It'll be a scandal for a while but then we can leak a photo of you showing your relatively bare chest and six pack. You do keep up with your crunches, I hope..."

I rubbed my stomach. "I try. Being a new father has been a bit taxing on my enthusiasm for weights but I do crunches regularly."

"Good. I don't imagine you have a photo from your time in San Francisco that might just exhibit your wonderful chest and abs, do you? I could leak it to a friend I have at the paper. They'd love to run a picture that had to do with the case. Great clickbait."

I thought to the photos Kate had taken of me with Sophie on the beach. Surely one of them captured me in my swim trunks, showing my chest and stomach. I did not have a beer belly.

I wasn't hairy, on my chest or especially my back.

"I'm sure Kate has a pic or two of me with Sophie. I'll check through our photos and send you something."

"Good. When people see your fabulous body, and compare

it to the tubby hairy guy on that video, they'll see it's not you."

"I hope so..."

It was then that Kate sent me a text. I pulled out my cell and checked.

KATE: I got a letter from Wards island where the psychiatric hospital is located. It's addressed to both of us and I think it's from Lisa but there's no signature. Who else would send us something from Wards Island?

"Oh, God," I said and Lara glanced up.

"What is it?"

"Kate got a letter from Lisa."

"What? What does it say?"

I texted Kate back.

DRAKE: What did the letter say?

KATE: You'll pay. That's it. Just 'You'll pay.' Drake, she's crazy.

DRAKE: She is. Don't worry. She's behind bars. All she can do is issue empty threats. Remember, we have five body-guards on contract. They're watching the apartment and will be with us whenever we go out.

KATE: They can't protect us from crazy...

DRAKE: They will. I'll be home soon. Try not to worry. But we should give the letter to the police so they know what she's up to. I'm sure the hospital already knows.

KATE: Okay. See you soon.

I glanced up at Lara. "Apparently, Lisa sent a letter to us and wrote '*You'll pay.*' That was it."

"She's nuts. I can't believe the hospital let the letter go through."

I sighed. "Maybe her family sent it?"

"Maybe. If so, it will be hard to pin it on her."

I frowned, feeling like Lisa was somehow going to win in all this.

"Don't worry," Lara said when she saw my frown. "We'll get through this. Trust in the system."

"I do trust it. I hope that the police and jury and judge will do the right thing and convict her and put her away."

"They will," Lara said and waved her hand. "Her defense lawyers will try to throw up as much mud as they can to see if any sticks, but in the end, I'm certain she'll be convicted. They'll put away for twenty-five years or more."

"I hope so."

We spent the next half hour talking about the process that would be taking place in the case and when I'd likely be called by the prosecution as a witness. The trial was still a month away, but we wanted to be prepared to deal with the buildup and aftermath.

Finally, I got up at about one forty-five so Lara could take her time and prepare for her next client.

"I'll leave you to it," I said and stood, slipping on my jacket. "You're pretty busy for a Saturday."

"I have a client who works late all week, so this was the only time I could meet with him."

"Do you bill extra on weekends?"

"Not with this client." She smiled and walked me to the door. "My arrangement with him is the same as with you. This client has me on retainer. A nice fat juicy retainer so we don't worry about things like that." She leaned over and kissed me on the cheek and squeezed my arm. "Go home to your pretty wife and beautiful baby. Forget about the video and the letter. Send me a great pic of your half-naked body and we'll destroy the defense's claim that the video is you. Once they see your body, they'll know."

"I hope so," I said and gave her a smile.

"Make sure to send me a scan of the letter before you give it to the police, okay? For my files."

"I will. See you."

"Take care, and Drake?" she said and came to me at the door. "Don't worry. All of this will blow over. You just have to be patient."

"I'll try."

Then she closed the door and I went down to the street where John was waiting by the car.

Of course, John wanted to see the letter. Once we got back to the apartment, John came up and reviewed the letter.

59

"I'll let people in the security detail know to keep a lookout for any of Lisa's family members. Just in case."

"Thanks," I said. "I'll call the police."

Then John left and I took out my cell and called Detective Gates, who was my contact in the police department. I told him about getting the letter and what it said.

"Can you bring the letter to the precinct? I'd like to keep it in evidence. We'll return it when the case is over."

"Sure," I said. "I'm glad to get rid of it, to tell the truth."

"I'm sure you are. I'll speak to the hospital about Ms. Monroe and see what they have to say. I'm surprised she was able to send you a letter, given the situation. She may have had a family member send it for her."

"Whatever the case, I don't like that my wife is threatened by someone in a psychiatric hospital."

"I understand. Thanks for calling. You can drop the letter off at the front desk. I'll let the duty officer know to expect you."

"Thanks."

And that was it. I took the letter to the precinct, John driving me there and back, and dropped the letter off with the duty officer.

Then, Kate and I tried to put the letter and the threat it contained out of our minds.

KATE

LATER THAT WEEK, when Drake was out playing racquet-ball with Dave, Karen Mills came by and sat with Sophie while I went to see my studio space. Mike, my bodyguard drove me there.

"Let me check it out first," he said and went inside before me, checking the space out. A few of the other artists gave him dark looks, wondering why he was there so I decided I'd have to have a little talk to them after Mike left.

"All clear," Mike said to me and gave me a nod. "I'll be outside. Luckily there's a bench across the street. I can watch the building from there. If you need me, I'm on my cell."

"Thanks, Mike."

I watched him take the stairs back down to the street and went back inside the studio. Then, I went to each of the spaces and spoke with the other residents, letting them know that I had a bodyguard due to a physical threat to me and that he would usually check the place out before I arrived to make sure it was secure.

I apologized but most of the other artists were pretty laid back about it.

Finally satisfied that I had done my part to smooth the way, I went into my own space and sighed. I went to the window and sure enough, there was Mike, dressed in his overcoat, sunglasses, reading a newspaper, glancing up and down the street every now and then to check things out.

Before we went to California, we'd sold my studio space in Chelsea so I was lucky to get back on the schedule at the old place and was even happy to see the old faces I remembered from before.

When I went out into the main area for some paper towels, I saw Jules standing by the main entrance, tying his shoes.

"Hey," Jules said when he saw me. "You're back."

"I am," I said and smiled when he leaned over and gave me a pat on the shoulder.

"I heard about your accident and that you went to Cali. How come you're back? Too much sunshine?"

I laughed. "No. We both felt like Manhattan is our real home. We loved California, but Drake's son Liam is living here with his grandmother and so we wanted to be close to him."

Jules nodded. "Good to have you back. We have a few new faces. I'm going for coffee. Want some?"

"If you could get me a chai tea, that would be great."

"Sure," he said and waved his hand when I reached into my pocket to get some money. "Dude, I got this."

"Thanks," I said, smiling that he called me Dude. I watched him leave, then went to my space, excited to see it again and get back into the swing of things. I loved my studio space. I felt energized when I entered and looked out the window at the busy street below. I saw Jules walking down the street to the local Starbucks and sighed, taking my canvas and my paints over to the easel so I could get back into my painting.

For the next fifteen minutes, I fixed my paints and got everything set up so I could spend a couple of hours working on the piece. Jules returned and brought in my chai tea. He glanced over my canvas, made a few appreciative remarks on it, and left me alone.

I turned on my radio and listened to a local music station -- modern hits of the past decade. In between songs, the news came on and I was shocked to hear one of the reporters mention Drake by name.

"They call him Doctor Dominant, and he's quite the romantic." Then, she read from one of Drake's letters to his submissives.

A letter to my sub.

You trust me completely to know what you need.

And I do know what you need. I know what to whisper in your ear to make you need me even more. I know how to touch, where to touch, when to touch.

I know you.

I've known every part of you – every naked inch, inside and out.

You can relax completely with me. You can feel everything possible with me. You can respond with total abandon with me.

It is what I most desire.

I can't wait to bind you with my soft leather restraints and make you cry out my name as you come, again and again. Then I will kiss you, smothering your moans with my mouth...

I remembered it well -- it was one of the reasons I wanted to meet Drake and talk to him. I secretly fantasized about meeting someone like the writer of those letters -- someone who knew me so well and made me feel desired and cared for. He really got into a submissive's mind and made them feel cherished.

That was something Drake did so well. Once again, I felt lucky to have him.

But I didn't like the fact that it was more publicity about Drake and his relationship with Lisa. She must have provided those letters to the reporter. Or someone did who wanted to distract from Lisa's guilt.

I knew if I didn't know Drake and I saw a picture of him and read those letters, I'd want him. I also knew that there would be dozens of young women who would send Drake love letters and invitations to become their Dominant. It happened before we left Manhattan and while Lara tried to keep it from me, I found out anyway. I found it amusing, but I had to admit it made me feel a little jealous. Not that I worried Drake would ever cheat on me. He wasn't that kind of man. But I was jealous that other women would get the chance to see into Drake's mind the way I had.

He was *mine*.

I wanted to keep him all to myself.

I sighed and turned the station after the news report on the letters and the trial finished.

About half an hour later, my cell dinged. I checked and saw a text from Drake.

DRAKE: Hey, Mrs. Morgan. What do you feel like for supper? Fancy some steak and salad?

I texted him back.

KATE: Sounds good. How are you doing, Doctor Delish? I heard one of your letters being read over the airwaves.

DRAKE: What? Don't tell me they're going to resurrect those old letters again...

KATE: Yes. One of your letters to your new submissives. Someone must have sent a copy to the station and they had real fun reading it on air. You should have heard the banter between the news reporters. They really liked your prose. There was a great deal of snickering and giggling.

DRAKE: I'm sure they had fun. UGH. What else will come out? I hope someone else doesn't leak any real video. This fake video is pretty bad. But Lara wants to leak a real pic of me naked from the waist up in my swim trunks to prove that fat dude with the hair isn't me.

I smiled at that, thinking that now, not only would the women of Manhattan get to read Drake's very sexual and sensual and Dominant letters to his submissives, they'd get to see his very delicious body, next to naked in his swim trunks.

KATE: *I don't know if I want to share your glorious body with the world. It's mine. All mine. You promised me that you were mine -- every inch I seem to recall you telling me. I want to hold your every inch to that promise.*

DRAKE: *I will gladly let you hold my every inch, anytime, Ms. Bennet. How about tonight?*

I laughed at that, imagining him holding it against me.

KATE: *Tonight sounds divine. Make sure you don't let Sophie sleep too long or else she won't be sleepy at her usual bedtime.*

DRAKE: *I'll make sure she wakes up on time. How's the studio? Feel like old times? Don't tell me that flaky guy is there -- what was his name? Jules with the long hair?*

KATE: *Yes, Jules is still here. He provides comic relief for the place. Seriously, Drake, Jules is really sweet in a very laid back SOCAL way. He really belongs in California.*

DRAKE: *Tell him to stay away from you or there'll be swords at dawn between us.*

KATE: *LOL if you knew Jules, you'd never worry about me. He has all these artsy-type skater girls hanging around his studio. I'm probably an old woman to him. In fact, I suspect he doesn't even see me as a woman. He actually called me Dude.*

DRAKE: *Guys today call everyone Dude, Kate. There is no way Jules doesn't think of you as a woman. That would never be possible. You're a delicious MILF.*

KATE: *OMG don't say that!*

DRAKE: *Seriously delicious MILF. More like MIIF.*

KATE: *??*

DRAKE: *Mother I Intend to Fuck*

KATE: *DRAKE MORGAN!*

I laughed as I re-read his texts, glad that he seemed to be in a good mood, all things considered.

KATE: *I better get back to work. See you at five-ish.*

DRAKE: *Love you.*

KATE: *Love you back even harder.*

DRAKE: *Believe me, when it comes to loving you back, I'm harder. ;)*

KATE: *:) I hope so.*

I turned off my cell and slipped it back into my bag, smiling to myself as I did. I loved Drake so much, I felt like I could face anything as long as he was there, waiting for me to get home, sleeping in my bed, eating meals with me, making love to me, being the father to my child.

I went back to my current painting and examined it, then set to work trying to accomplish what I hoped with the piece. When the news came on, I was about to change the station again but of course the report included a piece on the Richardson murder trial and despite my earlier plan to avoid the news, I decided to listen. More evidence had been leaked -- most likely by the defense trying to paint a picture of Lisa as a poor abused child, exploited by two adult men. It included an excerpt from Lisa's school counsellor when she was a teenager, and how she was particularly vulnerable to manipulation by father figures because of her experience of childhood sexual abuse.

It made me almost physically ill to think about Lisa being abused as a child. I couldn't imagine it, as pampered and protected as I had been growing up. I didn't even know about sex until I was ten when a babysitter talked about the dogs in the backyard mating. I thought they were playing piggy-back, but she said they were making babies. It was then I got the whole talk about the birds and the bees, not really believing it at first.

I turned down the sound, not wanting to get too upset about the case, distracting me from my art. Soon, I forgot about the news story about Lisa and was back into it. An hour passed, and then my cell calendar alert chimed, letting me know that it was time to leave. I was deep into the painting and really felt like staying for another hour, but I wanted to make sure I was home on time. I put away my canvas, cleaned up my brushes and paints, and closed the door behind me, glad that I was lucky to have the studio space to come to when I wanted.

Of course, I had my space at home, but I liked getting out of the apartment and going to a dedicated studio. When I was at home, I always felt distracted, like I should be doing anything else but paint. Cleaning, especially. So, going out each day for a couple of hours was a way to force myself to focus on my art. When I was at the studio, there were no distractions except the radio or internet and so I got a lot of work done without feeling guilt.

I exited the building and went onto the sidewalk outside, and of course saw Mike right away when he hopped out of the car and opened the rear door for me.

"I feel so bad making you wait," I said when I went up to the car.

"It's my job, ma'am."

"I know, but still. It must get very boring."

He shook his head. "I listen to podcasts on my iPhone. Right now, I'm learning to speak French. When I sit in my car, I get to practice. It's a great job for what I want."

"That's good," I said. "*Merci beaucoup.*"

"*Pas de problème.*"

I smiled and got into the back of the car.

When I arrived home, I ran up the stairs to the apartment and went inside. After removing my coat and boots, I entered the kitchen to find Drake standing at the stove, stirring something on the burner. Supper was almost ready, and I could see two steaks resting on a tray by the stovetop. Sophie was seated in her high chair next to the kitchen island.

"Hello, sweetie," I said and went to her, kissing her cheek. She smiled at me, and continued to play with her baby crackers, shoving them into her mouth. "Were you a good baby for your daddy?"

"She was a very good baby," Drake said and came over to me, wiping his hands on his chef's apron. He kissed me, and then pulled me into his arms. "She woke up early and instead of letting her stay in her crib in case she fell back asleep, I got her right up. She'll be extra sleepy tonight at bedtime."

He wagged his eyebrows at that and I laughed.

"I see there's nothing wrong with your libido," I said and squeezed him.

"Nothing at all," he said and pressed his groin against me.

"What are you cooking?" I asked when he pulled away and went back to the pan, which was sizzling.

"Sautéed mushrooms with garlic, butter and white wine. They'll go great with the two strip loins I grilled."

Then, Drake turned off the burner under the mushrooms and together, the three of us ate our supper.

We spent some time together as family in the living room, watching a children's show on television then reading Sophie a book after her bath. Drake and I both tucked her into her crib, and she went down without as much as a peep, her eyes closing almost as soon as her cheek hit the mattress.

"Our evil scheme to make our baby go to sleep earlier than usual was a resounding success," Drake whispered to me as we closed the door to her room.

"We're not evil," I replied, laughing softly. Then I turned and faced Drake, slipping my arms around his neck. "We need mommy and daddy time. It's essential for proper func- tioning and will make us even better parents."

He kissed me and brushed hair off my cheek. "You're right, of course. I need my Kate time. Speaking of which..." He ran his hand down my back and squeezed a buttock. "What would you like first? A nice bubble bath, followed by a full body massage, and then maybe sleep?"

"Sleep?" I said, mock frowning. "When you put your hands on my body after a bath, there's no way I'd be able to go to sleep..."

He grinned, one corner of his mouth turning up. "I'm counting on it, because I had something else entirely in mind than sleep."

"You do, do you?" I said, acting coy. "What could you possibly mean, Dr. Morgan?"

"You know exactly what I mean, *Katherine*..."

That told me everything I needed to know.

"Yes, Sir," I said solemnly. "I know exactly what you mean."

Inside, I was smiling to myself but I knew enough to keep my smile to myself. "What would you like this one to do first?" I glanced up at his face, not quite meeting his gaze, batting my eyelashes in a way that I hoped was alluring rather than saucy.

"Hmm," he replied, looking down at me from under his eyelashes. "I think I'd like you to run us a nice bath and then I think I want to tie you up and have my way with you."

"Oh, *Sir*..." I closed my eyes, for the thought of Drake taking control made me almost giddy. "That makes this one very excited."

"Good," he said and thrust his hips and his very notable erection against me. "Because the thought of tying you up and making you come over and over again is making me very hard."

I smiled and leaned my cheek against his shoulder. We stood in an embrace for a few moments, both our bodies warming to the feel of the other. I was already wet and swollen just thinking about Drake tying me up.

"Mmm, Ms. Bennet, I love it when you tremble with desire. It's such an incentive to me to think up ways to make you shudder."

I smiled and breathed in his scent; a heady mixture of his cologne and his maleness. "When you call me Ms. Bennet, it takes me out of scene..."

"I know," he said and laughed lightly. "I can't help but be torn between Ms. Bennet, Mrs. Morgan and Katherine. I love all three of you."

I glanced up into his eyes and saw the warmth and love -- and desire in them.

"I'm yours, whichever one you want me to be."

"All of them at once, then. Just be you." He kissed me deeply, squeezing me tightly against his body. "Oh, God, I love you."

Then he devoured my mouth, his hands sliding over my body and I was caught up in his desire.

He pulled me to the bedroom, his eyes dark with passion, and I didn't resist for just the vision of him aroused and in need woke up the same desire in me. When we got to the bed, he pushed me down so that I lay across the mattress, my hands over my head. Then he stripped off my clothes, his motions a bit rough, needy, until finally, I lay naked beneath him while he remained fully clothed.

It was a familiar situation for us -- me naked, him fully dressed. I enjoyed being on display for him because I loved the expression in his eyes -- bald possession. He owned me, body, mind and soul. I was his completely.

His mouth moved from my mouth to my chin and then my collarbone while his hands slid down my body, cupping a breast, squeezing my buttock, pulling me up against his erection. When his mouth got to my belly, I flinched, a gasp coming out between my lips without my knowing it. My hands flew to my flesh and I instinctively covered my scar.

Don't ask me why I did, for we had made love many times before when it was even more fresh, but at that moment, I was became unaccountably self-conscious. The scar had faded with time but was still pink, the scar an ugly gash down my belly. It wasn't the usual bikini line surgical scar in a normal C-section. It was from my navel down and was ugly, the flesh on either side puffing out so that it resembled a small butt. At least, that was what I thought when I examined myself in the mirror after a shower. The surgeon hadn't sewn me back up carefully because they kept me open a long time in an attempt to stop my bleeding. As a result, the muscles had been cut and had separated -- at least, that's what my massage therapist told me when I asked her about it.

"What?" Drake glanced at me, his brow knit. "What are you doing? Don't cover yourself up."

"I'm sorry," I said and it took considerable effort to remove my hands from my belly. "It's just silly self-consciousness..."

"Don't apologize. You know I've seen you naked before many times since the accident. I've seen your scar. In fact, I've licked it and kissed it."

"It's ugly."

He rose up and lay fully on top of me, taking my hands in his and holding them above my head.

"I *love* your scar." He kissed me, tenderly. "Because of that scar, you're alive. You and Sophia are alive because of that scar. That scar is beautiful to me because it saved your life."

He stared into my eyes, and the expression in them was so intense that it made me tear up.

"You only say that because you love me," I said.

"Yes," he said and squeezed my hands in his. "Yes, of course I only say that because I love you. Another man wouldn't feel that way about your scar because he doesn't love you, but I do. I love you more than anything in this world. You are the world to me. That scar saved your life and I thank God every day for it. I wish it never happened and you had a normal birth and delivery, but the alternative was you dying. Sophia dying. I'd be happy with any scar that saved your life. Kate, I would have gladly given my own life to save yours and Sophia's. Don't you understand that?"

He continued to stare into my eyes, and my tears spilled over finally.

"Yes," I said, finally.

Then he kissed me again and the passion and intensity in his kiss told me he wasn't just being nice. He wasn't just telling me that to please me. He truly felt that way deep inside. Instead of tying me up the way he planned, he made desperate love to me, needy love, ripping off his own clothes and throwing them on the floor beside the bed, then devouring my body with his mouth and hands. When I was close to orgasm from his tongue and fingers, he entered me, thrusting deep until I spasmed around him. His own orgasm followed almost immediately and he cried out as he ejaculated, groaning in my ear, his eyes squeezed tightly, his face red.

It wasn't the careful, methodical, session of bondage and multiple orgasms I was used to with Drake. It was desperate and passionate and fast.

After we both recovered a bit, he looked in my eyes once more.

"Don't ever feel embarrassed about your scars," he said in a firm voice. "Never. They're beautiful, like you. They let you live."

He kissed me once more, tenderly now, his hands cupping my face, his thumb stroking my cheek.

"I usually just accept my scar as evidence that I survived, but I suddenly felt so self-conscious. I don't know why. Maybe it was the video I saw of Lisa on the internet earlier today."

"There's a video of Lisa on the internet?"

"Yes," I said, remembering it. "She's wearing a bikini and her body is perfect. People were commenting that she could have been a model. Long legs, slim, beautiful."

"She's a murdering psychopath," Drake said, his tone derisive. "She's ugly inside and believe me, that moves her from attractive to unattractive in anyone but the crassest of men."

"Still, I remembered how beautiful she is and for some reason, I just felt sick about my scar. It'll continue to fade but it'll never go away completely. I'll never be able to wear a bikini again in public."

"You should wear one just to give the universe and any shallow person who might care about it the finger. If anyone dared say anything about it, I'd punch them out."

"Drake Morgan!" I laughed and wiped my eyes. He sounded like my knight in shining armor, ready to defend my honor, that my heart warmed. "You'd do no such thing."

"I would. I did it before," he said and I thought immediately about Sefton at the art studio and the day Drake punched him in the nose when he rushed onto the elevator unexpectedly. "I'd do it again if I thought anyone hurt your feelings about the scar or threatened you. Seriously, Kate."

Then even he laughed, because Drake was the most laid-back man when it came to confrontations. He was so calm usually. You couldn't be a neurosurgeon doing delicate robotic maneuvers and get easily flustered.

Later, after we had showered and were lying in bed, basking in the afterglow of our lovemaking, Drake rubbed my cheek with the backs of his fingers.

"I talked to Lara while you were out," he said, his voice sounding grim. "Someone provided one of the news stations with several images of me dressed up in my leather pants, bare chest, tying up a woman I was having sex with. I'm pretty sure it was Lisa. Anyway, she's all bound up, and I'm leaning over her menacingly. Of course, it's all part of the game, but the casual onlooker won't understand."

"Were you threatening her?" I asked, a catch in my throat. I rolled over onto my stomach and gazed into his eyes. "I thought you were just supposed to tie her up and fuck her."

"I did, and I wasn't really threatening her," he said and frowned. "It's all a game intended to heighten arousal. She liked to feel forced, and that's why she liked bondage. She wanted to feel like she had no control over the pleasure she felt and how her body responded."

"I know the feeling," I said, familiar with that particular response. I traced a pattern over Drake's bare chest. "When I'm bound up, I feel free. Like feeling pleasure at what you're doing to me is no longer my fault or my responsibility. It must be my Catholic upbringing. I must feel like I'm bad, deep down, for enjoying sex. Bondage frees me to be sexual. I can't help it because it's no longer my choice -- other than the fact that I have chosen to be tied up of course." I grinned at him and he nodded.

"That's the main dynamic to bondage. It's consensual and done for mutual pleasure. But the average Joe and Jane on the street thinks it means the woman is being forced against her will, abused and dominated, diminished. That's rape. Bondage and Dominance are really done for her pleasure, but the public is caught up in this notion of consent meaning there can be no resistance or force. It's totally psychological. Someone who really enjoys forcing a woman

-- tying her up against her will -- is a psychopath. Some people don't get the difference."

I rolled over onto my back and stared at the ceiling, my body feeling well used. Drake would usually tie my hands and feet to the bedposts and use several sex toys and his mouth to make me come three times before fucking me when we did a normal scene. If anyone was to watch us, they would know immediately that it was all freely chosen and freely offered and was only about pleasure. There was no force involved or lack of consent. I trusted him completely to do what he wanted with my body because I knew he loved me and only wanted my pleasure. It was entirely consensual and by choice.

But seeing Drake tying up Lisa would appear to be all about force and lack of consent if all you saw were the pictures. Her lawyers would play that up, saying that instead of doing so voluntarily, she was doing it because she was coerced, taken advantage of by two older men.

Drake rolled over and pulled me against his body, folding me in his arms and wrapping the down quilt around us both, my back to him. Then he switched off the light.

"I wish all this was over," I whispered in the darkness.

"It will be, soon," he whispered back and kissed my neck. "Then we can find some new normal."

I nodded and turned to face him.

"Good night, my love," I said and he kissed me on the lips once more.

"Good night," he replied and that was how I fell asleep.

I WOKE IN THE NIGHT, my heart racing and blinked in the darkness, trying to get my bearings. I'd had a nightmare of Drake in a dark dungeon with Lisa and Lara, both of them telling me that I just didn't understand that Drake needed more than I could give him. When I finally realized it was a dream and not reality, my heart rate decreased and my eyes adjusted to the night. I turned over and watched Drake, who was lying on his stomach with the pillow over his head, which was his normal mode from years of trying to sleep during the day while he worked shift. My gut was still in knots about the dream and about Lisa, wondering whether Drake and Derek Richardson should have understood at the time that Lisa was mentally unstable and should not have been involved in a B&D relationship. Drake assured me that Lisa was totally positive about their scenes. She was casual about her relationship with Derek and seemed to be his equal, free to speak her mind when she was not in scene. Derek seemed really fond of her, indulgent even.

But underneath that confident facade was a budding erotomaniac, if we were right about her now. She fixated on Drake and imagined a relationship between them that didn't exist outside her fantasy world.

How could Drake, who was trained in psychology and psychiatry, be so wrong about her? It had to be because Drake went by appearance and Lisa was a master at presenting a confident self-assured and competent appearance.

I knew that Drake wouldn't have been with her if he thought for a moment that she was mentally unstable.

Still, it made me feel anxious for him and for us. Not that

Drake was in any legal danger. He'd done nothing wrong. But all of this -- the trial, the publicity, the news reports, the pics and videos, were all affecting his reputation.

I could only hope, as I lay there and watched him sleep, that he was right -- it would all blow over as soon as the trial ended and people moved on to the next outrage.

DRAKE

IN THE MORNING, after a shower and after feeding Sophia her breakfast, I stood at the island in the kitchen and watched while Kate made some coffee. I'd dressed in something casual so I could blend in at the courthouse. The last thing I wanted was to be recognized.

"I'm going to head out to the courthouse and catch the trial," I said, watching Kate's face carefully to see her response.

She scrunched her nose up. "Really? You want to go and watch?"

I shrugged. "Derek was a friend. I'm curious about how the prosecution will build its case."

Kate came over to me and wrapped her arms around my neck. "Aren't you afraid that the paparazzi will be waiting for you, shoving a mic in your face, asking about why you abused poor Lisa?"

"I have a canned response," I said and hugged her. "No comment."

"You really won't say anything?"

"I wanted to say that we were sex partners years ago and that everything had been completely consensual. Any relationship after that was purely professional. If she claimed otherwise, it was because she was mentally unstable. But Lara insisted that I not comment except to say that Richardson was a friend and I hoped that his killers got the justice they deserved. That's it. I'll stick to it."

Kate didn't appear convinced. "It won't bother you to have people point and stare and take videos of you?"

I shook my head. "Nah," I said, although it did bother me, of course. "Better me than anyone else. I can take it." I mock-pumped up my biceps and grimaced like a weightlifter.

She laughed and shook her head, her face becoming serious.

"You've taken more than enough already. It might be better for you to stay home and forget the trial. When you show up, people will talk and point cameras at you."

"I feel like I owe Derek this much." I kissed her, warmed by her concern for me. "I'll be fine."

"How long will you be?" she asked, adjusting my collar.

"I'll be back this afternoon. I'm meeting Lara for lunch to discuss the case. If you need me, I have my cell."

"Okay," Kate said and ran her fingers through my hair. "Sophie and I will go out for a walk to the park and then maybe get a coffee at Starbucks. We'll be home this afternoon."

"You want to go to your studio? I'll stay home this afternoon if you want to."

"That would be great."

We kissed again and then I went to the closet and got my coat and boots. Once dressed, I got to the front door and Kate followed me over with Sophie in her arms.

"Say bye bye to Daddy," Kate said and waved at me.

Sophie waved and of course, I had to kiss them both once more each for good measure before I left.

OUTSIDE THE AIR was moist and cold, typical for October in Manhattan. It rained overnight and was almost cold enough that it could have been snow, but not quite. It woke me up in a way that a hot shower couldn't. I walked down the street to the parking garage where I kept my car. Before I drove off, my cell dinged and I checked my messages.

It was from Michael Owiti.

MICHAEL: *Drake Morgan, how are you? I've been following the news about the trial and hope everything is okay with you and Kate and of course, that beautiful baby of yours Sophia. I'm writing to let you know I've been hired to head up the new pediatric neurosurgery unit at the Southampton Children's Hospital.*

I replied immediately.

DRAKE: *Fantastic news about Southampton. I bet you'll be happy to be in charge and back in the UK. Will Claire be with you?*

MICHAEL: *She's not coming. We've split. Say no more.*

I couldn't help but raise my eyebrows at that. He and Claire split?

DRAKE: *Understood. Let me know next time you're in New York City and I'll be there.*

MICHAEL: *Good to hear. I was hoping you'd come with me and start up a robotic surgery unit. I'd love one dedicated to children and since you're doing your fellowship I thought it would be a great fit.*

DRAKE: *Had to put that on hold, because of the trial. Maybe get back to it after. But starting a pediatric neuro-surgery robotic unit sounds like a dream. Don't tempt me like that!*

MICHAEL: **tempts you* Seriously, consider it. I have the funding. There's nothing I'd like more than working with you on this. Keep it in mind. Talk to Kate. She'd love it in Southampton. Great weather and city.*

DRAKE: *I will. Talk later.*

MICHAEL: *Give her my love. And kiss that baby for me!*

I smiled as I put my cell away, and sighed. As much as I would love to go to Southampton and set up a pediatric robotic neurosurgery unit, I couldn't see Kate wanting to move again after we'd only just returned. Besides, she was so happy to be back in Manhattan and close to Ethan, I couldn't see her being willing to move again.

Then John drove me to the courthouse and dropped me off a few blocks away. I waited while he got out of the vehicle so he could follow me a discrete distance behind. I was filled with a sense of wistfulness as I walked to the court-house, wishing Kate would want to go to Southampton, but

I put it out of my mind. It wouldn't be fair to ask her. Not after moving back to Manhattan.

I slipped on some sunglasses so I could blend into the crowds on the street in the hopes that any reporters hanging around the courthouse wouldn't see me and try to get a comment. The sidewalk was crowded outside the court-house so I tried to avoid the center of the steps leading up to the entrance where the reporters were standing. Court was scheduled to start soon and I wanted to get in and through security as fast as possible so I could find a seat somewhere in the rear of the courtroom. I managed to slip inside without any reporters recognizing me and went through the metal detectors and signed in before entering the court-room, which was almost filled. I found a space at the back of the court, and took a seat on the bench beside an older couple, who were whispering to each other while they watched the proceedings.

The woman turned to me and smiled, apparently not recog-nizing me, which was good. I wanted to be as unnoticed as possible. I had even considered growing my beard and had let my whiskers get longer than usual. Plus, I wore a pair of jeans, a baseball cap and my battered leather bomber jacket instead of my usual car coat and scarf. I wanted to look as little like myself as possible. Hopefully, no one would look at me and see anything other than a curious bystander taking in a murder trial. That was my hope, at least. As much as I told Kate I didn't care about the paparazzi, I didn't want to make the news headlines or pictures of me appear in any of the newspapers or websites covering the case. It would only make things worse, so I hoped my disguise as an ordinary, slightly-scruffy Joe off the street worked.

The court filled up and soon, every seat was taken, the rows filled with ordinary people and with a few who were clearly reporters, either dictating into their cells or writing down notes in their notebooks. I leaned back and watched as the assistant district attorney and his staff entered the court, stopping to speak with the guard on their way and then taking their place at the appropriate table. Next to them was the defense's table. The defense attorney was already there when I arrived, with a young man who I assumed was an assistant, seated beside her. Finally, a door at the side of the court opened and Lisa was brought in. She wore a conservative suit with a white blouse, her dark hair pulled back into a ponytail, her face devoid of makeup and looking anxious and fatigued. I knew people would feel sympathy for her because she looked frail and in need of protection.

They didn't understand than underneath that facade was a woman who was cold and calculating. Manipulative. Everything about her appearance and demeanor was meant to manipulate the audience, to garner their sympathy for her. Poor abused woman taken advantage of by cruel older men. Her lashing out was in self-defense because she feared for her life.

I knew that would be the approach the defense took. But Derek was just not into violence. If he disciplined Lisa, it was because that was their game. She had sex with other men and played the bad nympho who couldn't get enough. Derek and she both had big orgasms as a result of their game. It wasn't my game. I didn't get off imagining Kate with another man. In fact, it upset me to think of anyone else touching her. But I was liberal enough to understand that it turned some men's and women's cranks. To each his or her own, as long as no laws were broken and it was all consensual.

The defense would have to build a case that Lisa had been coerced and systematically abused so much so that she feared for her life and when confronted by Richardson, Jones had struck out to prevent him from harming Lisa -- and himself. The would argue that Lisa having taken a hammer and striking Derek with it several times after he was already down was just her losing control out of fear.

It was so far-fetched that I couldn't believe anyone would swallow it.

But that was the defense's argument. It was up to the defense to provide evidence to support that contention and the prosecution to knock that evidence down and show that the murder was premeditated. The Assistant District Attorney would argue that Lisa had planned to kill Derek and make it appear as if he had gone out of the country. She and Jones would hide his body and live high off the hog, stealing possessions and selling valuables to fund their own new life.

Only, they didn't count on Derek's staff coming to check on the cabin just in case Derek returned from overseas and wanted to stay there.

That much had already been leaked over the course of the past year while the prosecution and defense prepared their cases. I'd followed the case of course and had Lara to help me understand the whole process and what each tidbit of evidence that leaked meant.

Lara was sure the jury would convict Lisa of first degree murder as Jones's accomplice, but it was possible that she would succeed in playing the victim card and make it look as if Derek was the deranged madman who had to be stopped before he hurt her even more.

Lara thought that Lisa should accept a plea bargain for a lesser charge of manslaughter, but apparently, Lisa was having none of it. She wanted to prove her innocence.

Ridiculous. I wouldn't be surprised if Lisa decided to act as her own lawyer. She really thought she was smarter than everyone else -- typical of malignant narcissists and sociopaths.

The door at the rear of the court opened and the Judge entered. We all stood and waited until the Judge was seated and the trial began.

After some housekeeping business about the trial and how it would proceed, we listened to the prosecution deliver its opening statement.

I watched Lisa as the Assistant District Attorney gave her statement, detailing the events of the murder and making the argument that the evidence would prove beyond a reasonable doubt that Lisa and Jones had conspired to kill Derek Richardson, and then carried out the murder, luring him out to the cabin, killing him, then burying his body in the forest near the cabin. They then lived at the cabin, using Derek's money and stealing his possessions to fund their lifestyle. They used his cell to send messages that made it appear he had gone to Singapore to spend some time vacationing, and would be relocating there, starting a new business. Several transfers of money took place over the next weeks to Jones, and a number of possessions had been sold on eBay including some valuable jewelry and watches.

I thought back to when I contacted Derek the second time about Lisa, after I realized Lisa was going to be a problem. I never heard back from him that second time and had no idea that he was probably already dead.

While people had made inquiries about Derek's whereabouts, Lisa and Jones relied on the fact Derek often took unannounced trips to the far east for business and pleasure and had spoken often of wanting to start fresh somewhere like Singapore. So, no alarm bells were raised when Derek left the US and people stopped hearing from him.

Derek was just being Derek -- freewheeling billionaire who left his empire to be run by his money managers. They were only too happy to keep milking their cash cow and didn't care that he only communicated by text and never by phone. That was just Derek wanting to disconnect from all technology while he spent time on the beaches of Thailand, or took a trip on a freighter so he could avoid the news of the day, which he found distasteful and stressful.

Lisa knew him well enough that she could mimic his texts and no one was the wiser that he had disappeared -- permanently.

It was only when a staff member went out to the cabin and discovered that Jones had been living there that the jig was up. At that point, Lisa was in jail awaiting trial for the attack on Kate but Jones was taking orders from her, planning for the day that she got out of jail and they could continue their lavish lifestyle.

According to the prosecutor, those were the facts of the case. There could be no doubt that Lisa and Jones had each struck Derek and that the attack killed him. There could be no doubt that they hid his death and buried his body on the grounds around the cabin. There was no doubt that they used his credit cards and bank accounts to transfer money to themselves and carry on a lavish lifestyle, stealing his identity online to enrich themselves.

The evidence would prove beyond a reasonable doubt that Lisa and Jones murdered Derek. They lured him to the cabin and killed him then hid the evidence. The only question was how long of a prison sentence Lisa would get. Nothing else was in doubt.

The defense attorney countered the prosecution's claims, one by one. She argued that although there was evidence that Derek died in the cabin, the evidence would not show whether the death was the result of a premeditated murder or an act of self-defense. She argued that the defense would provide evidence and testimony that Lisa was a battered woman who merely tried to protect herself from a vicious attack when she was found with her lover at the cabin. Derek had become enraged and had attacked first. He had a history of abusing women and the defense had images and videos of spanking women and of engaging in bondage. Derek was active in the BDSM lifestyle. Lisa was afraid of him. Jones had defended her, grabbing a knife on the spur of the moment to stop Derek's attack on a defenseless and fearful Lisa. When she realized Derek was going to attack her, Lisa found a hammer and struck Derek with it to stop him from killing her. She fought for her life. Then, in fear that no one would believe her, she and Jones buried Derek's body and continued to live there, in a fugue state caused by years of abuse at the hands of older men.

Self-defense. A battered woman who had suffered for years under his power and domination.

The opening statements over, the prosecution brought in its witnesses and experts to build the case against Lisa. The first witness was the beat cop who was sent to the premises to check out a B&E reported by one of Derek's security guards after the staff alerted him of someone living in the cabin. The police officer arrived on the scene, called to the cabin by a very distraught security guard, who found Jones at the cabin and was probably very lucky to have escaped with his life. Jones wasn't fast enough or deceptive enough to think of killing him and so the guard was able to call police and even though Jones left and went to stay at his mother's, he was eventually caught. Initially, when confronted with evidence that Jones had been staying at the cabin, Jones claimed that Derek had given him permission to stay there, but the groundskeeper was adamant that Derek had never done so and he always told the groundskeeper and his wife when either he or his guests would be using the cabin.

Derek had not done so and so the groundskeeper had insisted that the man had no permission to be there. Detectives found some of Jones's possessions, left behind in his haste to escape, and were able to identify him. They traced him to his mother's home in upstate New York through his phone's GPS, when it pinged a tower closer to her house. They showed up at her door asking about Jones's where-abouts and his mother denied he was present, but in panic, Jones bolted, running out the back of the house into a heavily wooded neighborhood. Police chased him and took him into custody and that's when it all came crashing down.

Police got a search warrant to inspect the cabin and grounds, found forensic evidence, including blood and DNA evidence that suggested someone had been seriously harmed in the cabin. When confronted with that forensic evidence, Jones had spilled, laying most of the blame for Derek's death on Lisa's shoulders. He was only too happy to blame her, even telling the police detectives where the body had been buried. The cross-examination of the police officer was minimal, merely going over the details without challenging any of them.

The detective in charge of the case provided his own testimony about the day he interviewed Jones and what the forensic team found in the house and on the grounds when they started to dig. Again, the cross examination was minimal and did nothing to call into question any of the testimony.

The prosecution called the medical examiner to the witness box and she told the court about the condition of the body when it had been exhumed from a shallow grave in the woods surrounding the cabin.

"Mr. Richardson had been beaten and stabbed. He died from blood loss after receiving twelve stab wounds with a very sharp and thin knife and several hammer blows to the head and chest, so his death wasn't immediate. Based on the amount of blood loss and based on the evidence at the crime scene, he took some time to die."

The defense passed on cross examination, apparently not feeling any need to challenge any of the testimony or evidence.

A member of the forensic team that inspected the cabin

testified about the trace blood evidence found at the scene. The jury was shown photographs of the floor and walls taken using Fluorescein, which displayed trace evidence of blood even after it had been washed away and wasn't visible to the naked eye. The forensic technician testified that based on the size of the stains and the fact they were spread over a large area in the cabin's main room, Derek had put up a real fight and had been chased, repeatedly being struck with both a hammer and fish boning knife. Both murder weapons had been found at the scene, and while both had been cleaned thoroughly, it was still possible to find trace blood evidence on them, linking them to the murder.

By the time noon came around, the prosecutions first three witnesses had finished their testimony and the defense had cross-examined the witnesses. Apparently, the defense was not going to dispute the physical evidence. They were going to approach the case as one of self-defense. Lisa's lawyer asked each one of the prosecution's witnesses if it was possible to tell from the physical evidence who attacked whom first, and of course, the answer was no. There was no way of knowing, outside of the testimony of those actually present, who attacked whom first. The defense claimed that it was Derek who attacked Jones, from anger that Lisa was involved with another man. Jones was merely defending himself and Lisa against Derek's rage.

Anyone who knew Derek would know right away that he wasn't jealous at all of Lisa. They had no relationship at the time of his murder and hadn't been involved for several years. But it was the defense's contention that they had carried on a secret relationship during those years and that Derek had been obsessed with Lisa, jealous of her every friendship with other men, imagining that she was cheating. He had threatened her before with violence and so she was acting out of fear for her life when she picked up a hammer and attacked Derek with it.

Lisa wept silently when her lawyer cross-examined the forensic tech and medical examiner, making the point that no one could tell beyond a reasonable doubt whether Derek or Jones attacked first. In fact, it was far more likely that Derek did out of jealousy when finding Lisa alone with Jones at the cabin.

"Isn't it true that in cases of domestic violence, it's usually the man who threatens the woman? In your years of experience as a homicide detective, how many cases have you investigated where the husband or boyfriend was the aggressor vs. the wife or girlfriend?" she asked, her tone authoritative.

The detective shrugged. "Only a few, but that doesn't mean it isn't possible. Every year there are a dozen or more cases in which the wife or girlfriend kills their partner out of jealousy or for money."

It was up to the prosecution to prove beyond a reasonable doubt that Jones and Lisa conspired to kill Derek. It was the defense's job to create that reasonable doubt in the minds of the jury so that they would fail to convict.

I couldn't imagine that the jury would fail to convict or that the defense would succeed and was surprised that Lisa didn't take a plea and go to jail for a shorter period on a lesser charge, but apparently, she was going for a finding of not guilty.

Was she self-deceived? Did her lawyer really think she could get Lisa off using the battered woman defense?

The court was recessed until the afternoon and so I got up before anyone else did and made my way out of the court-room and went as quickly as I could down the hallway to the rear exit, hoping no reporters or interested observers recognized me.

"Drake!"

I turned at the sound of Lara's voice, glad that it was her instead of anyone else.

"Phew," I said and wiped my brow dramatically when she got to my side. "I thought you were paparazzi."

"No, thank God. Just your attorney."

"Were you in the court? I didn't see you."

"I slipped in just before the judge."

I texted John so he knew I was coming out and could have the car ready.

"So," I said, opening the door for her. "What do you think so far?"

She smiled. "I think this is going to be a slam-dunk case and Lisa will be put away for the maximum."

"You do?"

We went down the steps to the street, and I was glad to see that the group of reporters were busy talking to their camera people and didn't see me, or didn't recognize me if they did see me.

"I do. I have no doubt the jury will convict. The question is what kind of damage to your reputation will Lisa do in the process?"

"Oh, God." I'd been focused on the evidence and hadn't thought about that -- at least, not during the testimony. "I don't know what more damage she can do. I'm off the board at the corporation and foundation. I'm not doing my Fellowship. I'm not even practicing. What else could she do?"

Lara made a face. "Not that I'm superstitious or anything, but hush, Drake. There's a lot of damage she could do. Just bringing your name back into the public eye like this is going to damage your reputation. But we can weather this, if we stick to the script. Okay?"

"Okay." We got to the car and John opened the passenger door for Lara. She smiled and got inside. I slipped in beside her and fastened my seatbelt.

"Let's go get some food and talk strategy and tactics," she said.

"Sounds like a plan."

And so we did.

KATE

DRAKE GOT home from lunch with Lara around two in the afternoon, when I was a bit sleepy and Sophie was playing on the floor with her Thomas the Tank Engine train set. He came into the living room, his cheeks cold from the October air outside and kissed me.

"Hey, beautiful, how are you? How's my two girls?"

"We're fine. We had a nice walk this morning and had our lunch, and now, I'm just waiting for her to get tired enough for her afternoon nap. How did the trial go? What does Lara think?"

Drake plopped down on the sofa beside me, his arm around my shoulders. "It went fine. No one recognized me in my *casual dude in jeans and a growing beard* disguise. We heard opening arguments and the prosecutor had a few witnesses on the stand. There was cross-examination as well."

"Who did they call?" I asked.

Drake recounted how the morning went and who testified for the prosecution.

"It seems pretty straight forward that Lisa and Jones planned to kill Derek and steal his money," I said. "They were planning on leaving the US for a country with no extradition treaty, weren't they? Mali, wasn't it?"

"There were two tickets to Mali in the cabin, yes," he said. "Lisa claimed Derek bought them for the two of them. She said he was planning on taking her there to start over."

"It's a lie, of course," I said, amazed at how she was such a compulsive liar. "You can't believe anything she says."

"No," Drake said, picking Sophie up, who had walked over with a toy, wanting to sit on his lap. "Narcissists can't stand to be seen being wrong or making a mistake -- and worst of all, being rejected. She'll say and do anything to protect her fragile ego. The problem with her is that she thinks she's smarter than she is."

"She's obviously smart," I said, remembering the pictures I'd seen of her online. "And beautiful. She's a doctor. You can't be stupid and get through med school."

Drake shook his head. "She's smart but sometimes, she thinks she's smarter than she really is. She doesn't know forensic science as well as she should or they wouldn't have killed him in the house. She should know that the police could find traces of Derek's blood at the scene. She cleaned up but you can't clean up every trace of blood. The chemicals from the blood cells remain. I saw the pictures of the trace blood evidence and it must have been a horrific scene. Blood everywhere -- on the walls, on the floor. On the kitchen countertop."

"Sounds really violent," I said, imagining it in my mind's eye.

"A fish boning knife. Long and thin."

I scrunched up my nose in horror. "Oh, God. One of those?" Jones was a big guy while Derek was of average height and build. From what I had seen on television, he was no match for Jones -- especially Jones with a knife.

Drake nodded, an expression of disgust on his face. "Yep. He didn't die right away. They chased him around and Lisa hit him with the hammer half a dozen times. It must have been a horror show."

"God," I said, my gut in a knot about it. "I knew she was dangerous when I saw her at O'Riley's but I never would have thought she'd actually try to kill someone, let alone me."

"I should have quit right away," Drake said, his voice regretful. He sighed. "Maybe none of this would have happened."

"You couldn't know. None of us could know she was crazy."

"Couldn't we? Maybe Derek didn't know her as well as he should have. Maybe I shouldn't have blithely agreed to top her, not knowing anything about her background and history. Usually, I relied on Lara to vet the subs I topped or signed a contract with. I didn't because I assumed that Derek, who I thought was a responsible smart guy, would have done so. I wonder if he knew about her past. If I had known, I wouldn't have become involved with her. Someone with a traumatic past involving real abuse should probably approach the lifestyle very cautiously. For some it might be healing. For others, it might just screw them up even more. There are bad guys in the lifestyle who prey on women like Lisa."

"Usually they don't get murdered by those women," I added. "She was a piece of work, Drake. Probably only someone really trained in psychopathy would recognize her behavior and be worried."

"I should have been," Drake said softly. "There's no excuse, considering I studied psychiatry. I even considered psychiatry as a specialty."

"Don't blame yourself." I reached over to squeeze his bicep. Sophie put her head down on Drake's shoulder, sucking away on her pacifier and Drake turned to me, his eyebrows raised.

"Looks like somebody is ready for a nap," he said softly.

"Looks like it. Do you want to take her or should I?"

"I will," he said and stood up carefully, carrying her up the stairs to the bedroom. I waited on the sofa, turning on the television to watch the headlines. Luckily, there was nothing on the news about the case. I didn't relish seeing any pics of me or Drake on the screen. Reporters often referenced my case when they first talked about Lisa, since she had been convicted of attempted murder. Luckily, the reporters all used an old photo of me from several years earlier. While I had been stalked a bit during Lisa's first trial and had a few pics taken of me, so far I'd escaped their attention during the lead-up to her new trial. I wanted to keep it that way. I'd taken to wearing my hair up in a bun rather than down, and when I went out in public, I dressed down as much as I could so I blended in with the rest of the crowd.

I didn't want anyone sticking a mic in my face. In my mind, the trial couldn't end soon enough. Once it was done, there was yet another trial on charges of reckless endangerment for encouraging Jones to commit suicide.

Drake came back down and sat beside me, pulling me closer to him. "She went down easy," he said. "We are so lucky."

"We are," I said and smiled up at him.

"Are you going to the studio?"

I nodded and stretched. "I want to finish this piece I'm working on. That way, the series is done and I can send some slides to the gallery and see if they're interested in an exhibition."

"That would be great," he said and pulled me onto his lap. "Give me a kiss before you go. I need some Kate time."

I kissed him and laid my head on his shoulder and we sat like that for a few moments, listening in the background to a news report on one of the news networks.

"One day, all this business with Lisa will be over and we can go back to our real lives. I feel like we're in limbo right now. You can't do anything until the news dies down after the trial is over."

"All we can do is put our heads down and wait."

I kissed him again then stood up from the sofa. "I'll go for a couple of hours and should be back in time for supper. This time, I'll cook it. How about a stir fry? We have that broccoli and some chicken in the freezer."

"Sounds good. I'll read over some reports Dave sent me on new projects. I don't get to approve anything but at least

I'll know what the foundation is doing without me around."

"Poor Drake," I said and bent down, kissing him once more. "It's so unfair to you."

"It's for the good of the foundation. I can still see the good it's doing. I don't need my name or face connected to it to be fulfilled."

"You're too good," I said and grabbed my bag before going to the front closet to get my coat and boots. I glanced at the window and saw that it was starting to snow. I texted Mike to let him know I needed a ride. Drake got up and came to the front door. "Give me one more kiss," he said and leaned forward.

I did, slipping my arms around his neck briefly.

"Have fun," he said and released me, opening the door. "What do you say to an artist going to their studio? Break a leg doesn't sound right."

"Make good art?" I said, laughing.

"Make good art," he replied and closed the door as I went down the stairs to the street level.

Outside, the sun was covered by thick grey clouds. There were a few hours of sunlight left but the days were getting shorter and the air was crisp. Fat snowflakes drifted down from the sky. I loved this time of year because it reminded me of the start of the happiest time of my life -- meeting Drake and falling in love, our trip to Africa and then our wedding. The birth of Sophia hadn't been the happy event that I hoped it would be, but we survived and now we were a happy little family -- despite the trial and all the fallout for Drake.

Of course, once I got onto the street, Mike was leaning against his vehicle. When he saw me, he stood up straighter.

"Mrs. Morgan," he said and nodded.

"Hi, Mike. I'm sorry to bother you. I'm perfectly capable of taking a taxi or the subway. I keep thinking I'm perfectly safe the way I always thought I was and then I see you and reality sets in and I realize I need a bodyguard."

"Sorry to be bad news," he said with a shrug and a small grin. "Best to live in the real world when it comes to safety. Most people don't need a bodyguard, but some do. Try to forget I'm here. I know that's not easy."

I gave my head a shake and pointed down the street. "Do you mind if I walk part of the way, then take the subway the rest? I need some fresh air."

"Suits me fine," he said and adjusted his earpiece. "I like to get some exercise given that I sit a lot of the time."

I set off and walked down 8th Avenue towards the studio. I tried to forget he was behind me, and plugged my earphones in, listening to some classical music while I took in the sights. It felt good to get out and blend into the crowd, to feel the energy of the city around me. I could almost imagine that all was right with my little world.

Almost.

Until I passed a newsstand with newspapers emblazoned with pics of Lisa and Derek side by side and the headline, *Accused Billionaire-Killer Stands Trial.*

I removed my figurative rose-colored glasses and put on my real sunglasses, hoping that no one recognized that I was her second victim.

WE TOOK the subway the rest of the way and Mike followed me along the street and then up the stairs to the studio. After he checked it out as usual, he left me alone and went back to the street.

It upset me that I couldn't feel safe even in the studio, but Lisa was still able to reach outside of the prison and influence people. Who knew what she might do to try to punish me and Drake even further? She'd been able to convince Jones to kill himself. She had family in Manhattan and they were adamant she was not only innocent, but that Drake and Derek Richardson were evil men who were the ones who should be in jail, not Lisa.

At her first trial, Lisa's older brother had caused a scene, shouting at one of the police officers who had given testimony about Lisa's behavior when she was finally picked up. He had to be forcibly removed from the courtroom. I tried to avoid the trial, but Drake watched coverage and attended court when he could. It was the brother's behavior that convinced him to keep a security detail for us even though Lisa was in prison. When I complained, Drake mentioned Lisa's brother.

"You never know what someone like him might do in anger. He might feel I deserve a beating and come after me. He's a security guard. He's capable of whupping ass."

"Drake Morgan!" I had said in response. "It's not like you to say something like that."

"Just trying to be real," he'd said and gave me a kiss and a pat on my cheek. "I want you safe. I want to be around to enjoy you -- and Sophie -- for a long time."

I gave in and agreed to have a bodyguard whenever I went out alone. Drake had one as well, because he was a target, too. The two of us were no longer anonymous in Manhattan because of the publicity around the trial. It upset me and partially ruined my return to the city in which I was born and had lived all my life, but that was the reality.

I tried to put it out of my mind. I had to push thoughts of the trial, of bodyguards and personal security out of my mind so I could focus on my art.

I wouldn't let Lisa and her nutcase brother make me stop living my life.

THE TWO HOURS I allotted myself to work in the studio passed with me barely noticing the time. I made a great deal of progress on the current piece I was working on – a detail of a scene of a watering hole I'd drawn out while in Africa, the animals crouched down around its border, drinking. I don't know why it appealed to me so much, but it did. It spoke of the reliance on water and how the scarcity of it during the dry seasons pushed the animals to their limits, testing their ability to survive in harsh conditions. It seemed like a metaphor for us, Drake and me. We usually had it really good. Drake was wealthy, healthy and intelligent. He was exceptionally well-trained and skilled. Yet, all of that was put to the test when he met Lisa and she almost killed me and put Drake's past in the spotlight. He was losing all the things that made him Drake – his practice in neurosurgery, his fellowship at NYP, his place on the board of the foundation and corporation his father had started. Now, he was a stay-at-home dad living off his wealth rather than fulfilling his personal promise. All because of Lisa Monroe and her erotomania.

Both of us were being tested by these new environmental conditions. In nature, only the strongest and healthiest survived, ensuring a strong and healthy future generation. In the human world, that wasn't the case. Sometimes, it was the worst of us who survived and thrived, if you could call it that, while the best died young. I tried to put Lisa and her acts out of my mind, but she kept creeping in at any time of the day and no matter what I was doing, ruining my otherwise peaceful day.

Damn her.

I couldn't wait until all this passed and Drake and I and Sophia were able to live our lives the way we wanted. That would only happen once the trial was over and Lisa was put in jail for the rest of her life.

I cleaned my brushes and put my canvas away, then locked my space. I sent Mike a text, letting him know I was finished, and left the studio. On the street, he was waiting, his newspaper tucked under his arm.

"Mrs. Morgan," he said when I reached his side.

"Hi, Mike. Ready for a trip home on the subway? I want to get there fast."

"Lead on," he said and waved his arm.

WHEN WE ARRIVED BACK at the 8th Avenue building, I said goodbye to Mike and went up the stairs to the apartment. I slipped off my boots and coat and went into the kitchen where Drake was busy fixing Sophia some supper. As usual, she was in her highchair and was pushing around some animal crackers on her tray.

"Hi, baby," I said and gave her plump cheek a kiss. "Have you been a good girl for Daddy?"

She gave me a huge toothy-mushy-cracker smile and shoved another animal into her mouth.

"She's been a very good girl," Drake said from the stove. "She went down without a peep and woke up about half an hour ago. We played on the floor for a while with Thomas the Tank Engine."

"That's good," I said and went to his side, leaning up to kiss his cheek. "I guess I should start cooking."

"I'll help." Drake rubbed his hands together. "Give me a knife and tell me what to do."

I went to the refrigerator to get the vegetables out for the stir fry. After I placed them on the counter in front of Drake, I did hand him a chopping knife and cutting board.

"What's new? Any developments in the trial?"

"As a matter of fact, yes," Drake said and began chopping the broccoli while I fixed the rice. "Lara called before you arrived and filled me in on the trial this afternoon. Seems that the defense is going to call me as a hostile witness."

"What?"

Drake nodded, his expression grim. "Yep. They want to

question me about my relationship with Lisa and Derek. Part of building the case that Lisa was abused and battered and was acting in self-defense when she hit him with the hammer a half dozen times after Jones stabbed him as many times with the fish boning knife and after making him transfer money to them both."

"Do you have to?" I made a face, not relishing the fact Drake would be pulled into the limelight again.

"I have to. We knew this was coming," he said. "I hoped Lisa would accept a plea bargain and plead guilty but for whatever reason, her lawyer really believes she can get Lisa off on a battered woman defense."

Drake shrugged, but I could see how unhappy he was.

"I'm sorry," I said and went to him, wrapping my arms around his waist, resting my head against his back. "What a pain to have to go through it all again. Why can't they take a deposition and let the jury read it?"

"They want to put a face to the name of the man who corrupted poor Lisa since Derek is dead. They can't harass him, so I guess it's me."

"What kinds of things will they ask you?"

He shrugged and turned around, slipping his arms around me. "When we met, what we agreed to, what we did, what happened afterwards. Lara's going to take me through the probable questions they will ask so we can practice my responses. Not that I won't tell the truth, but so I know how to phrase it so I don't bias the jury."

"The jury won't understand that it was all consensual. They'll just hear bondage and think violence and abuse."

"I'll be questioned by the prosecutor and she'll correct any misunderstandings in cross examination."

"I hope so."

I sighed and went over to feed Sophie her supper while Drake finished chopping. As usual, Sophie was glad to feed herself, eagerly picking up the pieces of soft food in her fingers and holding her fork in the other hand. I smiled while I watched her. She was a good eater.

"You better make sure to bring John along with you when you testify."

"John waits outside. It's pretty safe in court." Drake finished chopping some red bell pepper. "He'll push any pesky reporters out of the way and lead me through the throngs of paparazzi to the limo."

"They'll love it," I said, and took the chicken out of the freezer. "The news will carry video of you leaving the courthouse, claiming you're a real-life Grey. You'll probably get more fan mail." I thought about the letters and texts and emails Drake had received after the last trial from young women hoping to become Drake's next submissive. He'd had to change his email address, phone number and twitter accounts so he no longer received them.

"Oh, God, I hope not."

We worked together for the next fifteen minutes to fix the stir fry, with me cooking and Drake watching over the rice and preparing the sauce.

Finally, when the food was ready, we dished out our servings and Drake sat beside me. Then, he got up abruptly and went to the refrigerator. "I got this for us," he said, holding up a bottle of white wine. "It's South African. I hear it's all the rage now."

He brought over two wine glasses and poured us each a glass.

"To my beautiful wife," he said. "May we weather this coming storm, and look forward to smooth sailing afterward."

"Hmm," I said and clinked my glass against his. "Sounds like you need a vacation."

Drake laughed and took a sip. He made a face of appreciation and then set his glass down. "I wouldn't mind a vacation, actually. My schedule in California was pretty grueling. Somewhere warm and sunny with white sand beaches and everything done for us. How does that sound?"

"Sounds wonderful. As soon as the trial's over, we should go for a couple of weeks. Maybe before Christmas?"

"Before Christmas. I want to be here for Christmas and New Year's, unless I can convince Maureen to let me take Liam along with us, and unless Dad and Elaine decide to come along as well."

"I'll talk to him about it and maybe we can plan. It would give us something positive to look forward to."

"You wouldn't miss the snow and Macy's and the Christmas tree lighting ceremony?"

I shook my head. "Nope. White sand, surf and all-inclusive services with a Santa in Bermuda shorts sounds like heaven."

"I'll talk to Maureen and see if she'll let me take Liam over

Christmas. She'll probably want to get him to come visit them on his vacation."

"Well, if she does, there's no reason for us not to go somewhere as a family. Maybe we can go somewhere close to him and he could come for a quick visit."

"Sounds like a plan."

We finished our dinner, thoughts of a nice vacation to somewhere warm making me feel more optimistic.

DRAKE

I LAY in bed beside a sleeping Kate, and remembered, my mind going back to the first time Derek suggested I top his submissive.

We were at a masked party at his mansion in Yonkers. Everyone wore a mask of some design to hide their identity, but everyone had been vetted before being admitted. Everyone also signed an NDA about the events and people who attended.

"You like bondage, if I remember correctly from seeing you at Perry's party last month," he said to me as we stood at the bar in his mansion and watched the guests talking in small groups. Derek was a man of about my age and height, a bit more grey in his hair than I had, and dark brown inquisitive eyes.

"That I do," I said and raised my glass of vodka tonic with a lime wedge. I usually didn't have more than one drink when at a dungeon party. I wanted to be completely in control so one drink before was all I allowed myself. Derek was similarly cautious, drinking a single glass of white wine. We were both sons of wealthy businessmen who carried on in our father's footsteps. Derek's father was in securities and of course, my father Liam was both a trauma surgeon and medical implements inventor and manufacturer.

"I want you to top my sub while I watch," he said, his voice hesitant, as if he was uncertain that I'd be interested.

I raised my eyebrows and considered. Usually, my subs were all found through Lara, whose judgement I trusted. She knew what I wanted and what I liked -- someone submissive without any interest in masochism or humiliation. Basically, I wanted a woman who enjoyed being bound and controlled, but who ultimately wanted pleasure, not pain.

"I'm pretty tame when it comes to BDSM," I said. "If you want to watch something rough, you've got the wrong man."

"I had you researched," Derek replied. "I know what you like. I'd like to watch you top my current sub. That's what I like."

"And?" I asked, not wanting to get into any heavy SM scene or thinking one took place after I was done with my parts. "After that? What happens between you and her?"

"After that, I punish her by denying her an orgasm while I take mine. Then, we have great makeup sex where she's ever so submissive and on her knees. Don't worry," he said and shook his head, giving me a look that said no problem. "She's not into pain and neither am I. Just the game. The mental game."

"I understand."

I did understand the mental game. It was my specialty. I liked to find out what made a woman really hot, what really turned her on, and then I liked to give it to her. Did she like to feel like a bad girl? A nympho? Did she like to watch herself be fucked hard? Did she want to crawl on her knees and please a man? As long as it didn't involve children, pain, scat or animals, I was fine. Whatever mental game that got a woman off, I'd play it as long as I was in control. The most aggressive I ever got was mock-rape, and then, there'd be no pain, only mental excitement about being forced and getting off anyway. For some women, it was a way to master their fear of the real thing. For others, it was a way to overcome their past experiences. I wasn't judgmental about why.

"Here's the scenario," he said. "After both of you sign contracts, I leave you with my sub, you take her upstairs to her bedroom and tie her up, fuck her, and I catch you in the act. You continue to fuck her while I watch. Then, you leave. That's it. Sound good?"

"Sounds good on my part. Do you have papers ready?"

"They're in my office."

We left the large room where the party was being held and took a narrow hallway to an expansive office, with floor to ceiling bookshelves and an ornate desk in front of a bay window. On the desk was a contract that I would read and sign to ensure I knew the sub's limits and agreed to abide by them.

I read over the contract and noted that the submissive was willing to engage in pretty much any kind of sexual contact and bondage. After discussing it with Derek, I signed the contract and we left the room.

I saw Derek nod to a small crowd of people standing off to our right and a young woman walked over, pretty even under the mask that covered half her face, her dark hair long and flowing, her lips reddened and swollen -- obviously injected, her breasts pert and round under a push up leather bustier. She wore a skirt slit at the side, showing off a shapely thigh.

She was attractive enough to get me hard thinking of tying her up. Given there was no pain involved, just bondage and exhibitionism, I'd find the scene to be quite enjoyable.

"Mia, this is Master D. Why don't you two talk. I have to take a phone call."

"Yes, Master," she said, her eyes downcast.

When Derek walked away, Mia turned to me and looked me directly in the eye. I was surprised at her impertinence for she should have stayed in submissive mode. Was she looking to be disciplined right away? Maybe she needed to feel my dominance before she could comply.

"Your manners," I said softly.

She held my gaze for a moment longer and then looked down. "My apologies, Sir."

Some submissives enjoy being disciplined before sex. It made them feel released from any guilt at enjoying the sex that followed. Mia must have been one of them. It reinforced the power exchange between the Dominant and submissive.

"You're allowed one transgression, but be assured that if you don't obey, you'll be punished."

"Yes, Sir," she said with an emphasis on Sir. Her tone was a tad more impetuous than I would like. I didn't want to manage her as much as get my pleasure from her body and the scenario. I had a feeling she was quite the handful.

Of course, I was right but I had no idea at the time how right.

Our scene was brief, and consisted of us speaking in the main room, then leaving to go to her bedroom where I tied her up and had sex with her. On cue, Derek walked in and stood in the shadows not far from where we were on the bed. I continued to thrust to orgasm after Mia came very vocally. Once both of us had finished, I withdrew from Mia's body and removed my condom, dropping it in the wastebasket beside the bed.

"So, the little slut convinced you to tie her up and pleasure her, did she?" Derek said from the shadows. At that, Mia became all apologetic.

"Please forgive me, Master," she said. "He tricked me into coming upstairs with him. I didn't know he'd tie me up and rape me."

"Leave us," Derek said, his voice hoarse with desire. I pulled on my clothes, my part in this little scenario finished, and left them alone. I had no idea what transpired after I left, but I trusted my sense of Derek that he wasn't into pain either, or humiliation, but that both he and his partners were titillated by exhibitionism / voyeurism. Based on what I'd read in the contracts and what we'd discussed was truthful and that Mia -- Lisa -- would suffer no abuse when Derek was alone with her.

That may have been a mistake. I didn't think he seemed like a sadist, nor had I heard that about him when I first met him and talked to others who knew him in the community.

Regardless, I now knew more about Lisa than I cared to. She had been mentally unstable before she met Derek and became involved in the BDSM community. She was mentally unstable when I did several scenes with her. She remained mentally unstable, although obviously very smart and calculating. It wasn't my fault, but it was my responsibility to ensure my sexual partners were healthy and mentally stable. I'd obviously failed in that sense, trusting my gut too much instead of my ability to do my research. I should have said another time and let Lara handle things between us as I always had before.

That was my mistake and now we were all paying for it -- Derek, Jones, myself and Kate.

I TURNED over and watched Kate sleeping beside me.

With her eyes closed and her hand tucked under her pillow, she appeared so innocent and trusting. She had no idea when we met that night at Ethan's fundraiser what she was getting herself into. I sensed an interest in me that night, but of course, tried to shut off that interest. She was Katherine. Ethan's beloved daughter. I had no right to her. I should have left her as she was -- young, beautiful, innocent.

Instead, I discovered that this young, beautiful and innocent woman was curious about submission. I was a goner from that moment on. Not only was she beautiful and curious about submission, she was also smart and principled.

She was perfect -- for me. I realized I couldn't go back and right my wrongs, take back my yes to Derek, but I could try to make it up to Kate for the rest of our lives. That's what I intended to do once the trial was over and we were free of the daily headlines about Lisa, Derek and my relationship with them. Once that part of our lives was finished, I hoped that everything could get back to normal. I could quietly go back on the board at the foundation, at least, and I could finish my fellowship at NYU. I could start up my practice again once the news died down. Kate could finish her MA and continue painting. Maybe Liam could come and live with me during the week and stay with Brenda or Maureen -- if she returned to the US.

We could be a happy family.

Then I remembered Michael's offer of heading up the robotic surgery unit at the Southampton Children's Hospital but that was pretty much impossible. I couldn't ask Kate to move once again.

My most fervent wish as I lay there, listening to Kate breath slowly, her sleep peaceful, was for life to get back to normal for us. I loved her and Sophie beyond all reason and I would do everything I could to make sure we could be together.

I WOKE in the morning and saw that the bed was empty. The noise on the monitor told me that Kate was up with Sophie, who was talking in the background, naming her toys and babbling happily as she did in the morning. It was Kate's day to get up with her but I wanted to see my two girls and so I got up and pulled on my pajama bottoms and robe so I could join them.

"There's my girls," I said when I entered Sophie's bedroom. She was lying on her back on the change table, a toy bunny in her hand, one long bunny ear in her mouth. She smiled at me, a wide toothy smile and my heart melted. Kate glanced over at me, her smile adding to the effect.

"Good morning, Daddy," Kate said and continued her actions, wiping Sophie's bottom and putting on a fresh diaper. "You're up early. It's my day so you could have slept in."

"And miss seeing my two girls first thing in the morning on a sunny day? Not a chance."

Kate turned to the window and smiled. "It is sunny. We should take advantage of it and go for a walk."

I kissed her and then kissed Sophie. "I have the trial this morning. Maybe I could meet you and Sophie in Central Park at noon and we could have some lunch and take a walk? Then you could go to the studio."

"Sounds perfect."

"I'll go take a shower and get ready," I said and kissed them both once more.

LATER, after my shower, I held Sophie in my lap at the kitchen island while I ate my breakfast of toast and coffee.

"What's happening in the trial today?" Kate asked, pouring herself some coffee.

"More of the same, I guess. The prosecutor will continue to build her case against Lisa and the defense lawyer will cross-examine and try to poke holes in it."

"When will you testify?"

I shrugged. "I'll get a call. I imagine after the state has presented all its forensic evidence and interviewed all its experts."

"I'm sorry you have to do it," Kate said and came over to me, taking Sophie from my arms. "It'll soon be over. A few more weeks."

"Let's hope so. Either way, we'll go somewhere warm and get away from it all."

Kate smiled and bounced Sophie on her hip. "I'll talk to my dad today and see what he says. I'm sure I can talk him into a vacation."

I stood and drank down the last of my coffee. "I hope so."

I kissed them both again, and then texted John, to let him know to bring the car around. After getting my coat and boots, and pulling a baseball cap low over my eyes and wearing sunglasses, I left the apartment, hoping I could maintain my anonymity as I had the previous day. Outside, John, opened the rear passenger door for me.

"Good morning, Dr. Morgan," he said.

"Good morning, John. And I've told you, please call me Drake." I got in the back and once John was inside, we drove off towards the courthouse. I didn't relish having to avoid the reporters and paparazzi, but I'd escaped their notice before and hoped my luck would hold up.

The streets of Manhattan were busy at that time of day and there were a few delays so I arrived a bit later than I would have liked. Still, I managed to make it into the courthouse without being detected. John parked several blocks away and we took a less-traveled route to the side entrance, where he left me after he saw I got in safely. Once inside and past security, I took a place at the back of the courtroom. I was just in time for the judge's arrival but unfortunately, when I sat in the back row, Lisa's brother glanced around and saw me. He did a double take, and then shot me an angry glance that unnerved me a bit. A big man with thick arms, he looked like a dock worker or construction worker instead of a security guard. He was big.

Crap. Now he knew I was there. I'd have to make sure I left before he did so I wouldn't have to face him. I knew from reading the gossip columns about the case that he blamed Derek -- and me -- for Lisa's 'corruption' and felt that if anyone should be going to jail, it was me since Derek was dead and couldn't be punished further. He looked so angry all the time when being interviewed on television, glancing at the camera, like he was trying to call me out. I was glad to have John waiting for me outside the courthouse.

Once court was in session, the first few witnesses -- several police officers -- described their part of the case and how they had gone about collecting evidence. We listened to a forensic team member report on the location of the body, and how Derek's corpse had been buried in a shallow grave just a dozen feet into the woods beside the cabin. Finally, the medical examiner talked about the wounds and esti-mated time of death.

Just before noon, Lisa's brother Jeff got up and left the

courtroom, passing me as he did. When he walked by me, he pointed at me and spoke almost under his breath.

"I'm not done with you," he said and then disappeared outside the door.

The woman beside me, middle aged and clutching her bag on her lap, turned to me. An expression of shock spread on her face that would have been humorous if it had been for any other reason.

"Who *are* you?"

I shook my head. "No one."

I leaned back as the heads of a few people seated around me turned to look my direction.

Damn...

When the court recessed about ten minutes later, I texted John and said I'd be out right away. We'd listened to the final cross-examination of the medical examiner, and the state had asked the judge to recess for lunch while they waited for the next witness.

I stood up and left the courtroom quickly, taking the side door out of the building instead of the front doors. I hoped to avoid any reporters who might be hanging around wanting to talk to observers. I saw John on the street waiting beside the car, and felt a sense of relief flood through me. Before I could reach the car, I felt someone grab my shoulder and jerk me around.

The next thing I knew I was on the ground, seeing stars after a fist slammed into my cheek.

KATE

THE CALL CAME in around 12:10, just as I was mixing some yogurt and fruit for Sophia's lunch.

She was sitting in her highchair beside the kitchen island while I worked on the counter, stirring my leftover vegetable soup and cutting fresh peaches for the yogurt. We'd spent the morning walking through the streets around the apartment, getting fresh air and enjoying the late October sunshine. There had been a break in the rain, so I wanted to take advantage of it.

I picked up my cell and saw that it was from John, Drake's bodyguard, and my stomach felt like it fell through my body to the floor.

"John, what is it?" I said, panic filling me. "Is it Drake? Is he all right?"

"Dr. Morgan is all right but he was attacked outside the courtroom by Lisa Monroe's brother. He lost consciousness for a few moments and so we brought him in to the ER at

New York Presbyterian for a check just to be safe. He's feeling better, but is a little woozy."

"Does he have a concussion?"

"Yes," John said, his voice soft like he didn't want Drake to hear him speaking. "But the neurosurgeon on call in the ER said it was minor and he should be fine."

"What on Earth happened?"

"Apparently, Lisa's brother Jeff hid in a group of people outside the courthouse, waiting for Dr. Morgan to leave. I didn't see him and he cold-cocked Dr. Morgan out of the blue. Dr. Morgan, fell back, hitting his head on the pavement. He's got a real bruise on his cheek and a black eye, plus a cut on the back of his head that required stitches, but otherwise, he's fine."

"Oh, God," I said, covering my mouth with my hand. "What the hell? Why did he do it?"

"I guess he flipped out seeing Drake in the courtroom."

I had wondered if Drake should avoid the courtroom, but had thought he should avoid it more because of publicity -- not because one of Lisa's relatives would become unhinged and attack him.

"I'll come down as soon as I can. Why didn't Drake call me?" I asked, only then thinking of it. "You're sure he's okay and you're not just saying that so I don't panic, right?"

"No, no," John said. "Trust me, he's fine but he's down waiting for an MRI just to be safe. He asked me to call you and said he was sorry that you'd have to miss your session at the studio this afternoon."

"That doesn't matter," I said, shaking my head at Drake's apology. "I can go there any day. I'll call my sitter and see if she can come by on short notice. Luckily, she's a retired nurse and has a really flexible schedule."

"Okay," John said. "He should be out of his MRI within half an hour. The neurologist said he'll probably stay overnight for observation, just to be sure."

"Thanks for calling," I said and glanced around. "Tell Drake I'll be there as soon as I can."

"I will."

I ended the call and immediately dialed Karen Mills, hoping that she was home and available. The phone rang and rang, and I was almost ready to hang up when she answered.

"Hi, Kate, what can I do for you?"

"Sorry to bother you on such short notice, but Drake was attacked and is at the NYP ER. I was hoping you could come by and sit with Sophia while I go and see him."

"Oh," she said and I heard noise in the background. "I'm out shopping, but let's see... I can pay for my things and be there in fifteen minutes, if that's okay. I'm just a few blocks away from your place."

"Great, and thanks so much, Karen. You don't know how much I appreciate having you as a sitter. Seriously. I think I'd go crazy if I couldn't go and see Drake."

"Don't mention it," Karen said. "I'll be there as soon as I can. How is Drake?"

"He's getting an MRI done right now," I replied, quickly

scooping some yogurt in Sophie's dish, mixing in the fruit. "Apparently, he has a mild concussion but they're doing the MRI to rule out anything else."

"Who attacked him?"

"Lisa Monroe's brother," I said and related the story of how he attacked Drake.

"I'm paying now, so I'll be there as soon as possible."

"Thanks again, Karen. You're a gem."

"I know," she said with a light laugh.

I ended the call, feeling relieved that I'd be able to go to the hospital myself as soon as possible and make sure Drake was truly okay.

While I waited for Karen, I spent the next fifteen minutes finishing lunch and then getting ready to go to the hospital. If Drake was going to be in overnight for observation, I wanted to bring him his pajamas and robe as well as slippers so he didn't have to wear the horrible hospital clothing. As well, I tucked his iPad into a backpack along with his toothbrush and fresh boxer briefs and socks.

"Well, Sophie," I said and watched her play on the floor with her toys, "I'll go see Daddy and make sure he's okay."

Karen arrived a few moments later, and when Sophie saw her, she smiled and held up a toy brontosaurus. Karen removed her coat and boots and went right over to Sophie, picking her up and examining the dinosaur.

It warmed me to see how much Karen seemed to enjoy Sophie and Sophie was comfortable with her, too. I could relax when leaving her with Karen.

"Thank you so much, Karen," I said as I pulled on my coat and boots. "I'd have to take Sophie with me if I didn't have you."

"Don't you worry about it," Karen said, taking Sophie over to the living room so she could play. "Go and look after your husband and don't worry about the time. I can make supper for Sophie and me. You can stay as long as you want."

"You're a Godsend," I said and went to Sophie, giving her a quick kiss. I sent Mike a text that I would be going to the hospital and asked if he could give me a ride. He responded that he was outside waiting with the car.

Then, I left the apartment and practically ran down the stairs to the street. Mike was already there with the car door open when I left the building.

"Hi, Mike," I said, so glad that I could rely on him to get me where I needed to go.

"Mrs. Morgan. Sorry to hear about Dr. Morgan. John called me. Dr. Morgan's at New York Presbyterian. We'll be there in fifteen."

"Thanks."

Then I sat back and watched the streets of Manhattan pass outside my window, relieved that Drake's concussion was minor but still on edge. I wouldn't feel truly better until I had seen Drake myself, looked in his eyes and heard him speak.

WE ARRIVED at NYP and I left the car and waited for Mike to join me. He followed me down the halls to Admitting where I asked about Drake's location. They'd put him on a neurology observation ward and so we made our way there. My stomach was in knots as I walked up to his room, wondering what I'd see. The ward had several rooms with beds facing into the central hall where the nursing station was located so the nurses could watch the patients. Drake was in the third room from the end, and was lying on the bed, the head raised slightly, his eyes closed. Beside his room, his bodyguard John stood, his arms crossed. When he saw me and Mike, he came over to us.

"How is he?" I asked, glancing at Drake.

"He's resting quietly. Jeff Monroe is a big man and he has a very powerful punch. Dr. Morgan had no chance to even prepare for it. It knocked him out immediately and he fell like a stone, hitting his head. We're lucky he wasn't hurt even more than he has been."

"Poor Drake," I said, my throat tight.

"I'm so sorry, Mrs. Morgan," John said, his voice truly sorrowful. "I let him down. I didn't see Monroe because he came out early and was standing in a group of pedestrians. I didn't know he'd threatened Dr. Morgan."

"He did?" I asked in shock. "When?"

"He said something to Dr. Morgan when he left the court-room a few moments before the court was recessed."

"Is Jeff Monroe being charged with assault?"

"Yes," John said, nodding his head. "Police took him into custody."

I took a good look at Drake's face through the window and

my heart skipped a beat. Jeff Monroe had hit him hard and his eye was blackening, the tissue around it and on his cheek bruised and red. Drake had a bandage on his head and his arms were on top of the covers. He looked peaceful and I wasn't sure if I should wake him so I went back to the nursing station and waited for one of the nurses to come over to me.

"I'm Kate. Morgan, Dr. Morgan's wife. How is he?"

She gave me the once over, probably expecting someone who looked less like a disheveled mom and more like a wealthy urbanite, given Drake's wealth.

"He's fine," she said dismissively. "We're watching him for twenty-four hours to be on the safe side."

"Can I wake him up or should I let him sleep?"

"Up to you," she said and turned back to her work. I wondered why she was being so short with me. The ward didn't seem particularly busy, but maybe she was just stressed at being responsible for neurology patients. Maybe she didn't like having two big burly bodyguards cluttering up the hallway.

That, or she had an opinion on Drake and it wasn't good.

"Thank you," I said pointedly, but she didn't respond. I tried not to let it get to me. Maybe it was nothing. Maybe I was being too sensitive.

I went back to the observation room, to find that John had left. Mike had taken a chair from the hallway where several were stacked, and was sitting outside Drake's room.

"You're standing guard, are you?"

He nodded. "Yes, ma'am. John took a break while we're here."

I sighed and went inside the small room, sad that Drake and I were in such a predicament that both of us needed bodyguards.

I went closer to Drake's side and watched him quietly for a moment, trying to decide if I should wake him or just let him sleep. I decided to wait to wake him and took the chair by the side of the bed, moving it as close as I could, trying hard not to make too much noise. While I waited, I gazed at him -- at his face and body.

His face was pale against the pillow, and the paleness made his bruise and scrape appear even worse. I played the scene over in my mind of Drake getting punched by Jeff Monroe and it made me tear up to think of how much I loved Drake at that moment, my heart swelling as I listened to him breathe. We were all so vulnerable to those who might hate us. One moment, we're alive and vigorous and the next? Harmed, possibly near death, our lives at risk.

I had never felt in danger before Lisa attacked me and was a bit dismissive when Drake first suggested we get a security team to provide us with protection. While Lisa worried me, I never imagined she would actually harm me. I'm sure Drake felt the same about Lisa's brother, but if there was one thing I had learned, it was that people were unpredictable. You really couldn't know what they might be capable of.

I felt thirsty so I left Drake's room and spoke with Mike. "I'm going to the cafeteria to get a cup of tea. Can I get you something?"

He shook his head. "I'm fine. Just finished lunch when you called."

I left the ward and made my way down to the cafeteria to get a cup of fresh hot tea. While I was there, I picked up a muffin and then went back to the ward, not wanting to leave Drake alone for too long. On my way back, I passed the small gift shop and thought I'd stop in and buy some flowers for Drake's room. He'd only be in overnight, but I thought it might make him feel better to see some flowers. Of course, as I was checking out the various arrangements, I saw a television perched above and to the side of the cash register. The television was tuned to a local news station and on the screen was a picture of Drake lying on the sidewalk, plain clothed police restraining Jeff Monroe, while John bent over an unconscious Drake. It made my gut clench to see how vulnerable he looked and what a scene he'd been in. The headline read, *"Brother of accused killer attacks her ex-lover."* I could only imagine the gossip tabloids once they got hold of the story.

I went back up to the ward and saw that Drake was still asleep, so I tiptoed quietly into the room and sat back down by his bed. I sipped my tea and while he slept, I remembered I needed to send a text to my father and Elaine to let them know what happened to Drake and how he was doing, not wanting them to find out from the news reports they would see on television. I only hoped that they hadn't already seen the story yet, but if they had, I was sure they would have called. It would still be a shock but would be worse if they saw it first on television. I didn't want that. I sent a text to my dad, just in case he was snoozing, as he often did just after lunch. I didn't want to wake him up in that case.

KATE: Just a quick note to let you know that Lisa Monroe's brother Jeff attacked Drake outside the courthouse at noon when the court had been recessed. He's got a mild concussion and is at NYP overnight for observation. I'm here now and he's fine.

My father texted me back right away, so he was awake.

ETHAN: So sorry to hear that, sweetheart. My God, what happened to his bodyguard? I thought Drake hired a security firm to provide you both with security.

KATE: Monroe hid in a group of people and attacked Drake just before he got in the car. It wasn't John's fault.

ETHAN: Well, you give Drake our love and keep us posted about how he's doing.

KATE: I will. Love you.

ETHAN: Love you back XOXOX

I put my cell away and sat back, content just to watch my husband while he slept.

For the next fifteen minutes, I sat by Drake's side and read my texts, checked my email and scanned my Twitter feed. When Drake finally stirred beside me, I put my cell away and waited for his eyes to open.

DRAKE

THE PUNCH CAME out of the blue. I never saw it coming and it hit like nothing I'd ever felt before. One moment, I was focused on getting to the vehicle to go back home to Kate and Sophia and the next, I felt someone grab my shoulder and jerk me around and then...

BAM.

I woke up, lying on my back, my eyes still closed. Around me, I heard shouting and a searing pain ripped through my head. When my vision cleared, my bodyguard John and Lisa's brother Jeff wrestled each other above me.

"I'll get you, you sonofabitch," Monroe shouted. Two plain clothed police officers at the courtroom for testimony intervened, the men grabbing and then holding Monroe back while John bent down to check me out.

"Are you okay?" he asked, peering down at me. He held up his hand in front of my eyes. "How many fingers?"

"Two," I replied, seeing them despite the wooziness I felt. "Vision's a bit blurry though."

"You may have a concussion," John said, shaking his head like he was angry with himself. "Please stay where you are. An ambulance has been dispatched."

As a neurosurgeon, I knew more than enough about the human brain to realize that I should lie still and wait for trained paramedics to arrive who would do a neuro assessment before moving me. I had an intense pain in my head though, and touched the back of my head to feel wetness. It was either from the street or, more likely from the viscosity of the liquid, it was my own blood. I reached my hand up to my eyes and sure enough, they were stained red.

"Damn," I said and showed John. "I've got some kind of cut. Do you have a first aid kit in your vehicle?

"I do," John said and jumped up, rushing to his car. The police dragged Monroe off and a crowd of onlookers gathered to watch my ordeal.

John returned and rummaged through the kit, finding some bandages, which he opened. He turned my head gingerly so he could apply them to the injury on the back of my head.

"My apologies, Dr. Morgan," he said, his voice angry with himself. "I didn't recognize him as a threat. He was with a group of people and peeled off at the last second when he was beside you."

"No, that's okay," I said, touching my cheek. "I didn't see him either. We never thought of him as a real threat in our briefings. His name never came up. You weren't in the court-room, so you couldn't have known he threatened me."

He shook his head again. "Still, I could have been more situationally aware. My apologies."

I waved my hand, trying to allay his concerns. It was an ambush that none of us were expecting.

The ambulance drove up just as John was wrapping gauze around my head to hold the bandage in place. The EMT came over, his kit in his hand, and got a report from John.

"The patient is Dr. Drake Morgan. He was attacked and fell onto his back, hitting his head on the sidewalk. He was unconscious for about two minutes but is now conscious and is oriented to time and place. He's bleeding moderately from a cut, and has some bruising on his cheek."

"Thank you," the EMT said and took over, kneeling beside me. He did a full assessment, asking me questions while the other EMT applied a portable BP monitor and flashed a pen light into my eyes to gauge any neurological impairment.

"That's going to need stitches," the EMT said to me. "If you were unconscious, you should come into the ER for assessment and observation."

I agreed and they brought over the gurney, assisting me onto it. It felt strange for me as someone who was usually on the other side of the gurney to become a patient instead of the one who treated them. I was so used to being the one in control, the one making decisions about a patient's treatment, not the one being controlled and treated. I tried to take a back seat and let them do their jobs.

"Can you call Kate?" I asked John before the EMT closed the ambulance doors.

"Will do, Dr. Morgan. I'll let Mike know as well."

John drove behind the ambulance to New York Presbyterian and followed my gurney to the ER, waiting outside my room while I was examined by the ER nurse and doc. They called in the neuro who was on call, who luckily was in the hospital at the time checking on patients. Dr. Poindexter came in, wearing his white lab coat, his name stitched onto his pocket, and regarded me over a pair of reading glasses.

"Dr. Morgan," he said, a smile on his face. "Fancy meeting you here."

I managed a smile, remembering him as a joker in the first degree. "Yeah, not my usual role in NYP."

He then did a full neuro exam, and after talking through what tests I'd have, he left the room and the nurses finished their own ministrations. For the next hour, I spent time in various hallways waiting for the exam, and having blood work taken. Finally, I was moved up to the neurology observation ward and after getting checked over by the nurses there, I closed my eyes and tried to rest.

Sometime later, I woke, my eyes opening and slowly focusing. Beside me sat Kate, her face pale from worry, her eyes warm.

Beautiful Kate.

"You're here," I said when my vision cleared. I reached out my hand and Kate took it in hers. She stood up, leaning over to kiss my good cheek.

"I am," she said, tears in her eyes.

"How long have you been here?"

"Not long. How are you feeling?"

"Banged up," I replied dryly, forcing a smile to assure her I was okay. "But otherwise fine. Don't worry. My concussion is mild, but to be on the safe side, they'll keep me in overnight."

"I spoke with the nurse," she said and straightened the bed sheet around me. "I brought your pajamas and toothbrush. Are you able to get up and walk around?"

"Oh, sure," I said and moved my bed more upright. "But I have a bitch of a headache that is worse when I get up completely."

"Can't they give you anything for it?"

I shrugged. "Tylenol, but it doesn't work completely. Plus, they don't want to mask any more serious symptoms that might indicate bleeding."

"Oh, Drake," she said and frowned. "I thought they ruled that out with the MRI."

"It can be minimal at first and progress. By tomorrow, I'll have another scan and check before they let me go. Until then, I can't do anything stressful, no reading, no television. Just lie here like a lump and let my brain recover."

"I brought your iPad thinking you could at least read," she said with a frown. "But we can talk."

"We can talk," I replied and smiled at her, squeezing her

hand once more. "Sorry that you're missing your studio time."

"Don't even say that," she said adamantly. "You're the most important thing in the world to me, along with Sophie. I can paint any time."

"Is Sophie with Karen?"

"Yes, she came right over as soon as I called."

"Good," I said and briefly closed my eyes, which felt tired just from being open for that long. "That's good."

"You tired?"

I could tell Kate moved the chair closer to the bed by the sound of it scraping on the floor.

"If you want to sleep, go ahead. I can amuse myself. I have a novel downloaded to my phone I've been meaning to read."

"That sounds good," I said and peered at her from under one eyelid. "I may sleep for a while if you don't mind."

"You sleep if you feel like it. I'm a big girl."

"Okay, nurse," I said with a smile, my eyes closed.

I WOKE SOMETIME LATER, my hearing gradually returning, but consciousness was slow to re-emerge. I felt like I was in a strange time warp, and that everything had slowed down. Finally, I came to completely and took in a deep breath. Kate was still sitting beside me, her eyes on her cell as she must have been reading that book she mentioned. She looked a little better than earlier, probably less worried now that she had a chance to talk to me and realized I was all right. I didn't say anything, just watched her, so glad to have her in my life, unable to think of a life without her and Sophie.

Every day when I worked in the hospital, and especially after working on the trauma team in California, I saw the results of the harm that could come to humans and the brain, either from diseases like cancer and epilepsy, or from accidents and violence. I never thought it would be me on the receiving end, having been lulled into complacency from a lifetime of freedom from serious injury.

After my father died in a plane crash, some of that sense of invincibility disappeared, but I still felt it was so unlikely, you couldn't change the way you lived to prevent something like a death in a plane crash. My false sense of my ability to protect my loved ones died when Kate was attacked, and I had felt vulnerable for a long time after, my faith in my own ability to deal with the risks in life eroded. That was why I hired bodyguards for Kate and myself. But I never suspected I would really become a target. I had this vague sense that I could become one, but it was just an overabundance of caution rather than a real sense of personal danger.

Now, even that was gone.

I thought about Monroe. He seemed irrational and unable to see that his sister had been found guilty of attempted murder, and was now facing a murder charge. Surely by now he must have realized she was a danger, and was a sociopath. Was he that blinded by his blood ties to her that he couldn't see it? Someone like Lisa went through life lying and cheating those around her. Sure, she might flatter them at first, get them on her side, and could be charming, but soon, the lies would start, the manipulation and then the harm. Her brother seemed unable to see clearly that this was on Lisa, not me or Derek Richardson. She had been an adult when she became involved with Richardson and with me.

It was her who did harm, not us.

I took in a deep breath and stretched and Kate realized that I was awake. She glanced over at me, her expression softening immediately. She slipped her cell into her pocket and stood up, leaning over to give me a kiss. Her lips pressed against mine and she held my face -- the good side of my face -- in her hand.

"You're awake."

"I am." I glanced at the clock on the wall. About thirty minutes had passed since I fell asleep.

For the rest of the afternoon, I either snoozed or talked with Kate about everything -- the trial, the attack, and my injury. By the time the workers started to bring dinner around, Kate had been with me for several hours.

"Do you want to get something for yourself and bring it up here?"

"I do," she said and left me alone. The worker brought in my tray and I moved the head of my bed up a bit more, checking under the domes to see what was for supper.

A lump of what looked like meatloaf, some pasty mashed potatoes, some mixed vegetables, and a cup of vanilla pudding. It looked like what I thought I'd get in prison, but my stomach grumbled. I'd missed lunch and was hungry.

I waited as long as I could for Kate to return but realized there was a limit to how long food like that would stay palatable and cold meatloaf was not something I wanted to risk. I ate my meal, and when Kate returned with a sandwich, some chocolate milk and cookies in hand, I was half done.

"What have you got?" she asked and peered at my tray. When she made a face at the food, I laughed.

"You'd never survive working at a hospital. Or living in a prison."

We ate together and talked more about the trial and the attack. It made me tired and my headache worsened.

"I should turn the lights down and rest," I said, grimacing at the pain.

"Do you want me to call the nurse?" she asked, frowning. "Maybe you need more pain meds."

"No, that's okay," I said and closed my eyes. Kate turned off the main overhead light and so the only light coming in was through the window. "I just need to close my eyes for a while."

For the rest of the evening, Kate sat with me and when I felt like it, I slept and when I woke, we talked. Finally, at around eight at night, Kate was ready to go back home.

"Sophie's already in bed," Kate said to me as she pulled my covers up and tucked them in around me. "I'll go home now so Karen can go to her own house. She'll come back tomorrow if I need her. When do you think you'll be discharged?"

I shrugged. "They'll do a follow-up scan and if that's okay, they'll discharge me after lunch. I'll get John to give me a ride home. Then I'll just have to take it easy for a while. Maybe a week to ten days, depending."

Kate bent over the bed and kisses me tenderly, her hands cupping my face.

"I hate to leave you," she said, her eyes moist. "We haven't been apart at night since I was in the hospital and I don't like it."

"Text me when you get into bed," I said and squeezed her arm. She kissed me again, and then got her coat and waved to me when she left the room, her expression sad.

I didn't like being separated from Kate either, but it was for the best. The knowledge that I'd be going home in the morning comforted me so that I was able to close my eyes and go to sleep.

I WOKE up around eleven to the sound of my cell phone dinging. I wasn't supposed to be using my cell for any work, but I decided I wanted to read Kate's text.

KATE: *Hey, you. I miss you in my bed Dr. Dangerous.*

DRAKE: *Dr. Dangerous? They're calling me that now? I'm not at all dangerous. Quite the opposite.*

KATE: *No, you're not. You're delicious. Delectable. Delightful. You're dangerous the way Rocky Road ice cream is dangerous -- you can't help but want more more more.*

DRAKE: *Mmmm. Rocky Road ice cream... Damn. Now*

you've got me craving ice cream. I wonder if John would go out on an ice cream run for me.

KATE: *You must be feeling better if you're hungry.*

DRAKE: *I always feel better after talking to you, Ms. Bennet. Did I tell you lately that I love you?*

KATE: *You did earlier today but you can tell me again if it pleases you.*

DRAKE: *It pleases me very much. I love you, Mrs. Morgan. Sleep tight. See you tomorrow.*

KATE: *I love you, Dr. Morgan. Don't let the bedbugs bite.*

DRAKE: *Give Sophie a hug and kiss from me and tell her that her daddy loves her very much.*

KATE: *I will. Good night my love.*

DRAKE: *Good night to you, my love.*

I smiled, feeling all warm and fuzzy from the conversation with Kate. Knowing that she was happy, and that she loved me made it easy to just close my eyes and drift off.

And so I did.

KATE

DRAKE CAME home from the hospital and after ten days of taking it easy, lying on the sofa, sleeping and occasionally watching television, he was almost back to normal. Because of the attack, Drake's testimony was delayed so he could recover. It meant that he would be attending court a few days before the end of the trial. We had hoped the judge would allow him to give his testimony in private due to the stress of a courtroom appearance, but that wasn't granted because a physician found he was healthy enough to appear in person.

On the day before his testimony, he went in to meet with the assistant district attorney prosecuting the case to go over the potential questions she would ask and those the defense would likely be asking.

Both of us knew the cross-examination by the defense lawyer wouldn't be pleasant.

He got dressed in business casual, and pulled on his coat on his way out. I went to him and slipped my arms around him before he left. He was preoccupied with the trial and I wanted to remind him that soon, all this would be over. That he had a loving wife and baby – and a young son to look forward to spending time with.

"Ah, Ms. Bennet," he said when he finally focused on me. "How glad I am to have you."

We kissed and he pulled me tightly against his body, which was warm and strong.

"This will soon be over. We'll look back and be glad that we got through it. One day, when we're in the Bahamas, we'll be lying on the beach beside each other, the sun on our faces, Sophie playing in the sand, and we'll smile at each other and remember this moment."

He kissed me. "I hope so. It better happen, because that vision is helping me get through today and tomorrow. I'm sure tomorrow's going to be a real shit-show, with Lisa's attorney grilling me about what an exploitative sadist I am to force poor innocent Lisa into a sexual relationship of dominance and submission."

"She'll try, but I hope the ADA is competent enough to re-direct the jury to see what a manipulative woman Lisa is and that she planned and carried out a cold-blooded murder with the help of Jones."

"I hope so," Drake said and sighed. For a moment, we stood in the embrace, enjoying the warmth of each other's bodies.

"I better go," he said finally and pulled out of my arms with clear reluctance. "I'll be back as soon as I can. Maybe this afternoon we can go out for a walk in Central Park. It looks like a nice sunny day. Might be one of the last ones we'll get before the real cold weather starts."

"Sounds good," I said and watched as he went down the stairs to the front door of the building. I closed and locked the door and then went to the bay window and watched while Drake got into the vehicle John had waiting at the front. As they drove off, I hoped that the stress wasn't too much for Drake and was once again angry that the judge didn't agree to let Drake do all this in private. It gave me a bad sense that the judge might be pre-disposed to blame Drake and Derek in part for Lisa's actions.

I went back to the living room where Sophie played on the floor with her tiny town people. The television was tuned to a children's show and I took the remote control, selecting a local news station to see if they were covering the trial. Sure enough, at the top of the hour when the news update came on, the announcers talked together about the trial, going over the previous day's testimony by defense witnesses, who all claimed that Lisa was a poor battered woman who was led down the path of evil by the men in her life who variously abused and exploited her innocence.

I was sickened to hear them paint this picture of her because it diminished real cases where this was the truth. There were battered women who occasionally took the law into their own hands to stop their abuser but this was clearly not the case with Lisa. She planned to kill Derek. The police were certain of it, and there was evidence to prove that. This charade about her being misled by Derek and Drake and killing Derek to protect herself was meant to hurt Drake -- that was certain. Her letter said as much. She wanted to punish Drake for spurning her. She probably knew she would be found guilty and sentenced to life without chance of parole for a very long time and so wanted to harm Drake as much as she could in the process.

Of course, they also talked about the attack on Drake and how his testimony had to be delayed because of his concussion. That meant that everyone who followed the trial and was interested could go to the courthouse and hear his testimony. I could only imagine it would be almost impossible to find a seat in the courtroom due to all the curious who wanted to watch Doctor Dangerous tell the court about his relationship with murdered Derek Richardson and accused Lisa Monroe.

Lisa's brother, Jeff, was released on bail but was prohibited from coming within one hundred feet of Drake due to a restraining order Lara filed on Drake's behalf. That meant at least he wouldn't be in the courtroom or anywhere near the courthouse when Drake arrived to give his testimony. He also had to stay that far away from our apartment, which made me feel somewhat safer, but there was no telling whether the man would ignore the restraining order.

I sat and listened to the two female reporters talking about the trial and the public interest in the case and thought how it had already changed Drake's life so much. It was unfair in the extreme. The report showed images from the attack on Drake taken by witnesses who were at the scene, including one of Drake lying on his back, clearly unconscious and a crazed Monroe being held back by two plain clothed police officers.

The news station just loved the footage from one bystander

who videotaped the aftermath and sent in the footage. During the first days after the attack, we saw endless loops of Monroe struggling with police while John knelt to tend to Drake and other police on scene tried to move onlookers back. Then the ambulance arriving and tending to Drake, eventually rolling him into the ambulance for all the world to see, a bandage on his cheek and head and as well as a neck brace. Then, of course, they skipped to a grainy image which was poorly lit, featuring a bound Lisa apparently being menaced by the pot-bellied hairy man who was definitely not Drake.

Even the two announcers commented that the image they had of Drake in his swim trunks did not resemble the man in the video and finally, I felt like maybe there was a crack in the narrative that it was Drake in that video. I was hopeful, but I doubted anyone who mattered in the fellowship program at NYU or in the administration at NYP would care about the distinction. Nor would board members and funders at the foundation or corporation.

Simply put, Drake was bad news. No one wanted to be associated with him, except for the O'Rileys and Dave Mills.

They were the only remaining friends that Drake had. The rest had slipped away and had not contacted Drake to wish him well.

So much for friends...

My cell rang and I picked it up to check the call display.

It was my father.

"How's Drake? I understand they're going forward with his testimony tomorrow."

I sighed. "He's better physically, but this will be stressful. I'm so angry at the judge for not allowing Drake to give his testimony in private so he didn't have to go to court. They've done it before for other witnesses, but the judge wasn't sympathetic."

"I know the judge," my father said, an acid tone in his voice. "Hogan. A bit of a stickler and is especially by the books with any crimes involving sex."

"But the crime didn't involve sex. It was a straight-up murder of Derek so Lisa and Jones could live in his cabin and use his money."

"I know, sweetheart, but because of the BDSM angle, the forces of righteousness are out in droves, their side claiming this case as their own, using it to advance their own agenda."

"It makes me sick. You know that those who are the strongest opponents to this kind of thing often are fighting a battle in themselves and the issue allows them to feel better about their own weaknesses. You know, the pastor who rails against homosexual marriage and then is caught with a male prostitute..."

"I know that all too well, having presided over a few cases in my time. It's sad that this happens, but it does. I'm sure Drake will do fine at the trial. He's a pretty cool cucumber."

"He was just attacked and has a concussion. His reputation has been smeared and he's lost most of what he loves -- his job at NYP, his fellowship, his position on the board of his foundation and corporation..."

"Things will get back to normal. Give it time."

I sighed. Of course, he was right.

We then spoke about a trip to the Bahamas as a family. I really couldn't wait to get away from Manhattan's grey cloudy days and drizzle, and go somewhere with sunshine, white sand beaches and warm air.

"I want to go back to the British Colonial Hilton in Nassau so Drake and I can relive our first weekend together."

"The weekend you two broke up," he said, a smile in his voice. "Here I thought I was bringing you two young people together and I find out you broke up already. Believe me, I was kicking myself."

"You did the right thing. It was me who did the wrong thing by listening to Dawn and not talking to Drake about it."

"The important thing is that you two are together, and in love, and have a life together with a real future. This trial is temporary. Things will eventually come to a new normal."

"I hope so," I said.

He gave me an update on Heath and then we said goodbye.

I sat on the sofa and watched Sophie chattering away with her toys while I muted the news report. I needed something to divert my mind from the trial. I hadn't been at my studio for several days, not wanting to leave Drake to care for Sophie in case she was difficult and he was stressed following the preparation for the trial. I could call Karen Mills and see if she could come by, but hoped that Drake wouldn't mind. My canvas and paints were at the studio in Chelsea so I couldn't work on them at home.

I called Karen, but her phone went right to voice mail, so I left a message asking if she would be available later today to take Sophie to her place so Drake could have the afternoon to himself. We had a portable playpen with a soft cushioned bottom and it could double as a bed.

Then I waited for Drake to come home, my gut in a knot about how the questioning would go and whether Drake would be overly stressed about it. Drake's neurologist warned him not to do anything that caused too much stress or his blood pressure to rise too much. Of course, as a neurosurgeon, Drake already knew that, but apparently, the judge didn't care that the courtroom might be stressful. I felt like I was going to go crazy waiting to find out how things were going, so I texted Drake to check on him.

KATE: *How are you? What are you doing?*

DRAKE: *I'm on my way to Lara's office to meet with her.*

KATE: *You never said you were going to Lara's. Isn't that too much stress? I'm worried about you.*

DRAKE: *I'm fine, my love. Don't worry about me. Lara just wants to go over the questions so we can be prepared.*

KATE: *That damn judge should have let you do this in private.*

DRAKE: *This will all be over tomorrow afternoon and we can forget about all of it. Think about Nassau.*

KATE: *Okay. How long will you be? Are you going to have lunch with Lara?*

DRAKE: *No. She has a lunch meeting. We're just meeting for fifteen minutes before.*

KATE: *Okay. I asked Karen Mills to take Sophie for a few hours this afternoon so I can go to the studio. I need to get out of the house because all I can do is think of the trial.*

DRAKE: *Kate, I'm fine. Sophie can stay with me. Really, I feel great. No headache. I'm totally chill, brah.*

KATE: *Brah??? Have you been talking to Jules? :)*

DRAKE: *No, actually. Just a dude who was in the waiting room with me. I asked him if my tie was on straight before I went into the ADA's office and that I was nervous. He said, 'You look totally chill, brah.'*

KATE: *OMG, that's a keeper. I'm going to use that the next time you look stressed. Chill, brah! Here I thought it was Bro...*

DRAKE: *Bro is so GenX. Get with it. This is the new Millennium. It's brah.*

KATE: *Guilty as charged. I'll see you when you get home. We can have lunch and relax, whatever happens. I still want Karen to take Sophie out so you can rest all afternoon.*

DRAKE: *If she can't, no problem. I'm fine. Really, Kate.*

KATE: *Okay. See you soon. I love you.*

DRAKE: *I love you, too.*

I put my cell away and tried to push my worries about Drake into the back of my mind, but it was hard. I felt all fidgety, waiting for Karen to call me back with her answer.

Finally, about fifteen minutes later, she did.

"Hi, Kate. I got your message," she said. "I can take Sophie, no problem. I'll come by at about two o'clock and take her for a walk through the park before putting her down for a nap at my place if that works for you. Poor Drake..."

"I know," I said, my sense of relief strong that Drake could spend the afternoon alone. "He says he's okay, but he's such a stoic and rarely lets anything show, but I know this is really upsetting to him. He's paid such a high price."

"Well, don't you worry about it. I'll be happy to take Sophie so you can go to the studio and Drake can rest. His testimony is tomorrow, right?"

I sighed. "Yes, unfortunately. But at least once it's done, we can move on."

"I heard a report on television today. The local station is really running with the salacious content. It's disgusting."

"I know," I said. "I guess it sells ad copy so what can you expect?"

"Exactly. See you around two o'clock?"

"Great."

I hung up, and sighed, happy that I'd be able to go to the studio and escape all the worries for a few hours. I'd be able to concentrate knowing that Drake could just lie on the sofa and sleep if he wanted, recover from the morning. He sounded in good spirits, but you never knew...

Of course, it was then that a news report came on with a breaking news banner. I turned up the volume, only to see the announcer talking about a video that had been released of Drake and some unknown woman that was too violent to put on television, but the announcer said it was available online for anyone who wanted to see it for themselves.

I knew at that moment that the video of Sunita and Drake had been released. Now that was going to make everything harder because there was no way to deny Drake had spanked and caned her and she had the welts on her leg and red ass to prove it.

Now, it was there for all the world to see...

DRAKE

My morning with Assistant District Attorney Canmore went as well as could be expected. She was sharp as a tack of course, and had won pretty much every case she tried with the exception of a few high-profile murder cases of very wealthy men. Lisa's family had connections in the NYPD, but those couldn't help her deny the evidence, since it was that very police department who provided it. And the evidence was damning. According to Canmore, the evidence was so good, so damning, that it was pretty much an open and shut case.

"Usually, I don't like to say that because it sounds arrogant and circumstances can always change on a moment's notice, but if there was ever one, this case is. We have emails, we have bank records, we have forensic evidence, we have a body, and we have the confession of one of the two suspects. The only thing the defense has is mitigating circumstances that might reduce her sentence, but she won't get off. No way."

"I hope so," I said, wanting to believe she was right but still having this low-level sense of doom hanging over me.

"Trust me," she said and waved her hand dismissively. "I've been doing this for years. The jury will convict on the evidence. She'll either spend 10 extra years or the rest of her life in jail. There's no way she'll be found innocent."

We spent the hour allotted to us going over the questions she would be asking and potential cross-examination questions the defense lawyer might ask. Of course, at the top of the list were questions about my relationship with Derek Richardson, how I met Lisa and how we became involved. She focused a lot on my refusal to continue the relationship because I didn't really enjoy exhibitionism and found a new submissive. I then talked about the next time I saw Lisa at NYU and recounted our meetings, how I had sought advice from Derek and how I had tried to withdraw from the fellowship program because of her attempts to force a relationship on me.

"Much of this was covered in her earlier trial," I said.

"This is a whole new case. The jury hasn't heard this testimony, or if they have read about it, they need to hear it again coming from you. You're a very believable witness, from what I saw of the videos of Lisa's earlier trial. Once the jury sees the evidence about Lisa and Jones, their plotting together to kill Richardson, they'll never trust a word that comes out of her mouth about your relationship."

"I hope so. She's pretty charismatic."

"All sociopaths are. Or in her case, psychopaths."

"Do you think she's a psychopath?"

"I do," she said. "Psychopath, sociopath, however you define it, she's on the far end of the spectrum, willing to kill or have others kill to achieve her goals. She belongs behind bars and I have every confidence that a jury will want to keep her there for as long as possible. Her story about past abuse, and her claim that she was merely defending herself against a violent lover who was jealous are laughable on its face."

I shrugged, willing to let the expert draw conclusions about the win-ability of the case. I had no idea, having not followed criminal cases at all during my lifetime.

When we were finished, I shook her hand and she led me to the door to the office. "Take the back hallway. Meet your guy outside the rear entrance. There'll be reporters outside hoping to get a look at anyone from the case. Given Monroe's crazy family, who knows what you might face."

"Good idea," I said and took out my cell. "I'll text my security guy to take the car around back."

We said goodbye and I wandered down the hallways outside Canmore's offices and waited out back, peering through a window to watch and see when John arrived with the car. Finally assured that the coast was clear, I got into the car and we drove off. I was planning to go right home but on the way, I got a text from Lara.

LARA: Drake, come over and meet with me for a few minutes this morning when you're done with the ADA.

DRAKE: Sure. I was on my way home but I'll get my driver to swing by your office. What's up?

LARA: Just want to go over things before you go to the court-

house tomorrow.

DRAKE: Okay.

I put my cell away and told John to take me to Lara's offices for a last-minute meeting. We changed course, turning around towards her building, but before we got there, Kate texted me, wondering how things were going. I responded and let her know I was going to Lara's for a meeting, promising to return as soon as I could.

She wanted to go to her studio that afternoon, and had asked Karen Mills to come and pick up Sophia so I could rest all afternoon. I tried to tell her she didn't need Karen -- that I was fine and could care for Sophie on my own, but Kate seemed really determined so I gave in. To be honest, I was starting to feel a little tired, the first buzz of a headache starting, but I didn't want to renege on my meeting with Lara so I pushed on.

Part of me admonished myself for doing so -- if I had been my own patient, I'd give myself hell for trying to do too much. It was probably a good thing that Kate had asked Karen to take Sophie for the afternoon. Kate needed a break and some creative time to lose herself and forget the trial. I needed to sleep.

We arrived at Lara's building and I went inside, riding the elevator up to her floor and saying hello to the receptionist. She stood and led me right into the small boardroom down the hallway.

Lara was already inside, a couple of files opened on the table.

"Drake, there you are, you poor man," she said and came

over to me, kissing my cheek and squeezing my shoulder. "You look a bit pasty. Are you sure you're feeling good enough to do this? We won't take long, I promise you."

"I'm fine," I said although I was feeling pretty rough. "What did you want to go over?"

"Have a seat," Lara said and pointed to the chairs. "Can I get Sarah to bring you some coffee or water?"

"No, that's fine," I said, impatient to get this meeting over. Then, I reconsidered. "Actually, can she bring me some water? I need to take a painkiller. I have a headache brewing."

"I'm sorry, Drake," Lara said, shaking her head. "We could have Skyped. I should have realized this would be too much."

"No, no," I said, holding my hand out. "I'll be fine. Just the water would be great."

"Okay," Lara said and used her cell, texting her staff about the water. "We'll be fifteen minutes, no more."

One of Lara's assistants came in and placed a bottle of water in front of me, a cup of coffee in front of Lara, then she closed the door behind her as she left Lara and I alone. I took out a few pills that I'd slipped into my jacket inner pocket, and drank down some water. Hopefully, they'd kick in within the hour and I'd head off a worse headache. I didn't want Kate worrying or changing her plans.

Lara and I went over my testimony, what Canmore and I discussed in our meeting earlier, and she coached me on how to frame my experiences in the BDSM community.

"You have to know that's all anyone will be able to focus on once it's been brought up. People will be curious and suspicious about it and what you like and why you became involved."

I nodded, for Lara and I had gone over this for the previous trial, but I supposed she was only trying to make sure I was as ready as I could be for this trial. She wanted to make sure that I phrased it right and didn't make myself look bad in the way I described my interest in bondage and dominance.

"The average person on the street knows about kink either through those books or via porn involving spanking or maybe hair pulling, rough sex. That, or they're curious and have seen some more intense porn, illegal porn. We don't want you to get mixed up into that at all. Really focus on how you were focused on the woman's pleasure."

"It's the truth," I said a bit defensively.

"I know it, and you know it, and your past partners know it, but the defense will try to frame it like you were controlling Lisa and she was only doing what you demanded of her."

"In her mind," I said. "There's no evidence. Whatever evidence they had at the start has been discounted."

"A lie gets half way around the world before the truth pulls on its shoes. All they'll remember is reading salacious extracts from the fake letters she and Jones concocted to make it look like you were the one controlling everything."

I sighed heavily and leaned back, closing my eyes and rubbing my temples. The pain killer hadn't yet kicked in and I was feeling pretty brain-fogged from the headache.

I opened my eyes and saw Lara watching me.

"Are you up for this? We could file for a further delay."

I shook my head. "No, that's fine. I'll be better tomorrow after a good night's sleep." I forced a smile and she finally narrowed her eyes.

"Drake Morgan, don't try to be a hero," she said, her voice low. "It will do no one any good if you pass out on the stand."

"You mean, it wouldn't get me any sympathy votes on the jury?" I cracked, grinning at the expression on her face.

"If you were my sub, I'd spank your ass," she replied finally, grinning herself. "Go home. Get some sleep. This will all be over soon and you can move on."

"I hope so," I said and stood, buttoning my jacket. "I'm just about at my wit's end with this trial and the fallout. I was hoping to start back on my Fellowship in January, but with all the publicity, I may put it off until next fall."

Lara stood and took my arm, leading me to the door to her office. "That's too bad, Drake. There will still be a fellowship program next year. There will still be pediatric neurosurgeon patients the following year. Try to keep your mind on the future and soon enough, this will pass and be nothing but a bad memory."

I kissed her cheek lightly and left her office, throwing on my coat and messaging John to come and get me.

I ARRIVED HOME JUST after noon, and trudged up the stairs to the apartment after telling John I wouldn't be going out until tomorrow. He'd likely set up a place to watch the building, coordinating with other members of the security team providing us 24/7 protection. It was probably overkill, but given what happened to both Kate and me, I didn't want to spare any expense.

I opened the door to the apartment to find Kate standing in front of the television in the living room, the remote in her hand, and Sophie at her feet playing with toys. Kate turned to me and raised her eyebrows.

"What?" I asked, hanging up my coat and shucking off my boots. "You look like you've seen a ghost. Something bad on the news?"

"A video."

"Another one? Does this guy have a pot belly and hairy back?"

"No," she said, her voice soft. "This one is you. You and Sunita."

Adrenaline jolted through my body. "What?"

I went to where she was standing and watched the television screen. On it, a still shot from a grainy video, displaying me with a woman who was obviously Sunita. She was wearing a leather lace up bustier, thin black lace panties, was blindfolded and had her hands tied above her head. On the fronts of her thighs were long red stripes from the cane I had used with her. It was the biggest regret of my life and I knew I'd never live it down. Once the public saw that video, they'd think the worst of me. All the subsequent submissives who swore on a stack of bibles that I wasn't a sadist would be meaningless.

"Fucking *great*," I said, exasperated. I watched with Kate, seeing myself on the screen, wearing nothing but a pair of low-slung leather pants with a thick black leather belt. My chest was bare and I was holding a cane, which was a common implement of discipline in the BDSM world. Lara had suspected I was a sadist and wanted to give me the opportunity to explore it, but it hadn't done anything sexual for me. In fact, it repulsed me. It turned off my desire rather than inflaming it.

None of that would matter now that this video had been released. Someone was trying their best to help Lisa and harm me. I wasn't sure who, but Sunita must have felt she was doing a good deed by turning that video over to the press. She probably made a pretty penny off it as well. If I had been that kind of person, I might have paid a whole lot more to stop the video from being played, but the station hadn't come to either me or my lawyer to make the offer.

I texted Lara, although I knew she was I a meeting.

DRAKE: The Sunita video is being played on the internet and talked about on a local TV station.

I waited, Kate and I standing there mute while the video of me caning Sunita played in a loop, the camera focusing on her blindfolded and gagged face while I struck her repeatedly.

My cell dinged and I checked my messages.

LARA: Oh, God... Usually, the station would have come to me for comment or the chance to kill the story with a nice juicy payment, but I guess not.

Lara was right. If we had known that the station had the video, we could have stopped the video from going public.

Obviously, the news station felt the video would earn them much more in advertising dollars and publicity than any money I could pay them to stop its release.

DRAKE: *What is our response?*

LARA: *I'm busy but I'll call you later. Take it easy, Drake. I'll take care of this. Don't stress too much, for your sake. You don't need anything else on top of what you already have on your plate. I don't want you stroking out over this.*

Again, Lara was the voice of wisdom.

DRAKE: *You're right of course. I'll shut off the television and relax. You can call me with anything you think I need to know.*

LARA: *Good man. Go, and hug your baby. Kiss Kate. Sleep.*

I put my cell away and turned off the computer and the television as Lara suggested.

"What are you doing?" Kate asked, wide-eyed.

"I'm taking my lawyer's advice and turning off the computer and television. I don't need this," I said and went to her, my hands cupping her face, which was pale with concern. "Neither of us need this. Lara will formulate a response. You go to your studio and paint, and I'll rest while Karen takes Sophie for the afternoon. This will all soon be over and we'll be back to the way things were before all this happened."

I kissed Kate and she closed her eyes and leaned into my arms.

"You're right," she said softly.

I hoped I was.

KATE and I ate a quiet lunch, our talk limited to our planned trip to Bahamas, to the hotel we stayed at that first weekend.

"I want to go scuba diving again," Kate said, smiling. "This time, maybe we should buy me a proper wetsuit so we won't have any problems with overheating."

I smiled. "I still remember how hard it made me to help you squeeze those breasts into that children's suit."

Kate smiled, a gleam in her eyes. "Dr. Morgan, by the way you're talking about that, I might think you love me only because of my breasts and not because of my mind or heart."

"Mind, heart, breasts," I said and reached over to stroke her cheek. "I love it all."

"I love you, Dr. Morgan. Every inch of you."

"Don't talk like that or I won't be able to rest this afternoon," I said. "I really should wait two weeks before we start up again."

"I'm sorry," she said and made a mock pout. "I don't want to make it worse."

"You could never make it worse," I said and leaned over to kiss her.

For the next two hours, while we waited for Karen Mills to arrive, we sat on the sofa with music playing and watched Sophie play with her toys on the living room carpet. We studiously avoided talking about the video or the case. It wasn't easy. I know both our minds were trying hard to go back to both, just because it was such a big looming part of our lives, but the music did help soothe me.

My cell rang when Kate was in the bathroom getting things ready for Karen. I checked the call display and saw that it was Dave.

"Hey, how are you?"

"Fine, all things considered. What's up?"

He hesitated. "I hate to be the bearer of bad news, but I can't delay it any longer. Three of our big funders cancelled their support today in the wake of the recent publicity. That takes a huge chunk of our revenues. We have to cancel a number of projects we had planned in the future and maybe cut short a few projects in the works right now if we can't find replacement funding."

I sighed. "Let me guess. Fundraising hasn't been all that stellar since this all started."

"In fact," Dave said, his voice soft. "We stopped new outreach and have focused on existing funders, to gauge their support."

"Why did you stop new outreach?"

"Our volunteers were getting hung up on and doors slammed in their faces at an unprecedented rate as soon as the title of the Foundation was mentioned. We had to stop sending them out. They get disheartened when they have to face that kind of rejection."

"What the hell happened?" I rubbed my forehead, a slight headache percolating.

"I guess that tell-all in the press about you and your father's foundation really did it. People hear Dr. Morgan and right away think of you. Even when we say you're no longer on the board of directors, the fact that you started the foundation gets in the way."

I sighed heavily. "What percent of our funding do we still have?"

Dave flipped some papers and then cleared his throat. "Thirty-five percent."

"Thirty-five percent?" I was shocked. That was a lot of money lost.

"Yes, we had to cancel about a dozen existing and future projects as a result."

I closed my eyes. "What's your recommendation, Dave? What should I do?"

There was a silence on the line for a moment. "I'd close it down. If you want, we can start another charity offshore that is in no way connected to you or Liam and still do the same work but you won't get the tax benefits of doing it in the US. But this way, you won't be named or involved other than as an anonymous funder."

I sighed. "Okay. Do what you have to. I don't care about the tax benefits. I just want to carry on what my father started. Do it. I'll be anonymous but will provide the lion's share of the funding to start. I want the foundation to do the same work that my father's did. You'll be in charge."

"Consider it done. It'll take a few months to get everything shut down at the foundation and restarted in a new charity."

"That's fine. I have nothing but time, considering I'm not working."

I hung up, and when Kate came back into the room, she looked so pleased that I didn't want to tell her the content of the conversation with Dave. I'd tell her later, when the time was right.

Finally, Karen arrived and took Sophie for the afternoon.

"We're going to walk through Central Park for some fresh air and when we get to my place, she'll have a sleep. I'll bring her back before supper."

"Sounds good," I said and waved at Sophie when the two of them left the apartment. Kate went into the office to get a few items she needed for the painting and then she was gone as well.

I was left alone, but try as I might, sleep eluded me. Instead, I lay on my back on the sofa and worried about the future, uncertain whether our lives would ever truly recover from this whole mess, and most of all, I was deeply saddened that I had to close the foundation. It kept my father's name alive but now, my name -- and my connection with the whole Lisa Monroe case -- had destroyed both.

KATE

OF COURSE, as soon as I got to the studio, I put on my small television so I could watch the news coverage of the trial. While it was good that Drake had decided not to follow the trial anymore because of his concussion and the stress doing so would cause, I couldn't stay away. I needed to know what was being said about Drake in the press so I could know how to deal with Drake and any fallout.

At the top of the hour, the image was displayed as the announcer went over the contents of the video, talking about how the video would seem to support Lisa Monroe's contention that she was an abused woman who had been controlled by two abusive older men.

How could they get it so wrong?

If anything, it was Lisa who manipulated Derek and Drake to get what she wanted. Lara had done some sleuthing about Lisa's past and family life. She wanted to be with rich older men who could provide her with the lifestyle she wanted. Her uncle was a police officer in the NYPD, but her mother had been divorced and impoverished, who traded on her beauty to find a man who would support her. Lisa wanted to find a rich man, and while she had ambitions to be a surgeon, they were more the result of her experiences with Drake than some inherent desire. She was smart enough to make it into medical school, and then be accepted into a neurosurgery residency, but her unstable mental health, her erotomania, got in the way.

According to police reports, Lisa and Jones kidnapped and held Derek prisoner with the idea of taking as much of his wealth as they could so they could live the way they wanted. The only thing that stopped Lisa from realizing her plan was her hatred and jealousy of me and her momentary loss of control when she struck me with the rental car. Sure, she had planned on it from the time she learned that Drake had gone to the administration about her, wanting to harm him through me, but until then, she really honestly thought she could coerce him into having a relationship with her. When she realized she couldn't she turned to plan B, which was to extort money from Derek, or worse, steal it outright and then kill him, covering up his death by making it seem he'd left the US for Singapore - which he had spoken to friends about doing anyway.

Based on what the homicide detective told Drake, when Drake contacted Derek about Lisa, concerned about her behavior towards him and that she was mentally unstable, Derek had reconnected with Lisa out of concern for her. Lisa tried to get back together with Derek because she felt she was making no headway with Drake. She and Derek had become involved again briefly, but when Derek began having problems with her accepting their new relationship, he had tried to break up with her.

In testimony given before his suicide, Jones said that Lisa had lured Derek out to the cabin and she and Jones kept him tied up and forced him to provide Lisa with his bank account information so she could transfer money to her accounts. When he tried to escape, Jones had fought him and that was the act that led to his death, with both of them attacking him with knives and a hammer. But she had been planning to stage his move to Singapore and had sent texts from his cell to his lawyers and accountant to that effect. She had always planned on killing him and when Derek finally realized it, he fought to save his own life but had ended up losing it instead.

Then, when Jones flipped on her, testifying against her, she coerced him into killing himself, encouraging him to do it.

That was the prosecutor's theory of the case, which the police detectives in charge of the case shared.

Lisa was a psychopath.

I sighed and switched the channel, watching a different report, my paints and canvas neglected. I had come to the studio to get away from the case and the news, but I was trapped by a terrible curiosity. I needed to know how the public would respond to the video and couldn't imagine it would be easy for Drake to overcome it. Those images of Sunita's bruised and battered thighs and calves were seared into my memory and most likely those of the public who witnessed them. The one incongruous detail was that during the beating, Sunita never cried out. The brief clip of the video I'd seen online showed her taking the caning without complaint. She had been used to it -- enough so that she kept quiet. Lara said that her former Master had trained her that if she cried out, he would strike even harder so she trained herself to be quiet and absorb the pain. She really was a masochist. To her, the pain was a reward or maybe a diversion from some deeper pain. She claimed she had been abused as a child and had become aroused by punishment.

I cringed as I watched the cane strike again and again, surprised that the local television channel was showing it, but any sexualized body parts were blurred out as was Sunita's face. The full video was available online at the station's website. To preserve their viewer's sensitivity, the channel had elected to only show a still image from the video but probably thousands of people had watched the full video.

"The video shows Dr. Drake Morgan, known as Master D in the BDSM community, repeatedly striking his submissive partner with a cane, leaving clear welts on her thighs and legs. His claim that he was not into pain, but into pleasure seems to be refuted by the video evidence. Dr. Morgan was not available for comment, but his lawyer insisted that this was a one-time event when he was learning his own personal limits and preferences."

"Dr. Morgan is what is known in the community as a gentle Dominant, more interested in bondage and dominance during sex than pain and discipline. He is more focused on his partner's pleasure -- or should I say, he was focused on that when he was an active member of the community. He is currently happily married with a beautiful wife and young daughter, both of whom were almost killed by Ms. Monroe when she struck Mrs. Morgan with her car..."

Thank God for Lara redirecting the focus onto Lisa's proven guilt in the attack on me.

I was worried it wouldn't be enough to divert focus from

Drake onto Lisa's and Jones's horrific murder of Derek. People were always drawn to the more salacious sexual gossip and details. The nuances of BDSM preferences and the difference between being a gentle Dominant like Drake versus a sadist was often lost.

When the news report was finally done, and seeing nothing else about the case, I turned off the television and put on some soothing music instead. Then, I tried to focus on my canvas, but it was difficult with images of Sunita's bruised thighs stuck in my mind...

FOR THE NEXT HOUR, I managed to resist the temptation to turn on the television and see what else the stations were saying about Drake. I did get some decent work done on my painting, and was feeling much more relaxed. Of course, it was at that precise moment that my cell rang. I should have put it on do not disturb so that I wouldn't get interrupted but I was always afraid something bad would happen to Sophie and I wouldn't know about it until too late. So I heard the cell ring and felt I couldn't ignore it.

It was Dawn.

"Kate," she said, her voice sounding so sympathetic. "I was just watching the news and saw that video. I'm so sorry."

"Thanks," I said, rubbing my brow. "It's the last thing we needed. More bad publicity about Drake's past. He's already sacrificed so much."

"He has."

I was surprised that Dawn had called and was offering up some sympathy. She had come around on the whole issue of

BDSM since dating Kurt, but still, I felt uncomfortable talking to her about my personal life. There was a part of me that couldn't forgive her for being so judgmental of my interest in Drake and BDSM.

We spoke briefly about the case, and she asked if I'd be up for lunch.

"I don't know," I said and scratched my head, trying to think of a good excuse to say no. "Drake was attacked and is recovering from a concussion. I don't like to leave him alone with Sophie until he's all better. Maybe once he's recovered completely, I'll give you a call."

"That's great," she said, and I cringed inwardly at the sound of hope in her voice. She really did want to reconnect, but I was still unconvinced.

"Look, Kate, I know you're still upset about everything between us," she said, her voice sounding emotional. "Believe me, I wish I could take it all back, but I can't. What I can do is apologize and show you that I can still be a good friend, when you need one. I'll leave it up to you, but I wanted to call and at least offer my sympathy for what you're going through."

"Thanks," I said and my heart truly did feel softened a little at her admission. "I appreciate it."

We said goodbye and I put my cell away, sighing, still wishing that we were the kind of friends we'd been before I met Drake. But we weren't. Both of us had gone in different directions and the bad feelings between us had only made the gulf between us even deeper. Thing was, I had no female friends. The closest was Lara, and she seemed to treat me like I was a little sister, rather than a real friend or equal.

Then, a knock came to my door. I went to open it and saw a young woman standing outside. She looked like one of Jules's friends -- long red hair in braids, a scarf tied around her forehead, wearing a short jean skirt, leggings and Doc Martens. Her nose ring and tattoo on her neck made her look like the coolest girl in school next to me, who was an older motherly type dressed in casual gym clothes.

"Hey," she said and pointed to the main room. "We're brewing some fresh fair trade organic coffee in case you want some. I made some brownies." She smiled and held out a plate of deep dark chocolate brownies with pecans sprinkled on top.

"Those aren't infused with pot or anything, are they?" I asked dubiously, bending down to peer at them a little more closely.

"Oh, no, they're just chocolate. No CBD or THC in these babies."

"Thanks," I said and picked one off the plate and took one of the square napkins she held out in the other hand. "I'd love one."

"Come join us for some coffee. No pot in it either, in case you're worried."

I laughed and followed her into the main room, where Jules and another guy, tall and lanky with long black hair pulled back into a ponytail stood admiring one of the sculptures Jules was working on. For the next fifteen minutes, I felt like a completely ordinary artist communing with others of my tribe and not a submissive whose Dom husband was going to testify in a murder trial, where the accused was a former sex partner and who was currently the star of a viral pornographic violent sex video on the net.

It felt nice for a change...

When I was finished with my brownie and had inspected Jules's latest work, listening to him talk about its meaning, I said my goodbyes and made my way back to my studio space. Before I could close the door, I noticed that Jules had followed me and was standing there, a strange expression on his face.

"Yes?" I asked, suspecting he wanted to talk about the news reports on Drake.

Of course, I was right.

"Um, I just wanted to say that I saw that video of your husband and I wanted you to know you have my full support."

I made a face but tried to smile. "That's nice," I said. "Your support for what?"

"You know, for you standing by him and all. It must be hard to see that kind of thing on the internet and on the news. People don't understand and get all freaked out when it comes to anything different to do with sexuality. Americans are obsessed with sex but at the same time are prudes."

I smiled awkwardly, not sure what to say. "Thanks again," I said.

"If you ever want to talk, feel free. I'm a good listener and I don't judge."

I nodded. "I will."

Then, he finally turned and ambled back to the main studio space and his current sculpture.

I closed the door and turned to face the studio, glad that conversation was over. There's no way I could talk to Jules about my relationship with Drake, or about the trial and the video. No way. But it was nice of him to offer. He was a harmless guy who was pretty laid back about everything. I was sure he'd have some gem of new age wisdom to offer me if I did talk to him, but that wasn't going to happen. I couldn't even talk to my former best friend about it. Lara, yes. Anyone else, no.

In truth, I didn't really need to talk to anyone about it. I talked to Drake and was able to tell him the full truth and nothing but the truth. He knew everything about me, knew me inside and out, knew how my mind worked and antici- pated my moods. There was nothing I couldn't say to him.

Well, except that I worried he'd never be happy again because of how his life had been ruined by Lisa and the trials.

He'd given up so much...

I would have to stay positive and not show any worry. I had to believe that given time, our lives would go back to normal and we could both be happy again. Problem was that I worried it might not be possible in Manhattan. The trial was too big a deal here and had been covered in all the papers and on the local news hour after hour. Drake's face had been plastered on every screen, his letters giggled over on gossip columns. He'd become well-enough known that reporters and paparazzi knew him on sight. Investors worried about his name on the banner of the foundation and corporation. The hospital worried about donors not giving if Drake was on faculty.

It was clear to me that things would never go back to normal for us. Who knew where we'd end up on this crazy ride of a life we had? I only knew I had to hold on to him as tight as I could and be there when we finally landed.

I LEFT the studio around five thirty, pulling on my coat and boots and tying a scarf around my neck. The sky was getting dark and it had turned cold during the afternoon. In fact, I suspected it was cold enough to snow. That prospect filled me with dissatisfaction. The idea of spending another winter in Manhattan seemed unbearable at that moment. I was glad Drake and I had talked about the Bahamas.

I wanted to escape -- more than just the weather.

My cell dinged and I pulled it out of my pocket and checked.

DRAKE: Hey there. When are you coming back? I miss you...

KATE: How are you feeling? Did you sleep?

DRAKE: Like a log. I really needed a rest. Now, I'm ready to face whatever life throws at me.

KATE: I was just locking the door to my studio space. I'll be home as soon as John can drive me.

DRAKE: Good. I miss you.

KATE: I miss you. Sorry to leave you alone.

DRAKE: No, not at all. I needed a sleep. I just want you here in my arms. That's all.

KATE: That's all? That's what makes me happy. Being in your arms.

DRAKE: That makes me happy. See you soon.

KATE: Soon.

I smiled to myself, glad that he was feeling better and that I could now go home to him and Sophia. It seemed like the worst was, if not over, at least closer to being over, so it had to get better from this point forward.

At least, that was my hope...

DRAKE

THE DAY I was scheduled to give my testimony started off well, but went downhill almost immediately.

I was woken by the sunlight streaming into our bedroom. Glancing at my watch, I saw it was already nine, which meant I had a few hours to relax and get ready for the afternoon when I would head down to the courthouse and give my testimony. I rolled over and saw Kate was already up. She must have woken when Sophie did and had already taken her downstairs.

I got up and had a quick shower, then pulled on my sweats and t-shirt, before making my way downstairs to find them at the kitchen island. Kate was wearing her nightgown and slippers, a sweater pulled around her shoulders. She smiled when she saw me, and that smile and the emotion behind it made everything worthwhile -- all the publicity and assault on my character, closing down the foundation. I could take it for the rest of my life as long as I had her and Sophia.

Sophie was currently shoveling oatmeal into her mouth, her

tiny fist clamped tightly around her baby spoon. She smiled as well when she saw me, her eyes crinkling, her cheeks rosy.

"Good morning to my two girls," I said and bent down to kiss Sophie and then I went to Kate and pulled her into my arms for a warm hug and kiss.

"Good morning, sleepyhead," Kate replied, a spatula in her hand. She was making scrambled eggs, and I saw a few slices of bacon in the pan. "I have some breakfast ready for you. Toast's in the oven staying warm.

"Have you eaten?"

"No," she said and stirred the eggs around in the pan. "I've had my coffee but I wanted to wait for you to eat. Have a seat."

I did, sitting beside Sophie, who kept feeding herself, her long golden brown curls tied up with a bow, making her look like a doll. A doll with oatmeal on her face. I grabbed a napkin off the counter and wiped her chin.

"How are you feeling today?" Kate asked, placing a plate of food in front of me. "Are you up for your testimony today?"

I shrugged. "I'm feeling fine, if that's what you mean. Don't know if I'm up for it or not. I'd rather do anything other than showing up at the courthouse, to be honest. Walk across hot stones, run the gauntlet at West Point, scale the mountains at Machu Pichu. But I'll do it."

She brought her own plate of food over and sat beside me, spreading a napkin onto her lap and digging into her eggs. "Just keep telling yourself that it'll be thirty minutes and then it's over. Finished. You can put this whole episode behind you."

"Onward and upward?"

"Exactly," she replied and held up her glass of juice. "To the end of the trial and us forgetting all about Lisa Monroe and her murderous ways."

"I'll drink to that."

We clinked juice glasses.

The three of us sat eating our breakfasts, enjoying the morning. Kate and I talked about our trip to Nassau and the logistics of getting Ethan there. He'd need a wheelchair-accessible suite of rooms on the main floor if possible.

"I'll call later and reserve rooms for us. I guess Heath has already done so. Do you think Liam will be able to come, too? I bet he'd love to go scuba diving."

"I'm going to start the delicate negotiations with Maureen as soon as I'm finished with my testimony. I don't see how she can refuse, unless she's already arranged for him to come to Kuala Lumpur for the holiday. If so, I really can't ask for him to come with us. He only sees his mother on holidays."

Kate reached over and squeezed my hand. "I know. It will still be disappointing. He's at Brenda's all week every week. You only get to see him occasionally."

"Chris and Maureen are the only parents he's ever known. Being with them is important. I can't complain."

I decided to call Brenda first, and see what was planned for Liam over the holidays. I dialed her number while Kate refilled my coffee mug.

"Hey, Drake," Brenda said when she answered the phone. "How are you? Sorry to hear about the attack. It was shocking to watch on the news."

"I'm better. I've been taking it easy for the past ten days, but I have to give my testimony today at the trial. After that, I'm done with the whole business."

"That's good. What's up?"

"I was wondering what Liam is doing over the Thanksgiving holiday. I'd like to take him to Nassau with us if he's free."

There was a pause on the other end of the line.

"Hmm," Brenda said finally. "I'm afraid I don't think that will be possible."

"Is he going to Kuala Lumpur? I thought he might be going. He hasn't seen Maureen and Chris for weeks."

"No," Brenda said. "He's not going. Maureen wants him to stay in town in case she flies in for the weekend."

"Oh," I said, frowning. "But it's not certain she will?"

"No. She's thinking she might fly back to Manhattan for a few days so she can see Liam, but it's up in the air in case Chris has something going on and she has to stay."

"Huh," I said, frowning. "I could always book a room for Liam and if Maureen doesn't end up coming back, he could fly with us. We won't be leaving until the day before anyway."

I heard her exhale like she was frustrated. "Look, Drake, I'm sorry, but I don't think Maureen wants Liam to go anywhere with you at the moment."

"Why?" I tried to damp down the anger that threatened to boil up. "I thought we agreed that Liam would spend time with me on weekends when he was off school."

"Maureen thinks that with all the publicity around the trial, especially given the recent, uh, videos that have been released, it would be harmful to Liam."

"What?"

"I don't agree with her, but she's the mother. She wants you to wait until the trial publicity blows over."

I felt my blood pressure rising, but took in a deep breath, trying to not let Maureen's unreasonableness get the better of me. I didn't need the aggravation considering I had to testify in the afternoon.

"Whatever," I said and exhaled, trying to let it go. "I'll still book a room and flight for him on the off chance she has a change of heart by then. The trial will be over so I hope the publicity will have died down."

"I wouldn't waste your money," she said softly. "I don't think Maureen will change her mind. She was pretty clear on this."

"It's my money to waste," I said a little too harshly. Then, I felt bad. "Look, Brenda, I don't mean to sound mad at you. I know this isn't your choice or decision. I'm going to book for him anyway. I can cancel if things don't work out. It's no problem. Thanks for being so reasonable about all this. I'm hoping to come by and see Liam this Sunday, and take him out for brunch if that's okay with you."

"Sunday isn't a good day," she said, her voice soft. "Liam has a birthday party to go to. Maybe next weekend."

I closed my eyes, hoping there really was a birthday party and Brenda wasn't just making an excuse. "Okay. I'll call back next week to arrange a time."

"Take care, Drake."

"You as well."

I hung up and turned to Kate, whose eyes were warm, her expression sympathetic.

"Well, that sucks," I said and forked some cold eggs into my mouth. I chewed for a moment, trying to calm myself. Kate reached over and rubbed my shoulder affectionately.

"Things will calm down and you'll be able to see Liam more often."

"I hope so." I drank down my juice and tried to pull myself out of the funk I felt coming on. Beside me, Sophie chirped and I glanced at her, noticing her smile when our eyes met.

She was such a beautiful child. She was mine. I may not have Liam with me, but I had Sophie and I was determined to make her as happy and healthy as I could. While I was deprived of being Liam's father, I could be a great father to her. I turned to Kate and reached out, taking her hand and squeezing.

"I'll be fine at exactly 3:30, after my testimony is over. And then, what I want to do is turn off the television, switch off my internet, and spend the week with my two favorite ladies."

"We're all yours," she said and leaned over to kiss me.

I LEFT the house at 2:00, John driving over to Lara's office on the way. She wanted to come with me to offer moral support while I waited for the call to enter the courtroom, and then we were going to go out after and talk about how it went, and then put the case to bed with a drink. I'd be having non-alcoholic beverage just to be on the safe side, but Lara deserved a cocktail. Then, I'd go home and implement my plan to completely disregard the case from then on.

When we arrived at her building, I sent her a text and we waited for her to come down. Sure enough, within five minutes, she stepped out of the building, looking like a million dollars in her long black coat, high leather boots, a grey pinstripe suit and white blouse underneath, her platinum blonde hair pulled back into her signature tight bun. She looked every inch a dominatrix, and I could easily imagine her intimidating business men in her dungeon.

"There you are," she said and got into the car beside me, leaning over for an air kiss. "Let's go and slay some dragons, shall we? Put all this bullshit behind you."

"Sounds like a plan."

We made small talk on the way to the courthouse, for I'd gone over the questions with her several times and felt I was ready for the prosecutor and cross examination.

I told her about Michael's offer for me to go to Southampton to set up a pediatric robotic neurosurgery unit at the children's hospital.

"Drake, that sounds like a fantastic opportunity for you. Right up your alley."

"I know," I said with a heavy sigh.

"What's the sigh about?"

I glanced away, feeling bad. "Kate. She just got back to Manhattan, back into her studio, with Ethan nearby. I doubt she'll want to move to England."

"You haven't told her? But she has to understand..."

I shrugged. "I know she won't like it. I have to understand as well that Kate's very close to her father. She loves Manhattan."

"You love doing robotic surgery, and the chance to set up a new unit at a children's hospital... That sounds like heaven for you. Surely she would realize it would be crazy of you to turn it down."

"I want Kate happy, Lara. I almost lost her. I don't want to do anything that makes her unhappy."

"I'm sure she feels the same way."

I rubbed my forehead. "I'm going to talk to her about it soon. We'll see how things go with the trial."

"Don't put it off," Lara said. "Honesty and openness is the best policy."

"I won't. After this weekend. I don't want to ruin it."

When we arrived, the steps to the courthouse were crowded with reporters and film crews, hoping to catch a glimpse of witnesses. I was certain to be top of their lists.

"Let me lead the way. I'll fend off any reporters," Lara said as she got out. I followed her out of the car and adjusted my coat while the John closed the door. Then, he stood beside me and I noticed that another bodyguard whose name I didn't know stood a few feet away. It gave me a momentary sense of unreality that my life had come to this -- two body-guards, the paparazzi approaching with their microphones held out, their cameras rolling.

"Do you have anything to say, Dr. Morgan? Do you deny that the video is of you hitting the woman you're with?"

Lara grabbed my arm and pulled me forward.

"Dr. Morgan will issue a brief statement after he's finished giving his testimony. Until then, he has nothing to say. Thank you," she said, her voice firm, giving the reporters the evil eye.

Together, her arm through mine, we walked up the steps to the door and went through security.

"You're damn good at this," I said while we checked our personal items and went through the scanner.

"That's why you pay me the big bucks," she said with a laugh.

I did pay Lara big bucks to be my lawyer and previously, to be my matchmaker. We were friends on top of it and it was her unwavering support of me as a human being that I truly appreciated. She had my back. We'd been friends for years and I knew I could rely on her advice. It was never wrong.

We went inside and checked in with the clerk, who would alert the prosecutor that I was there and would be waiting for my turn to testify. Then, we sat in the long hallway outside the courtroom and waited for me to be called.

While we spoke in quiet voices, a woman came out of the courtroom and walked past us. She glared at me on her way by and I frowned, trying to place her, but I didn't recognize her. She walked down the hallway to the washroom and I turned to Lara.

"Do you know who that is? She gave me a really nasty look."

"No idea," Lara said with a shrug. "Probably just some audience member who thinks you're the devil incarnate."

"Probably."

"Well, whoever she is, this whole business is almost over," she said and gave my hand a squeeze. "After we have a celebratory drink, you can go home to your beautiful wife and baby and put all this behind you. How are you feeling? Stressed?"

"Yes, but I feel pretty comfortable with my testimony. If the defense doesn't give me too hard of a time, it should be no sweat."

"I know Simpson," Lara said. "She's pretty good, all things considered. She'll make a few digs at you, be cautioned by the judge, and do her best to leave a smidgen of doubt in the minds of the jury that her client is not completely culpable. Her only goal now is to get a reduced sentence rather than an acquittal."

The two of us spoke together quietly about the trial and the evidence presented so far. It looked to me like it was a slam-dunk case, but I was a civilian and had no idea how the jury would respond. All I could do was tell my part of the story and leave it up to the skill of the prosecutor and hope the jury found her guilty.

When the clerk called me and the guard opened the door to indicate I was supposed to enter the courtroom, I turned to Lara and raised my eyebrows.

"I guess my time in the fishbowl is here. Wish me luck."

"You'll do fine," Lara said. "Soon, we'll be drinking at Bernie's on 7th and this will all be behind you."

With that, I entered the courtroom.

IN THE END, my testimony went far easier than I thought. I walked down the row to the witness box, was sworn in, and I deflected most of the questions Lisa's defense lawyer asked, denying that we had any kind of romantic relationship and were nothing more than colleagues at NYU, and that it was Lisa, not me, who pursued such a relationship. That I didn't even recognize her when we met again at NYU and when she pushed for a relationship, how I went to the administration to quit and was encouraged to stay.

While I was speaking, I noticed the woman who had left earlier returned and sat in the back row. She wasn't with Lisa's family so I figured Lara was right -- she was just an audience member who had a hate on for me.

The questions finally came to an end, and I felt fine with how I had performed. When I was dismissed, and walked past Lisa and her lawyer, I felt finally free.

I almost made it out of the courtroom without incident.

Almost.

Then, the woman from the back row stood up as I passed her and threw an object at me.

"Pig!" she screamed "Rapist! Sadist!"

The object, a balloon filled with urine, broke and the vile smelling liquid sprayed in my face and covered my jacket. The guard rushed to where she stood and stopped her from lunging at me, but she continued to scream, calling me every manner of epithets.

I was hustled out of the courtroom and she was hustled out another door.

Lara stood when she saw me, and made a face of disgust.

"Oh, my God, Drake. What the hell happened?"

"Some woman threw a balloon filled with urine at me on my way out."

She shook her head. The court security guard pointed down the hall. "There's a men's room down there, in case you want to clean up. Sorry I don't have an extra shirt here you could wear."

"Thanks," I said, noting the tone of sympathy in the man's voice. "I'll be fine. The sooner I get home and shower, the better."

"Yes, Sir."

While Lara waited, I went down the hallway and spent the next few moments cleaning the urine from my face and hair, dunking my head under the tap in the bathroom. I managed to get most of it off, but clearly, there was no way I was going out with Lara for a drink in my current.

When I emerged from the bathroom, Lara was talking to a couple of uniformed security officers. When I joined them, we spoke about the incident and they informed me that the videotapes would be reviewed and the prosecutor would decide whether to charge the woman with assault.

"Who threw the balloon?" I asked.

The ranking officer shook his head. "It was one of the defendant's relations. An aunt."

"She left the courtroom and went to the washroom," I said. "She gave me a nasty look when she walked by."

"She must have brought the balloons along with her and planned to do that when you testified. No one would have thought twice if they found party balloons in her bag."

"How in God's name did she pee into a balloon?"

One of the security guards shrugged. "She had a funnel in her bag. Must have used it to fill the balloon."

"Sheesh," Lara said and rolled her eyes. "What a crazy family."

"I know," I said. "A violent bunch."

After we finished discussing the event with the security officers, Lara and I were able to leave. Together, we walked down the hallway to the front entrance. When we got to the front door, I saw a crowd of reporters and onlookers waiting for me.

"Is there any other exit we can take? Considering I'm covered in piss, I'd rather not face the cameras."

"Let's go out the back. I had planned on you giving a statement, but all things considered, it might be best to avoid the cameras."

"Sounds good to me." I texted John and he agreed to meet us at the side alley. Then we left and I was never so glad to be escaping out the back door of any building.

In the car on the way home, I got a text from Kate.

KATE: *Are you okay? I was watching the news and there was a report that a woman threw a balloon filled with urine at you.*

DRAKE: *I'm wet and stinky, and my pride is hurt but otherwise I'm fine. Needless to say, Lara and I won't be going out for a drink.*

KATE: *I guess not! We have a bottle of champagne if you want to imbibe here. Invite her over.*

DRAKE: *I will.*

With that, I put my cell away and turned to Lara.

"Feel like coming over to the house for a glass of champagne? Kate invited you, if you want."

"Sounds good," Lara said with a smile. "After the past couple of weeks, both of us deserve to celebrate."

I leaned back in my seat and watched the streets of Manhattan pass by, glad that the trial and my involvement in it were finally -- *finally* -- over.

KATE

Drake arrived back at the apartment with Lara just after four thirty in the afternoon. When he entered through the front door, he was smiling, and he and Lara had been sharing some joke. It made me happy to see that he was in good spirits despite the latest attack.

"There you are," I said and went to the front door to greet them. I turned to Drake who was removing his jacket and shirt like it was poisoned. "Forgive me if I don't kiss you."

"No need to explain," he said. "I'm going to put my clothes in a bag and get them dry cleaned. But now, I'm going to take a shower. Maybe you could get that bottle of champagne out of the cooler and pour us all a drink."

"I will," I said and grabbed a large plastic garbage bag from the kitchen pantry. I let Drake drop his clothes into it and watched while he ran upstairs in his bare chest and slacks, which had missed getting the urine treatment.

I placed the bag outside the door in the hallway, not

wanting it to remain in the apartment. Then, I turned to Lara.

"How is he?"

Lara waved her hand and removed her coat. "He's strong," she said, and I took the coat from her then hung it up. Lara took my arm, leading me to the kitchen. "He'll be fine," she said and squeezed my arm.

"Thanks for looking after him through all this."

"He's like my little brother," Lara said. "Where's Sophia?"

"She's napping right now, but she's due up any time."

"I'd love to see her."

"Do you want to sneak up and check in her room?"

"Yes, let's do it."

She followed me up the stairs to Sophie's room. I opened the door. Inside, the room was dim, the blackout shades down against the afternoon sun. Sophie's crib was against the wall. Because she was older and taller, we had the crib set up like a day-bed with the mattress down low and the railing up about a foot so she could easily crawl out.

She was sleeping on her stomach, her butt in the air, her stuffed toy beside her.

"She's beautiful," Lara whispered, her arm around my shoulder.

I nodded, not wanting to wake Sophie.

We left the room and I closed the door.

"You are so lucky," Lara said as we went down the stairs to the main living area. "You have your man, you have your baby and you have your art. I'm so glad for you, Kate."

"I am lucky."

"Too bad Drake's career is tanking here in Manhattan. It would be so good for him to take Michael's offer."

I frowned. "What offer?"

"Michael Owiti's offer to go to work for him, set up a pediatric robotic neurosurgery unit."

"Michael made Drake an offer? To go back to Nairobi?"

"No," Lara said and put her hands on her hips. "I'm going to tell you something but you have to promise me not to tell Drake I told you until he tells you himself. Promise?"

I nodded.

"Michael's heading up the pediatric neurosurgery department at the Southampton Children's Hospital in England and wanted Drake to set up a robotic neurosurgery unit."

"He didn't feel he could tell me?" I felt a sick sensation in my gut. "When did this all happen?"

"He told me about it today, but the offer happened a while ago. He must feel torn about the job and didn't want to force you to make a decision. Don't say anything. Let him tell you. At that point, you can confess that I told you. Okay?"

"Okay," I said doubtfully, hurt that Drake had already talked to Lara about this news but not me.

"When will Sophie get up?" Lara asked, her voice sounding a bit sheepish. "I'd love to play with her a bit."

"She usually gets up at around 4:30."

Lara sat at the kitchen island. "Now, how about that champagne?"

"Coming right up." I went to the wine chiller and removed the bottle of Dom Pérignon from the bottom shelf. "We keep a bottle on hand in case we ever have anything to celebrate."

I chose three champagne glasses from the shelf in the kitchen where we kept the liquor. While Lara watched, I removed the foil from the stopper and popped the cork into a napkin. My mind was focused on Drake's news, wondering if and when he was planning to tell me about the offer.

I had no idea what to think about it. Southampton? That was across the Atlantic Ocean...

There was no way my father would want to make the trip very often. We'd just gotten back into the apartment on 8th Avenue. I only recently started back at the studio. I felt a little sick about it.

"You're good at that," she said, clapping when I poured the first glass for her.

"I used to play bartender at my father's parties when I was old enough. He taught me how to open a champagne bottle."

I poured myself a glass and downed it, needing the warmth

to offset the sadness I suddenly felt about the prospect of leaving Manhattan.

It was just then that Drake started down the stairs, freshly showered and drying his hair with a towel. He was wearing pajama bottoms and a robe, looking every inch the wealthy man of leisure that he was.

"Don't say anything," Lara said, reaching out to touch my arm. She raised her eyebrows. "Let him tell you."

I nodded.

Lara turned to Drake when he entered the kitchen. "Just in time," she said and held up her glass. Drake took his and the three of us toasted each other before taking a sip.

Drake drank his whole glass down at once.

"Ahh," he said when he was finished. "I needed that. And it tastes like another."

I laughed and poured him another glass of champagne. "It's going to be that kind of night, is it?"

"It is," he said and only sipped at the next glass. "I'm going to stay in all weekend and do absolutely nothing.

"Will you listen to the coverage?" Lara asked, eyeing Drake over her glass. "The closing arguments are tomorrow. I don't know how you can stand not going to court so you can hear it."

"Will they be broadcast?" I asked, curious myself.

"No," Lara said. "But I imagine there will be lots of news coverage."

"I may go," I said, glancing quickly at Drake. "I usually wouldn't want to, but I'd like to hear the closing arguments myself."

"We could go together," Lara said. "I have an in with the clerk."

She winked at me and I laughed. "I'm sure you do."

"You really want to go?" Drake asked, frowning. "I thought you wanted to avoid the trial and anything to do with it."

"I did, but this is the end and it would be interesting to hear them argue their cases. Would you mind?"

"Of course not," he said and drank more of his champagne. "As long as no one recognizes you. I thought you'd want to avoid any publicity."

"No one knows me," I said. "There are so few pictures of me in public. The one they use when they talk about me is from several years ago. I could wear my hair up, fake glasses and casual clothes. No one would know who I was."

"I'll get you in, if you really want to go, but maybe we shouldn't sit together. Some reporters know me and would likely ask questions about who I was with. If you want anonymity, that would be best."

"That's fine. You don't need to get me in, if that works better. I'll go incognito wearing my ordinary mom disguise."

"If you really want to," Drake said. "You can be our spy. People know my face by now, so as much as I'd like to hear closing arguments, there's no way I'm going. Who knows what another nutcase family member might do?"

We all nodded, thinking about the two attacks on Drake

from Lisa's crazy family members. For the next half hour, the three of us drank our champagne, and talked about the trial, going over the main testimony and evidence, then how we thought the jury would decide the case.

"Guilty of second degree murder," Drake said.

"Agreed," Lara replied and finished her second glass of champagne. "I do think she'll get a light sentence. There's been a lot of talk in the press about women and abuse. A lot of sympathy for victims who later do violent acts. I think the defense lawyer has been pretty good at playing that up in the jury's mind."

"It doesn't excuse her," I said, angry at the thought that someone as conniving and manipulative as Lisa would be seen with anything but contempt. She wasn't a victim, although she played one very well.

"The most important thing is that she'll most likely get at least another ten years minimum -- more likely fifteen -- tacked onto her existing sentence," Lara said firmly. "She won't be out of jail before she's fifty. And based on what I've seen of her, she'll likely get in trouble in jail and spend even more time there. Someone like Lisa can't help but try to control others around her. She'll get in trouble inside as well as out of jail."

"She should stay in the rest of her life," Drake said.

I turned to look at Drake, surprised at his tone, which was acid. "She should, but that's not going to happen."

It was then we heard a little voice on the baby monitor.

"I'll go get her," I said and left Drake and Lara. When I got to Sophie's bedroom, she was sitting up in her bed, playing with a tiny plastic person that was part of her tiny world toy. She had the farmer in one hand and a cow in the other and was sucking on her pacifier.

"You ready to get up?" I said and went to pick her up. She was wet so I changed her and then carried her down the stairs to the main floor.

"Here she is," Drake said and came over to us, kissing Sophie's cheek and taking her from my arms. "Daddy needs a hug and kiss from his best girl."

Lara and I watched Drake with Sophie. He seemed so happy to see her and hold her, kissing her cheeks and stroking her hair.

"She looks like you, Kate," Lara said, smiling at them. "Same hair and eye color. She's going to be a pretty little thing."

"She's beautiful," Drake said and came over to sit at the island.

We spent the next hour taking turns holding Sophie or watching her eat a snack in her highchair. Finally, after we'd all eaten some tortilla chips and salsa, Lara picked up her bag and stood.

"Well, as much as I'm enjoying this little sojourn, I have to get back to my office and finish up some paperwork."

"You can't stay for supper?" Drake asked, offering Sophie another piece of cut up banana.

"Not tonight. Once the trial is finished and the verdict is in, we'll go out and really celebrate. How's that sound? My treat?"

"Sounds good," I said and smiled, walking her to the front

door. I got her coat out of the closet and handed it to her. "How soon should I get to the courthouse if I want to watch the proceedings?"

"At least fifteen minutes early, probably more if you really want to pick your seat. Thirty might be best, given the publicity around the case."

"Okay," I said and opened the door for her. "Thanks for being a support to Drake through this."

"Don't mention it. He's my friend as much as my client." She leaned in and gave me an air kiss, squeezing my arm. "Look after him."

"I will," I said and watched her take the stairs.

Then, I turned back and watched Drake playing with Sophie at the kitchen island. He loved her so much -- that much was clear. It had to be an emotional time, watching the trial and seeing Lisa sitting there. She'd almost succeeded in killing me, and potentially Sophie. She did succeed in killing Derek and encouraging Jones's suicide.

I really wanted to see her face when she was sentenced. Part of me wanted to avoid the trial, but I was feeling stronger now, the farther away from my own ordeal we got. The truth was that I wanted to see her go away for a very long time.

With the release of the video showing him striking Sunita, I hated to think what his supervisors at NYU and NYP would think of having him on staff or in the fellowship program.

I went over to the kitchen island and joined Drake. Together, we watched Sophie eat her snack.

"Care to go for a walk? The sky is still sunny. She could use some air."

"Sure," I said and we got ready for a walk along 8th Avenue. Drake texted John, who would wait for us on the street. We carried Sophie and her stroller down the stairs and with John walking behind us and Mike walking ahead, we took Sophie for her afternoon walk. The air was crisp and cool, the sidewalk crowded, but there was a small park-like playground down the street from us that we took Sophie to almost every day. There, she could play on the swings and run around in the grass while we watched. A half an hour of her playing outside had her cheeks rosy, so we decided to make our way back to the apartment.

When we returned, I started supper while Drake and Sophie played on the living room carpet. Drake had on an after school program for kids and Sophie played happily until supper.

It was a peaceful domestic scene and I smiled to myself to see how happy Drake was to be a father. It made all of the heartache and pain of the past two years, including the attack and trials and all the related publicity, worthwhile. I decided not to mention what Lara had revealed about Michael's offer. Drake would tell me when he felt like it.

SOPHIE WENT down at around eight, a little later than her usual bed time. After supper, she had a quick bath and I put her in her jammies and then she sat down in the living room with her father for her usual routine of reading picture books. Drake seemed to want to keep her up a little longer, reading her book after book and she was happy to oblige, turning pages and pointing to various animals and people in the book, saying their names. When she finally started tugging at her ear, I knew she was ready for bed.

I picked her up, insisting that it was time. "She's a sleepy-head, Daddy," I said when he pouted. "You'll have her all day tomorrow if you're up to it."

"I am up to it," he said and put the books away, tucking them into the magazine rack beside the sofa. "You really want to go to the court and watch the closing arguments?"

I nodded. "I really do. And then maybe a quick trip to my studio. But only if you feel well enough to manage on your own."

"I do," he said and stood up, leaning down to kiss Sophie on the cheek. "I'll be happy to. Maybe I'll take her over for a visit with Dad and Elaine. They'd like that. I'm sure Dad will enjoy hearing about the courtroom hijinks."

"He'll love it."

Then, I carried Sophie up to her bed and turned off the light. Her bedside light came on, which projected a thousand tiny stars on the ceiling. I laid her down in her crib, stroking her back as I usually did, and sang her a song, which I also usually did.

"Hush, little baby don't say a word, momma's going to buy you a mocking bird..."

She listened for a while and then closed her eyes, snuggling down into her bed, her cheek pressed against the blanket, her stuffed bunny under her arm. I tiptoed out of the room and slowly closed the door and didn't hear a peep out of her.

She was tired after her afternoon in the park and staying up late listening to her dad read her books.

I made my way down the stairs to the living room, where Drake was busy putting a mix-cd into the music system. Something soft and clearly from the sixties came on. I didn't recognize it but it sounded Brit Invasion.

"Is that the Animals?"

I went to his side and he shook his head, holding up a CD. "Zombies. Time of the Season."

I slipped my arms around him and watched as he flipped through his CD collection. "I like this."

"Who's your daddy?" he said and turned to me, pulling me into his arms.

"Who's my daddy?" I said with a laugh. "Is that what they called boyfriends back in the 60s?"

"It was," he said.

"Kind of creepy when you think about it," I said, adjusting his robe collar. "But I understand the sentiment. Someone strong and caring to look after you."

"We're going to play this in our upcoming practice, so I wanted to listen."

"Saturday night?"

He nodded. "We'll practice on Saturday afternoon, and then we have a gig at the O'Riley's on Saturday night. Maybe you could get Karen to come by for the late set and I could pick you up. We could play out a little scenario..." He raised his eyebrows.

"Mmm," I said and stood on my tip toes to kiss him. "I like the idea of picking you up."

"Hmm," he said and cocked one eyebrow. "I thought I'd pick *you* up."

"We could pick each other up. Go to an expensive hotel for a couple of hours. Maybe Karen would spend the night?"

"Oh, now that sounds good. It'll be just the right timing for me to have sex again. Two weeks without has been hell."

I nodded, having felt rather deprived over the past two weeks. "It'll be good for you to practice with the boys and then go out with your loving and very needy wife. Get your mind off things."

"I won't be able to sleep now, imagining it."

He smiled and we kissed again.

"You sure you have to wait the *whole* two weeks before you can have sex?"

"Technically, I should wait until Monday, but I think I could get away with Saturday night, considering my concussion was pretty mild."

"You're the acclaimed neurosurgeon."

We kissed again and stood in an embrace, enjoying the warmth of each other's bodies.

For the next two hours, we lay on the sofa together and listened to music. When ten o'clock rolled around, we went to bed and lay in each other's arms for a while in the darkness, the only light coming from a crack between the curtains at the window.

I waited for Drake to say something about Michael's job offer, but he didn't. Perhaps he'd decided not to accept it and so I didn't feel like revealing it in case I pushed him to say no. It hurt me a bit that he didn't tell me, but I tried to understand his point of view.

The offer of a job as the head of the robotic neurosurgery unit would be plum and right up Drake's alley. The fact he'd be working with Michael would be a plus, since the two of them got along so well. But at the same time, we'd just moved back to Manhattan...

"Good night, my love," Drake said, murmuring against my temple as I lay in his arms, my head on his shoulder.

"Good night," I said, fighting with myself to ask about Michael. "I'm so glad this horrible experience will soon be over and we can forget all about her."

"Me as well."

We kissed and then Drake turned over onto his side and I spooned in behind him, one arm around his waist.

The fact he didn't bring up Michael's offer stung a little bit, but I was sure Drake had a good reason. After forcing the issue out of my mind, I listened to his slow and steady breathing, and was thankful once again that I took a chance and went out with him that first night. It was with thoughts of the first trip to the Russian Tea Room that I fell asleep, Drake's body warm against me.

DRAKE

I SPENT a glorious day with Sophie while Kate attended court.

The three of us ate breakfast together and then Sophie and I said goodbye to Kate as she left the apartment for her journey to the New York Supreme Courthouse. She was dressed in her soccer mommy disguise, wearing a pair of fake glasses she'd bought one year as part of a costume for Halloween. She braided her hair and put on a toque, looking every inch a Millennial with her Doc Martens and parka. I wouldn't have recognized her if I saw her at a distance and I hoped that no reporter did either, because I knew she wouldn't want to have to talk to anyone on camera.

"Keep in touch. Let me know how things are going and if your cover is broken. Sophie and I will come and rescue you if that happens."

"I will," she said and kissed both me and Sophie. Sophie

seemed amused to see her mom wearing reading glasses and tried to pull them off.

"No, no," Kate said. "Mommy need these for her disguise." Then Kate took them off and put on some Ray Bans.

"Call me," I said and held up my hand to mimic a cell to my ear. "I can come pick you up."

"No, that's okay. I want to take the subway. No one will recognize me in these. Besides, I want to feel part of the city again. John will follow me the whole way so I won't be alone."

"Okay. Try to enjoy yourself, or at least, quench your curiosity."

"I will," she said and then she seemed to stop for a moment, frowning a bit.

"What?" I asked, and waited before closing the door.

"Is everything all right?"

It was my turn to frown. "Of course," I said. "I feel fine, Kate. Really."

"Okay," she said with a sigh. "I'll be glad when this is all over."

"Me, too."

She left, waving goodbye and I watched her walk down the stairs.

Then it was just me and Sophie.

"Well, kiddo, it's you and me all day. Whatcha wanna do?"

"Momo!" she said and pointed to the television.

Nemo.

Her favorite movie. I practically had the dialogue memorized after watching it so often during the past few weeks.

"Okay, honey," I said and took her into the living room. I put her down on the carpet with her blankie and toys and slipped in the DVD. Soon, the opening credits were playing and she was bouncing up and down with excitement, her Tiny Town people in her hands.

I went to the kitchen and made some coffee and grabbed the *New York Times*. I proceeded to read the headlines while I enjoyed the sunshine in the kitchen. That was the way my morning went, with Sophie playing with her toys and watching Nemo. Around eleven, I remembered that I wanted to take Sophie over and see Ethan and Elaine for a visit. I called Ethan's number, checking my email while I waited.

"Hello, there, Drake," Ethan said, and from the tone of his voice, I could tell he sounded pleased to hear from me. "What's up with my favorite son in law?"

"Ha ha. That's faint praise since I'm your only son in law," I said with a laugh. "I'm fine. Much better."

"How's recovery from your concussion?"

"Almost all better. Headache's gone and I feel pretty much normal."

"I hear you've been taking in some golden showers..."

I laughed out loud at that. "Yeah, not quite the greeting I

had in mind when I went to court. I survived, but my pride was severely wounded."

"I'll bet. I guess it's true what they say -- better to be pissed off than pissed on."

I snorted at that and we laughed for a moment. "Hey," I said when the laughter passed. "I'm alone with Sophie today while Kate goes to court to hear closing arguments and thought it might be a good day for us to visit. What do you think?"

"That sounds wonderful. I'm here all by my lonesome while Elaine is out at the shops, but she'll be back in time for lunch. Why don't you two pop on over and have lunch with us? I think Elaine was talking about her famous turkey melts and soup or something."

"Sounds fantastic. We'll be there by noon. We're just finishing up watching Finding Nemo."

"That again? She watched that the last time we were there."

"I know," I said with a laugh. "It's her favorite. She calls him Momo. From the time she gets up in the morning until bedtime, it's Momo."

"Back in my day, we had to amuse ourselves with Saturday cartoons, or reading comics or actually playing outside. Kids these days -- who can imagine what they'll be like as adults? Bored to tears, most likely."

"You sound ancient, old man."

"Watch your tone, young man!" Ethan said in reply to my good-natured ribbing. "See you soon."

"See you."

I hung up and smiled to myself, looking forward to speaking with him and having lunch with the two of them. They'd get to indulge themselves in Sophie and I'd get to enjoy watching them.

On the television, the final credits for Finding Nemo were rolling and so I went and turned it off. Then, I got out Sophie's jacket and boots, as well as her toque and tiny heart sunglasses. We got all bundled up, and soon, we were going down the stairs. John met me outside and opened the door to the vehicle. Since Ethan and Elaine moved to Brooklyn into a more residential area, it was more of an adventure when we went to visit. We drove across the bridge to Brooklyn and finally arrived at the townhouse just before noon. I got the stroller out and the diaper bag, and finally, Sophie herself and together we trundled into the small entry way to the yard. Elaine was waiting at the door, smiling, her arms open to take Sophie from me.

"There you are," she said, hugging and kissing Sophie. "We've been so excited to see you. Both of you."

She glanced at John, who remained on the street beside the vehicle.

"Come on in," she asked, jerking her head to the side. "What about your bodyguard?"

"John's happy to stay in the car and listen to audiobooks. He tells me it's why he took the job." I grinned at her.

"That's good. Come on in. Ethan's in his study, of course, on the phone with someone from his club, talking politics as usual."

We went inside and removed our coats and boots and hats

and heart sunglasses. I put Sophie down and she ran off, looking for grandpa. Then, Elaine and I went down the hallway to the back of the main floor where Ethan had his study. He was seated in his wheelchair behind his huge mahogany desk, Sophie sitting on his lap, examining the items in his desk drawer.

"You two have a chat while I get lunch ready," Elaine said. "I hope you like vegetable noodle soup and turkey melt sandwiches on panini bread."

"Sounds fantastic." a drawer and

Before I could say anything, Ethan offered Sophie a lollipop, which she happily took.

"Grandpa spoils you with those," I said, shaking my head although I wasn't truly mad.

"That's what grandpas are for, aren't they Sophie?"

She smiled around her lollipop.

We spent some time chatting while Sophie played with a set of toys we kept at Ethan's.

"You really don't want to listen to the news about closing arguments?" Ethan eyed me from over his reading glasses.

"Honestly? No," I replied, shaking my head. "I heard opening arguments, and I heard the evidence. I don't need to hear them summarize what they've already said. In fact, if I didn't hear another word about it, I'd be a happy man. There is something I want to talk to you about though," I said, deciding to broach the subject of Michael's offer with him.

"Shoot. You know I'm always here to listen."

"I do know and I appreciate it."

Then, I went over the offer Michael had made to me to head up the robotic surgery unit at the Children's Hospital. I told Ethan I hadn't spoken to Kate yet.

He nodded, pursing his lips like he was considering. "Sounds perfect for you. I gather you're worried about Kate not wanting to move again so soon. And because of me."

"Exactly. I know how hard it would be for her to say yes and I know she'd feel obligated to do so for my sake."

He stared off into the distance for a moment. "I don't want to see you two go, but given what you've said about the publicity around the trial, what happened with the foundation, and your fellowship at NYU, it might be a way to escape Manhattan's gossip mill for a while and then, when you're ready, and when all this has died down you could come back. With that position under your belt, you'd be able to write your own ticket pretty much anywhere in the world."

"Anywhere except Manhattan," I said sourly. "As long as the current crop of people are in the administration, I doubt they'll want me here. Bad for fundraising."

"Probably."

We sat in silence for a moment and he sighed. "Well, of course it's up to you and Kate to decide. I give you my blessing to go and wish you well with it. It's a great opportunity. Kate is young and will adapt wherever you two go."

"Thanks, Dad. I'll talk to Kate tonight and see what she thinks."

"How soon would you start?"

"The new year."

Ethan nodded and rubbed his chin. "That would give us Christmas at least." He sighed and pointed to his wheelchair. "We'll come and visit of course. The south of England is a lot nicer than Manhattan in winter."

"That would make it easier for Kate. She worries about you."

"I know she does. I don't want her making decisions about your plans because of me. She has to focus entirely on you, Sophie and herself. I only want the three of you happy."

"I know."

We sat in silence for a moment. Ethan turned to me. "You won't mind if I listen to the news?"

"Be my guest," I replied. I understood he would be curious. "I'm only interested in the verdict and sentence. And I instructed my lawyer to send me both in an email. I'm ignoring the news and papers for the next month."

"Good plan," Ethan said. "It's out of your hands anyway. Focus on what you can change."

Elaine popped her head in the door. "Lunch is ready."

"Let's eat," Ethan said and wheeled the chair out from behind the desk.

Sophie squealed in delight.

WE HAD A NICE LUNCH, and I stayed at their place for another two hours so they could get their fill of Sophie. I told Elaine about my job offer and she responded just as Ethan had. Sad to see us go, but understanding that it was too big an opportunity to miss.

"Kate won't be as excited about it as I will be, but I hope she's fine."

"I'm sure she will be, when she thinks about it."

"We should go," I said, gathering up Sophie's toys and her diaper bag after changing her. While Sophie was happy and enjoying herself in Elaine and Ethan's company, she would need to go back home so she could have a nap. "She has to go down for a nap soon."

"Oh, can't you stay longer?" Elaine said, sounding really sad to see us go. "We already have a crib set up in the spare bedroom. Call Kate and get her to come for supper. It's so nice to have you kids here. We get lonely."

Given the news about my job offer, I figured that both Elaine and Ethan would be sad, and so I figured it would be good to stay for dinner.

"I'll text her."

I did, perfectly happy to stay and do nothing.

DRAKE: *Hey, how's it going?*

KATE: *Good. I'm at the studio, finishing up my painting.*

DRAKE: *Feel like having supper with Dad and Elaine? They'd like me to stay and for you to come when you're done. I'm sure Dad would love to hear about the trial.*

KATE: *Sure. I'll be there in an hour.*

DRAKE: Great. See you then.

"Done. Kate will come here when she's finished at the studio."

"Great," Ethan said wheeled his chair into the living room.

"Come with me," Elaine said, pointing to the hallway. "We'll get her settled into the spare bedroom."

"Kiss Grandad," I said and leaned down with Sophie so she could give Ethan a kiss. "Time for a nap."

I got her a bottle of water and then followed Elaine down the hallway to the back bedroom where the crib was located. Elaine was closing the drapes so that the room was nice and dark. She'd turned on a tiny globe lamp beside the crib, which was very much like the one we had in Sophie's room. It would feel pretty familiar with the stars sparkling on the ceiling.

I laid Sophie down and she sucked on her bottle of water, her eyes already closing. Elaine leaned over and kissed Sophie's forehead and tucked her blankets around her. Then, we left Sophie alone.

When I closed the door, Elaine shook her head. "I'm amazed at how easily she goes down. I'd expect her to cry and fuss."

"Not Sophie," I said quietly. "She's a sleeper. We were lucky."

We went back to the living room where Ethan was in his chair watching the news. When I sat on the sofa beside him, he switched channels to a replay of a golf game.

"You don't have to change because of me," I said and pointed to the television. "What's up with the trial?"

"Closing arguments are over and there was no drama in the courtroom, thankfully. I guess Kate's disguise worked since there were no pictures of her entering or leaving the courtroom."

"That's good," I said. "She didn't mention anything so I assume it went okay. She'll tell us more when she gets here."

Elaine stood in front of us. "What do you boys say about a stir fry for supper? Chicken or beef?"

"Beef," Ethan said. "Make that hot Korean beef I love." He turned to me, expectantly. "You like spicy?"

"Bring it," I said and nodded to Elaine. "Kate loves Korean."

"I have to zip to the store to pick up a few things, but I'll be back shortly," she said.

Then, the two of us watched golf while Elaine went to the stores to shop for supper. It was nice to spend time alone with Ethan, and to talk about nothing more important than Tiger Wood's golf game and who would win the Masters this year. As usual, Ethan was full of insight from a lifetime of playing golf and watching the pros. I'd never really gotten into golf, preferring racket sports and running, but as a lawyer and then a judge, it was almost expected for someone like Ethan.

Elaine returned in about half an hour and went to the kitchen to get things started for supper. About an hour after that, Kate showed up, just when Sophie started to grouse in the spare bedroom.

"Hey," I said and kissed her when she came in. "How was your afternoon?"

"Great," she said and hung up her coat. "Do I hear Sophie talking in the bedroom?"

"Yes," I said and together, we went to the back and Kate picked Sophie up and checked her diaper after kissing her on both cheeks.

Kate changed her and we talked about the closing arguments.

"Anything different from what they said in the trial?

Kate shrugged and finished changing Sophie. "Not that I could tell. The focus of the prosecution was on the physical evidence tying Lisa to the crime scene, the forensic evidence and Jones's confession. Lisa's lawyer focused on how Jones's testimony was self-serving and shifted all the blame for planning to Lisa. How she was the victim in all this, due to her submissive nature."

"Ha!" I said with derision. "That's the biggest joke of all."

"I agree. I think the jury will agree as well. It's pretty hard to deny that she planned things when there are emails stating what she wanted. But they may be sympathetic to her when it comes to sentencing."

"Well, as long as she stays behind bars for a good decade or two longer, I'll be happy."

"Me, too."

We went to the living room where Ethan was waiting and Kate gave her father a kiss then put Sophie onto the floor with her toys.

We spent the rest of the time before dinner going over the trial. Ethan was eager to hear the details and we had the benefit of his knowledge of the law and how courts worked to help understand what was happening.

"There was nothing new," Kate said. "The evidence is pretty damning, as far as I can see. Why wouldn't her lawyer have urged Lisa to accept a plea bargain to a lower offense? Why go to court?"

"She's a narcissist," Ethan said. "She can't be wrong. She has to do everything possible to make people see how she's the one who's been harmed in all this -- not you or Drake or Derek Richardson or Jones. Her. She's the victim," Ethan said, warming to his subject. "In her mind, she probably really believes it. She can't accept responsibility for anything that makes her look bad. It's everyone else who is at fault. That's key to understanding a malignant narcissist. They will fight to the bitter end to defend their self-image. It's very sad but I've seen it all too often in cases like this. These people are accidents waiting to happen. They go through life harming people, leaving broken hearts and bruises on all those they encounter. And for the worst of the lot, dead people."

"Is it because of her past?" Kate asked, her expression concerned. "I mean, the abusive home?"

Ethan shrugged, and pursed his lips. "There is a gene that gives a predisposition to criminality if the boy is abused as a child. I don't know that it applies to women. Haven't read the research."

"I have," I said and they turned to listen. "All I know is that for some children, abuse will make their personality flaws worse. In Lisa's case, I suspect that she didn't get the minimum care and nurturing she needed to develop empathy. But she's very smart. Above average intelligence, so she was able to get scholarships and compensate for her lack of care in her childhood. But it's clear that she's a narcissist. Most definitely a sociopath."

"What's the difference?" Kate asked.

"A sociopath lacks empathy, but they are quite capable of understanding their own culpability in their actions. They just don't care. A narcissist cares exceedingly about not being seen as culpable. They can't accept responsibility for anything that makes them look bad. It's always someone else's fault. You can be a narcissist without being a sociopath. And vice versa. Add them together and wham. That's Lisa. She must be loved. She can't be unloved. She can't be wrong. It's someone else's fault and she's the victim even when she's bringing the hammer down onto Derek's head when he tries to escape."

"It makes me sick to my stomach to think of it," Kate said. We sat in silence and watched Sophie playing on the floor.

It made me sick as well.

"We're lucky we escaped with our lives," I said. "She almost got you and Sophie."

Kate turned to me. "She's completely delusional to think you'd run to her with me out of the picture."

"She probably just flipped when NYU kicked her out of the program. I don't think she planned on killing you except in that moment, but I could be wrong."

"I remember her expression at O'Riley's that night you were playing. If looks could kill..."

I reached over to Kate and took her hand. "Thank God you lived." I kissed her hand.

"Amen," Ethan said. "She's not getting out of jail any time soon. We can count on that at least. Depending on the jury, she'll be in for another decade or two. That should keep her away from you for at least that long. By the time she gets out, she'll be in her sixties."

"Does age change a narcissist?" Kate asked, frowning.

"No," I said, remembering the research. "They don't mellow. They stay that way their entire lives. When she gets out, we'll make sure to get a restraining order if we're still here in Manhattan. I'd like to think she'd be safe at that point, after twenty-five years in jail, but I don't think that. She'll be vengeful. She probably has already convinced her family to get revenge on her behalf. That's why I was attacked by her nutcase brother and possibly her crazy aunt."

I almost told Kate about my job offer at that moment, but then Elaine came into the living room wearing an apron, a wooden spoon in her hand. "Are you three talking about the trial? I thought we agreed to talk about something pleasant." She raised her eyebrows.

"Guilty as charged," Ethan said. "We did. It's hard to ignore, considering. But let's talk about something more pleasant. How about Nassau? Is that pleasant enough?"

"Perfect," Elaine said. "That's more like it. Personally, I can't wait."

"Me either," Kate said and smiled. "I want to see Sophie playing on the beach with her little floppy hat and sunglasses. That's one thing I miss about San Francisco. I loved the beach."

"Me, too," I said and for the rest of the night, we avoided talk of the trial like it was the plague.

When eight o'clock came around, and we'd finished Elaine's delicious meal of Korean Beef stir fry and a crème caramel for dessert, Kate started to gather up Sophie's toys.

"We better go," she said. "Sophie has to get to bed and so does Drake. He's playing with the band this weekend, now that he's almost officially recovered from his concussion. I want him well-rested."

"Yes, nurse," I said with a laugh.

"I'd love to come and hear you play," Elaine said. She turned to Ethan. "Maybe we could come and see the band? What do you think?"

Ethan nodded. "I heard you play once, back when the band first got together," he said and I was surprised. We'd never much talked about Mersey. "I'd love to come and hear you guys again. Seems to me you did a lot of Beatles. I was a Stones fan, myself."

"They play the Stones," Kate said, smiling. "The old stuff. Paint it Black, Under My Thumb."

"That music was big when we were over in 'Nam. Do you mind if we come?" he asked me.

"Of course not," I replied. "I'd love to have you. I'm sure the O'Rileys would love to meet you."

"It's a date," Ethan said. "It's good to get out of the house now and then. Take the old wheelchair for a spin. Is it wheel-chair accessible?"

I nodded. "Yes. It's on the main floor and there's a ramp into the building if I remember correctly."

"Great. I look forward to it."

At that, we all kissed and hugged and said our goodbyes.

On the way home, Kate turned to me and took my hand. "I'm so glad it's all over. We can put this behind us and move forward."

I kissed her hand. "Me, too."

In her car seat beside us, Sophie's eyes were closed and her pacifier was clamped between her teeth, the sound of the car lulling her to sleep.

We got home and put her to bed without much fuss, and then it was just Kate and me alone.

I sat down on the sofa and opened my arms, wanting her to come and sit with me.

"Come here," I said softly. "I have something to talk about with you."

She came over and slipped into my arms, her arms around my neck.

"Shoot."

Her face was expectant, and I didn't know how to word my news, except to come right out and tell her.

"Michael Owiti has taken over the helm of the neurosurgery department at the Southampton Children's Hospital. He wants to add a robotic surgery unit to the neurosurgery department. He wants me to be the head of the unit and get it set up."

She looked in my eyes. "And?"

"And I want your thoughts."

"When would the position start?"

"January."

She sighed. "You don't really want to leave Manhattan again so soon, do you?"

I could see tears forming in her eyes. She didn't want me to take the position.

"There's nothing here for me now. I can't work at NYP. I can't do my fellowship at NYU. We've lost so many donors at the foundation that it's being shut down."

"It's being shut down?" Kate's face reddened. "That's terrible!"

"Dave's going to set up a new foundation to do the same work, but without me attached in any way except as the main anonymous donor."

"Oh, Drake," she said and pressed her cheek against mine. "That bitch has ruined your life."

"It's not ruined," I protested. "I have you and Sophie. I have Liam. I have Ethan and Elaine. I have my new family."

"But you're a neurosurgeon. And you want to be a pediatric neurosurgeon. Doing robotic surgery. It's so not fair."

"Life isn't fair."

We sat together, her head on my shoulder, and I waited for her response.

"So, what are your thoughts?"

She didn't say anything for a moment.

"You don't want to go," I said and forced her to look in my eyes. "We won't go if you don't want to."

A tear fell down her cheek and she quickly wiped it away. "I thought you'd want to stay because of Liam. And I hate to leave my father. He's so frail..."

"I know," I said. "I don't want to leave Liam or Ethan. But setting up a robotic neurosurgery unit at the pediatric hospital? Kate, that's what I've always wanted to do."

She didn't say anything, just sat there with tears running down her cheeks, her eyes on mine.

"I'll say no," I said, my heart heavy but I knew where my heart really lay. It was with her. I wanted her happiness.

"Are you sure?" she said, her voice so soft I could barely hear it. I knew she was torn. But I wanted to know how she really felt. I didn't want to get over to England and have her depressed.

"I can wait. There'll be another opportunity that'll come along down the road." I kissed her and she nodded, wiping her eyes.

"I wish it was here," she said. "Then there'd be no problem."

"I know. Now, let's just forget all about it. I'll text Michael tomorrow and turn down his offer."

"Okay. But I have to tell you that Lara already told me about Michael's offer."

"She did?"

Kate nodded. "She made me promise not to say anything until you told me yourself. She didn't want me to influence you or make you feel guilty."

"You two..." I said, feeling bad that I had talked to Lara before talking to Kate. I just knew Kate would be upset at even the thought of moving away and leaving Ethan behind.

"I'm sorry I didn't tell you right away," I said and leaned closer. "I won't keep anything from you ever again."

"Neither will I."

We kissed and then we finally went to bed. I wrapped my arms around Kate, but we were both blue from having to face the decision. Part of me wished Michael had never made the offer, but he did and now, we'd have to just move on.

It would be hard but I would have to push it out of my mind and focus on my life with Kate and Sophie. And Liam.

It would be enough.

KATE

THE WEEKEND WAS DIFFICULT. I felt sad about Drake turning down the offer to go to Southampton, but at the same time, I had just started to feel back home again in Manhattan.

Of course, it was different this time -- the trial made it next to impossible for Drake to enjoy himself the way we used to. We couldn't just go out in public as easily because Drake inevitably got recognized and people would stare at us -- or worse.

But I was determined to make Drake as happy as I could, given he had made this decision for me.

Friday afternoon, I went to the waxing salon while Sophie slept. I wanted to get a Brazilian before date night, so I wasn't too irritated. It had been a while since I'd had one and I wanted to be smooth for our first night of sex since Drake had been attacked.

Friday night, Drake and I spent in front of the television, ordering in some Indian food and watching a movie we'd been planning to catch in the theaters but never managed to get there.

Drake slept in on Saturday morning and then went to O'Riley's that afternoon for practice. He was gone the rest of the day, and we would all have dinner before the first set at nine o'clock. Sophie and I spent the afternoon in the park and then came home for her nap. I'd called Karen on Friday and she agreed to come sit with Sophie Saturday afternoon, staying overnight so we could all go to O'Riley's and meet my dad and Elaine and then Drake and I could get a hotel room for a bit of a vacation. I had arranged a couple of hours at the spa by myself Saturday afternoon, and then I'd go out with my dad and Elaine to O'Riley's. They'd stay for the first set, and then would leave. I'd spend the rest of the evening at the bar, watching the second set and then, Drake and I would do our little scene of him picking me up and taking me to his hotel room.

It sent a thrill through my body just imagining it.

Earlier, before he left for the practice, Drake packed a bag for when he went to check in at the hotel. When I asked what he was packing, he wouldn't let me in the bedroom.

"It's a surprise," he said through the bedroom door. "You'll just have to wait and see when we arrive, but I promise you that you'll enjoy it."

"I will, will I?" I said, a thrill in my stomach at the prospect of a night alone in a hotel with Drake all to myself. "I better get into the right mindset first. I've booked some time at the spa so I can get ready and prepare myself for you."

Drake peeked his head out of the door. "Prepare yourself? What could you possibly mean, Ms. Bennet?"

"You can use your imagination, but let's say I will be perfectly turned out for a night at O'Rileys."

"If you talk like that, I may not be able to focus when we're playing tonight."

I winked at him coyly. "You'll just have to wait to find out."

He leaned forward and kissed me, then left.

Sophie and I waited for Karen, who arrived just before three. Sophie was pleased to see her, and barely said a peep when I finished dressing and went to the door, my overnight bag in my hand with my dress and other necessities. I'd change and get ready for dinner at my dad's and then the three of us would go to O'Riley's.

I hadn't had a date night for a while and I needed one -- and needed Drake -- badly.

THE SPA WAS FANTASTIC. I got a massage, then a manicure and pedicure at the salon. I went to my dad's and changed into my dress and we all drove to O'Riley's for dinner at seven thirty. Of course, Mrs. O made a huge deal of us being there and we all sat together at a large table in the rear of the restaurant and shared a traditional Irish meal of Guinness, Irish stew and meat pies. Everyone fawned over my father, for they had lost Mr. O'Riley years ago and missed having him at the table. My father sat at the head where Mrs. O usually sat and people asked him a thousand questions about his career on the bench.

Of course, the talk turned to the trial and Ken held out a hand to stop everyone.

"Drake, if you don't want to talk about it, we'll move on to other topics."

Drake shook his head. "No, it's fine. It's not like it's a secret what happened. I'm just glad my part is over so Kate and I can move on."

Mrs. O held up her glass of wine. "Then let's do just that. Move on to other subjects. Sláinte!"

"Sláinte!" everyone replied and that was that.

The meal finished, my parents and I found a table near the stage where my dad's wheelchair wasn't in the way, while Mersey prepared for their first set of the night. By nine o'clock, the bar was full of regulars and the atmosphere was happy as the drinks flowed.

The band came out while the lights were off and took their places, but the crowd was busy chatting and it wasn't until the lights went up on the stage that they paid attention.

Drake stood at the microphone, his bass guitar slung over his shoulder. He looked devastatingly handsome with his longish black hair falling in his blue blue eyes, a white shirt open at the neck and a pair of low-slung black leather jeans. My insides felt all warm and mushy when I saw him up there. He was mine -- a gorgeous man. Soon, we'd be making love at the hotel and a surge of lust went through me at the thought. Seeing him so sexy on the stage, especially once he started singing, just did it for me. I can't deny I was proud that he was mine and as I glanced around at the crowd, I imagined that many of the women were wishing he was theirs.

The first song was my favorite, of course -- And I Love Her.

I knew that Drake picked it for me, and when he sang, he glanced out around the crowd until he found me sitting at the table. Our eyes met and a jolt of love and lust went through me. I held my finger tips to my lips and blew him a kiss.

He smiled as he sang, and held my gaze while he said those words.

My heart melted when I watched him, thinking of how much he'd been through in the last two years since Sophie's birth and the fallout from the attack and trials. His reputation was in tatters, he had to withdraw from the fellowship, and take a backseat at the foundation and corporation. I felt tears brim up in my eyes and my heart swell as I thought about how much this had cost him. We'd both been through so much, and finally -- finally -- it was over. All we had left was the sentencing and Lisa would go away to jail until her next trial for her involvement in Jones's suicide but that had nothing to do with Drake or me.

We could put her completely out of our minds.

And that was exactly what I tried to do for the next hour as we watched the show. I smiled at my father, who nodded his head in time to Time Is On My Side by the Stones.

"This is my kind of music," he said with a laugh as I leaned in. "The good stuff. I know I'm an old codger."

I leaned forward and shook my head. "I like Debussy, so that makes me an even older codger," I managed to say in his ear.

It was too hard to hear each other talk so for the rest of the set, we just listened, enjoying the music and atmosphere and watching Drake and the guys perform.

When the set was over, we clapped with the rest of the audience and I turned to my parents, who seemed to really enjoy the music.

"How did you like it?" I asked Elaine. "You've never heard them before."

"They're darn good," she said, her eyebrows raised. "I had no idea what to expect. Drake has such a nice voice."

"He really does," I said.

"All the women in the crowd are probably wishing they were you," she added. "He looks like a rock star on the stage with those leather pants and that white shirt.

"They can't have him," I said with a laugh. "He's mine."

During the break, Drake came out and kissed me warmly. "So, how did we do?" he asked, glancing at my dad and Elaine. "Brit enough for you? I snuck in some Stones just for you, Ethan."

"First rate," my dad said. "You could have been a musician if you'd wanted, but it's a damn good thing you weren't, for your patients' sakes."

Drake knelt between my father and me, his arms around each of us. "I don't have any at the moment," he said with a heavy sigh. "Maybe next year once all this blows over."

My father frowned. "It shouldn't be like that. You should be judged on your skills and competence, not your private life. If you go to Southampton, you'll have lots of pediatric patients. Have you two decided yet?"

Drake turned to me, a sheepish expression on his face.

"You talked to both Lara *and* dad before me?" I asked, feeling a bit hurt.

"I wanted to feel him out before I brought it up with you."

"And what did you say, Daddy?" I glanced at him, watching his face.

"I told him it sounded like a perfect position for him, given his expertise in robotic surgery and given he wants to work in pediatric neurosurgery."

"But Drake's saying no," I said and shook my head. "It's too soon. We just got back and we decided that focusing on family is more important right now. Liam's here. You're here..."

"You two are most important right now," my dad said. "If your relationship doesn't come first, everything else falls apart. Think about it."

I frowned, but didn't say anything. Drake squeezed my shoulder.

"We decided to wait for another opportunity. One closer to home. This way, I'll get to negotiate with Maureen about spending time with Liam."

"You two have to do what's right for you," my father said.

And that was that.

I turned to look at Drake and he seemed perfectly fine with it. Drake nodded. "We have." He turned to me. "How are you enjoying the set?"

"I really liked the first song, personally," I said and smiled, glad that he seemed truly fine about not accepting the Southampton offer.

"Good. I better go and get ready. Thanks for coming tonight." He gave my dad's shoulder a squeeze and then leaned over and kissed Elaine on the cheek.

Then he leaned over to kiss me once more. "See you later." He gave me an intense look that said so much.

"See you," I replied, my stomach doing a little flip, wondering what he had in mind, but feeling a little sick to my stomach about the whole Southampton issue.

"Drake really loves you to turn down a plum position at the Southampton Children's Hospital, Kate."

I forced a smile I didn't feel all of a sudden. "He does."

The three of us chatted for a few more minutes and then my dad glanced at his watch. "Well, I guess it's time for this old codger to go home."

"It was nice to have you both come out for dinner and the set. We should do it more often."

"We should," my father said. He wheeled his way out of the bar, with Elaine and me in tow. I walked them to the coat check and then to the car, which was waiting at the door.

"Goodnight," I said and leaned down to kiss my dad once more and then gave Elaine a hug and kiss. "We'll talk soon about Nassau."

"Sounds good."

They drove off just as a few faint drops of rain fell. It was cold enough that it could almost have been snow, but thankfully, wasn't. I wrapped my arms around myself and glanced up at the sky, which was overcast, the lights of the city reflecting off them. A few cars down the curb, I saw a door open and John stepped out of the vehicle. He stood beside the car and watched me and I remembered that I had security following me everywhere I went.

I waved at him and then went back inside, sad that it had come to this.

THE TABLES WERE all crowded by the time I got back and so I sat at the bar and faced the stage, eager to see the second set and learn my fate once the night was finished. Before the guys could get on stage, my cell vibrated. I removed it to find a text from Drake.

DRAKE: Don't get frightened, but I just received a threat from Lisa's brother. I called John and then I spoke with the police and gave them the number. They'll do a trace on it to see if they can identify the caller, but I recognize the voice. They're going to Monroe's house and will report back once they speak with him. If it was him, it'll be a contravention of his bail and the restraining order and he could go to jail without a chance for bail until the trial. I'm going to come out immediately so we can get Sophie and take her to the hotel.

KATE: Oh, Drake... I'm scared. What did he say?

DRAKE: Don't be scared -- we'll be fine. His message was: "I'm coming to get you, you sick bastard. You're going to pay for what you did to my sister." I thought it might be some random troll trying to screw around with me, but it sounded *like him. We should be on the safe side and leave. The band's going to continue playing but without me.*

KATE: Okay. I'm at the bar.

I glanced up at the stage to see Drake emerging from the back room. He scanned the crowd and found me. Our eyes met and I nodded and held my cell up.

Drake turned to Ken and they spoke and Ken laid a hand on Drake's shoulder. It looked like he was reassuring Drake that it was okay for him to leave.

After they shook hands, Drake picked up his guitar, slid it into its case, and slung it over his shoulder. Then, he came over to me, threading his way through the tables.

"Are we going home?" I asked when he got to me, his hands on my arms. "Do the police want you to make a statement or anything?"

"I spoke with them already over the phone but they will want me to come down and make a formal statement," he said. "They'll want to see my cell and they should be able to tell if it's Monroe."

My heart sped up. "You think it was, right?"

"Yes, I'm afraid I do."

"Oh, God." I hugged him, my eyes filling with tears.

Drake broke the embrace and took my hand. "Let's go."

I retrieved my coat from coat check and we went out the back to where John and another of the bodyguards were standing. John had his hand on his hip, where I knew he had a sidearm.

They took the threat seriously.

"Dr. Morgan, Mrs. Morgan," John said, his voice all business. "Please get in the vehicle now. We'll stop off at the police station so you can give a statement and then we'll pick up Sophie and take you to the hotel."

We did, sliding into the back seat and fastening our seat belts while John got in the front.

"I just spoke with Detective Gates at the NYPD that they received a call from one of Monroe's family members that he was armed and had been talking about finding you and making you pay for his sister's incarceration. The family member tried to stop him, but was unable and so they called 9-1-1 immediately. The operator called NYPD with the threat information and they contacted me as the head of your security detail so now we know he was the one who send you that message."

"What should we do about Sophia?" Drake asked, his voice concerned. "Is it safe for her at home? Sophie's there with a babysitter."

"I sent a security detail to watch your house, front and back. If Monroe tries to get into your building, we'll take him down. He must know your home address and phone, both of which are publicly accessible. You might want to reconsider that."

"I'm a surgeon. I need to have my name and business number out there." He turned to me. "Not that I have any patients..."

"For the time being, until the publicity around the trial dies down, I'd change your number to unlisted and take down your home address where it's publicly available. Monroe probably got your address from your testimony at Ms. Monroe's trial."

"I will." Drake took out his cell and called Karen. In a moment, she answered. "Hey, Karen," he said, his voice soft. "How's it going?"

He listened for a moment and then nodded. "Unfortunately, the police say there's been a credible threat to me from Lisa Monroe's brother. Has anyone called you tonight?"

Drake frowned at that. "Okay, when did he call?"

Drake covered his cell and looked at John in the rear view mirror. "Some guy called the house about eight wanting to speak with me. Karen said I was out for the evening. She didn't tell the man where when he asked, and when she asked who was calling, he hung up."

"Sounds like our boy trying to see if you were home."

"We should go and pick up Sophie first, before we go to the precinct. Can I go by myself later? I'd rather get everyone settled in the hotel, then you and I could drive over."

"Probably a good idea," John said. "Just to be safe."

Drake spoke to Karen, telling her we were coming home early because of the threat. We decided to pick up Sophie and take her with us to the hotel.

"Sorry about this," Drake said to her. "We'll be there soon." He ended the call and put his cell away.

"What happens now?" he asked.

"The police will pick him up for uttering a threat, take him in," John said. "Until we know he's in custody, you should stay away from the apartment."

"Can they charge him for making a threat?" I asked.

John caught my eye in the rear-view mirror. "They can," he said. "They can detain him and get a psychiatric assessment done. If he's delusional, or they feel he's a threat to himself or anyone else, they could temporarily admit him."

"Oh, God," I said, a knot of fear in my gut. "He's gone off the deep end."

"That he has," John said. "From what the Detective said, Lisa and her half-brother were rather close. Maybe too close."

I glanced at Drake. "Unhealthily close maybe?"

Drake nodded. "All kinds of boundaries crossed probably. She may be manipulating him from jail."

We drove to the 8th Avenue apartment and John passed the curb in front of our building.

"I don't want to go in the front," he said. "It's too hard to control the scene with pedestrians and vehicular traffic. It's impossible to know if Monroe is hiding in wait."

He drove down the street to the back alley and parked beside the back entrance. Before we got out, John surveyed the alley and finally, got out and spoke on his cell to someone.

"I have a man standing by at both ends of the alley. We should be okay. Be quick."

Drake and I got out and went into the building from the

rear door. We took the stairs up with John in the lead. The fact that his hand was still on his sidearm made me nervous. There was no way Monroe could have gotten into the building but I supposed he wanted to be safe.

We unlocked the door and went inside to find a frightened looking Karen standing in the hallway.

"Drake!" Karen came over to us, her face concerned. "What on Earth is going on?"

"Like I said, Lisa Monroe's brother made a threat against me. He's probably the man who called you earlier."

"Oh, God," she said, her hand to her mouth. "I thought it was strange that he asked where you were. He said he was a friend but I didn't want to tell him anything because we hadn't talked about how to deal with calls. When I asked him for his name, he just hung up. I thought maybe he was a colleague or something."

"It's good you didn't tell him where we were."

I went to Sophie's bedroom and stuffed a few clothes for her and some diapers into her diaper bag. Drake came in behind me and picked her up, putting her jacket and hat on. She was very sleepy and kept her eyes closed in the dark, sucking hard on her pacifier. I was surprised she didn't wake, but she was very tired.

Drake put her in her car seat and after I grabbed some clothes and my laptop and stuffed them into an overnight bag, we all left the apartment.

"Call me and let me know how it all works out," she said when we got to her car, parked a block down the street from our building.

"We will," Drake said. "Thanks for everything, Karen."

"Don't mention it. Take care, you two. I'm so sorry this happened to you."

I waved goodbye and watched her get into her car.

Then we drove off to the Ritz, Sophie asleep in her car seat.

It wasn't the end to the evening I hoped it would be...

DRAKE

WE CHECKED into the Ritz Carlton across from Central Park.

I had planned to take Kate there and tie her up, make her orgasm about three times and then sleep in until noon, have breakfast in bed and a long luxurious bath and another fuck before we left and returned to the real world.

That was my plan and my hope for how the night and next day would play out, but it turned out completely different.

Sophie woke up when we got out of the car at the Ritz, and I took her and Kate up to the Premier Suite, which had a beautiful panoramic view from the top floor of the hotel. We got Sophie out of her carrier and tried to put her to sleep, but she was wide awake.

"Sorry to leave you, but I'll be back soon."

I kissed Kate and then gave Sophie a big smooch on the cheek. John and I took his vehicle and drove to the Midtown South precinct to report the threatening message. I met with Detective Gates, who took my statement and checked my cell, reviewing the message I'd received from Monroe. He'd already contacted Monroe's family, and they confirmed the number belonged to him, so we knew then for a fact Monroe had threatened me.

"We'll find him," Gates said, leaning back in his chair once we were finished and I'd signed the complaint. He handed me his card. "If you get any more messages from him or anyone, give me a call."

"Thank you, Detective."

John and I drove back to the Ritz and I thanked John for his professionalism.

"I'm just doing my job, Dr. Morgan," he said and waved me off.

"Well, I appreciate it all the same."

Then I went inside.

Sophia was still up when I arrived back at the suite. She was awake for another hour and after several books and a fresh bottle, she went down around eleven thirty. By then, Kate and I were tired and only wanted to lie together on the sofa and watch the news, the romance of the evening lost to our fears and worries about Monroe and his threat. He was still not in custody when John messaged me just before midnight, so until he was, we decided we'd stay at the Ritz instead of going back to the 8th Avenue apartment.

We had a suite, which was like a home away from home, if a little opulently furnished for my tastes, but it had a dining room, living room and a large bedroom for us and a second bedroom with a crib for Sophie. The suite had a magnificent view of Central Park, and we enjoyed the view of Manhattan at night while we snuggled together on the sofa.

So instead of the sexy night alone with my love, we spent the rest of the night together worrying about Monroe and whether he'd be picked up soon so we could get back to our lives. The man had been charged with my assault weeks earlier, but had been released on bail on the condition he obey the restraining order issued and so as soon as he was picked up again, he'd be in for good until his trial. And he'd be charged with another felony.

That was the only comfort in the situation.

I'd felt somewhat concerned about him after he was let out on bail, but I honestly never thought he'd really try and harm me again.

He was truly off the deep end.

"You ready for bed?" Kate asked, yawning. She covered her mouth, trying to hide it, but failing. "I'm not really in any kind of mood for sexy times, I'm afraid."

"Being worried about the threat of physical harm from a crazed relative of the woman who tried to kill you destroying your mood, Mrs. Morgan?"

"Something like that," she said, her tone guilty. "I'm sorry. You've been deprived because of the concussion."

I kissed her, smiling to myself. "Don't worry about me. I went almost three months before. I can last another day or so. But no longer," I said with a mock-menacing expression on my face. I touched the tip of her nose and then I broke into a smile. "I expect some very dedicated slave-girl services as soon as we're in the clear."

"Your wish will be my command," she said, unable to keep a grin off her own face.

We snuggled together for a while longer and then went to bed, a bit disoriented because of the change in plans, but at least we had a good meal with the O'Rileys and our family. I got one good set in with the band, and would have another chance to finish a full evening the next weekend.

Life, despite the more recent series of ups and downs, was good.

THE NEXT MORNING, I woke up and had a quick shower while the suite was still dim and quiet, wanting to check in with John to see if they had found Monroe. After wrapping a towel around my waist, I went into the living room and sat in front of the television, my cell in hand. I checked the news and then my cell for messages, but saw none so I called John.

"Hello, Dr. Morgan," he said when he answered. "How was your night? I hope you both were able to sleep."

"We're fine," I replied. "Just checking in to see if there's any news on Monroe."

"Not yet," he said, "but I'll put a call in to my contact at the precinct and get an update. I'll call you back ASAP. Until then, don't go out of your room or the hotel."

"Got it. Let me know what you learn."

I hung up and switched channels, but there was nothing on the local news except talk about the traffic issues because of a steam pipe explosion earlier in the week.

I peeked into the bedroom, which was still dim due to blackout curtains over the window. Kate was asleep so I went to the other bedroom and saw that Sophie was still asleep as well. I smiled to myself, happy that my two girls were fine.

I really wanted to go for a run, but that was out of the question. Until Monroe was in custody, I wasn't taking any chances. I quickly and very quietly dressed, and then I went back into the living room and called down to room service, ordering breakfast for the three of us. For the next twenty minutes, I worked on my laptop going over some information on my credentials at NYP, wanting to talk to the supervisor there about waiting for a year before being considered for reinstatement.

I heard a light knock at the door and checked through the peephole. Sure enough, a young female room service staff was standing outside with a cart containing several silver dome-covered plates, glasses and cups and what I really wanted -- a carafe of coffee. Beside her stood one of the guards who was on duty, watching our hotel room all night.

It felt a bit excessive, but John and I agreed that it was better to be safe than sorry.

I opened the door and the maid wheeled in the cart and placed it in the living room. When she was finished, I thanked her and gave her a generous tip.

First things first -- coffee. Black. Two sugars.

I sat in front of the television, drinking my coffee and waiting for my two girls to wake up and keep me company. In about ten minutes, I heard the shower running and knew that Kate was up and getting started. I put my cup down and went into the second bedroom to find Sophie asleep on her back, her arms thrown up beside her head, her pacifier still between her teeth. She was asleep and I wasn't going to wake her up. Maybe Kate and I could enjoy our breakfast together before she got up and could talk about the whole business.

Sure enough, in about ten minutes, Kate arrived, freshly showered and dressed. She came right over to where I was sitting on one of the sofas and bent down for a kiss.

"Good morning," she said. "I see there's breakfast."

"There is," I said and got up. Together, we went to explore the food. There was an opulent spread -- a hot serving dish with eggs and bacon, plus fried potatoes and toast. There was also a cold serving dish with fruit and yogurt, Danishes and muffins. Plus a carafe of coffee, one of fresh-squeezed orange juice and one of hot water for tea.

"Yum," Kate said and took a plate. "I could get used to this."

Together, we dug in and sat at the sofa, eating our breakfast in front of the television.

"Anything new on Monroe?"

"Nothing yet," I said. "I talked with John but they're still looking for him. He didn't show up at home so maybe he's hiding out at a friend's place or other family."

"I hope they find him soon," she said and forked some eggs onto a triangle of toast. "But not too soon, so we have an excuse to stay here and get room service morning, noon and night." She gave me a smile and I laughed.

"You know, we could afford to hire a housekeeper and cook, if you really wanted it."

She shook her head. "No," she said and drank down some juice. "We only ever had one cook for parties and occasionally a housekeeper would come in for deep cleaning at my home when I was growing up. It's a bit ostentatious for me to have a housekeeper and cook, but it's fun to indulge now and then." She smiled at me, her eyes crinkling up at the corner.

"If you ever change your mind, let me know and I'll sign the papers."

"Seriously? You'd agree to having a housekeeper and cook?"

"Of course," I said, for I would if it would make Kate happy. "If you feel it would give you more time with Sophie or with your art, yes."

She glanced away and considered. "I'd be embarrassed. Maybe a housekeeper once a week though. That would be nice. Then neither of us would have to mop or vacuum."

"Consider it done. I'm sure there's a service we could hire that could come in once a week. We could all go out as a family while they were cleaning and when we came home, all our dust and dirt would be gone."

"That's great. But I want to keep cooking together. I love it when we cook for each other."

"Me, too."

We kissed quickly and then returned to our breakfasts while the news came on at the top of the hour.

The jury had been deliberating for several days, and that

wasn't a good thing, according to Lara. The longer they took, the less likely they were to convict because it would mean the state's case had not been made clearly enough for an easy verdict. They had asked to see evidence again and read over testimony. Lara said it was often the case that jurors wanted to go back over the evidence and testimony but the longer they were out, the shorter might be the sentence.

Finally, what we had been waiting for – the jury reached a verdict and was going to reconvene in the courtroom. There were cameras on the street and a real buzz in the public. What would the verdict be? We watched entranced while the news reporters outside the courtroom heard the verdict over their earphones and informed the viewers.

The verdict was better than I could have hoped. Lisa would be spending twenty-five years in prison for the murder of Derek Richardson. Her trial for the death of Jones wasn't for months but it could only add to her sentence – or I hoped at least she'd get another decade or two.

I turned to Kate and smiled, then opened my arms. Together, we hugged and a moment of silence passed between us. I think that, at that moment, the burden of the past was partially lifted.

She was going away – for a long time. Once her other trial took place, I knew she'd be going away for even longer.

"I'm so glad," Kate said, tears in her eyes. "That bitch can no longer hurt us."

"I hope not," I said but I felt uncertain even then. I paid a heavy price for my relationship with Lisa. What else could she do? She could continue to spread lies about me. I had a feeling she wouldn't go gently into that good night.

Kate and I sat listening to the commentary for another half an hour. Then I heard a squeak from the back of the suite.

"That's Sophie," I said. "I'll go get her. You stay."

"Are you sure?" Kate said, making a move to stand.

"It's my day today. You stay."

"Okay, thanks," she said and sat back down, then continued watching.

I went to the bedroom and opened the drapes to admit bright sunlight into the room. Sophie was standing up in her crib and was smiling at me, her pacifier in her mouth.

"Good morning sweetheart," I said and went to her, picking her up and giving her a big kiss on both cheeks. "How's Daddy's favorite little girl?"

She pointed to the door, but instead, I carried her to the bed and laid her down, grabbing the diaper bag from the floor. Of course, by the time I got back, she'd crawled to the edge of the bed so I had to grab her playfully and pull her back into place. While I unzipped the bag, she twisted out of my hand and crawled once more over to the edge.

"Hey, you!" I said and grabbed her, pulling her towards me and tickling her once I got her back into place. "You stay put so Daddy can change your diaper."

She giggled when I tickled her, and finally, she let me get her onesie unzipped and her diaper off. As I changed her, we played the 'Wat dat?' game, as I called it. It was a point and name game that we played while I changed her. She would point and sometimes poke my face or her own and we'd name the part. Every time I changed her, it was the same.

"Wat dat?"

"Daddy's nose," I replied. Then it was my turn. "What's that?" I asked, pointing to one of her eyes.

"FoFi eyes." Then, she'd point at something on me. "Wat dat?"

"Daddy's mouth. What's that?"

"FoFi ear."

Sophie referred to herself as FoFi, as it seemed to come the easiest for her to pronounce. I loved hearing her say actual words rather than the babble that often came out when she was trying to talk. I couldn't wait to hear what went on in her mind in more detail once she could express herself more fully.

When I rolled the wet diaper up and was reaching to the trash can beside the bedside table, she wriggled away once more, squealing when I grabbed her and tickled her back into submission.

"You are a wiggle-worm," I said and finally managed to get her diaper on her, with no further wriggles away. I zipped up her onesie and she crawled off the side of the bed while I went to wash my hands. I watched from the bathroom door while she ran out of the bedroom and into the living room where Kate was seated, still eating.

"Hi, baby girl," Kate said, opening her arms for a hug.

Sophie babbled around her pacifier and climbed up on

Kate's lap. Kate then happily fed her some yogurt and fruit. It was such a happy domestic scene that only a few years earlier, I never thought I'd ever have or enjoy.

I almost didn't get a chance to enjoy it either, because of Lisa Monroe. And now, Lisa's brother was threatening me.

I exhaled and went back into the living room, thankful for what I had, determined to never, ever take it for granted.

I SPENT some time on my laptop that morning catching up on my email while Kate and Sophie played. Dave sent me the final papers that officially shut down the foundation, and seeing them, reading over the document, made me sad. I loved the foundation for it kept me connected to the memory of my father and the good work he did all his life as a trauma surgeon, volunteering with Doctors Without Borders. I hated that my past and my involvement in BDSM had forced me to shut it down.

I sighed and sent Dave an email, thanking him for taking care of it for me and asking him to keep me informed of his efforts to set up a new foundation.

Around eleven, my cell rang and I checked the caller ID. It was from Detective Gates.

"Just a quick call to let you know we apprehended Mr. Monroe without incident about half an hour ago and we have him in custody. He spent the night at a relative's place after one of his family members warned him that they'd called the police. We surrounded the house but there was no stand-off. He came out willingly, was arrested and is getting processed as we speak. You can relax. He won't be getting out of jail any time soon, at least until his trial finishes."

"I hope not then either," I said.

"I doubt he will, but we'll let the wheels of justice grind and find out whenever the case comes up. In the meantime, he'll be in custody so at least you don't have to be afraid to return home."

I glanced over to Kate. "My wife was just saying she could get used to the room service."

"I'm sure she could. I expect you heard the verdict?"

"That I did. I can tell you that it was a relief that she's going away for so long."

"Everyone did their job," the officer said. "Have a good day. If anything related to the threat comes up, please give me a call."

"I will," I said and ended the call.

"Well, we can go home," I said, raising my eyebrows at Kate.

"So soon?" She mock-pouted, although I was certain that she really meant it. "Can we stay another day at least?"

"We can," I said. "I already called down to the front desk, reserving the room for another night just in case. We have it until tomorrow at eleven."

"Good," Kate said and leaned back, her feet stretching out. "I want to eat waffles tomorrow. With real maple syrup."

"Waffles it is. What do you want to do all day?"

She stretched her arms up over her head. "I don't know -- maybe go to Central Park? It's a bit cold but it's sunny."

"Central Park it is. Maybe we can finalize our trip."

"Yes," she said. "I can't wait to go to Nassau. I want to go back to every place we visited that weekend."

"If I recall correctly, we didn't really have the greatest time. I thought everything was going well and then all of a sudden you were treating me like I was the oldest fuddy-duddy ever and couldn't wait to get out of my presence."

She leaned closer, resting her head on my shoulder. "I thought you were the hottest, most desirable man I'd ever met and felt sick to my stomach that I had to lie to you and leave early."

"I had so many plans for you, and then *bam*. You were gone back to Manhattan and I was alone -- again."

"I was physically sick over the next few days because of it. I honestly laid in bed and moped for so long, Lara was worried about me. Then I cried on her shoulder at a coffee shop and told her what happened."

"She saved the day," I said, remembering when Lara played the recording of what Kate said about me.

"She did," Kate said. "I remember thinking she wanted us to break up. Instead, she was forcing both our hands. When I saw you across the street from the deli, I only knew I wanted you more than anything."

"When I saw *you* sitting in the window seat in the deli, I only knew I had to have you as my own. More than anything."

We smiled at each other, leaning our heads together, forehead to forehead.

"I love you, Mrs. Morgan."

"I love you, Dr. Morgan."

We kissed tenderly. On the floor, Sophie bashed her Tiny Town characters into the toy car, her pacifier clamped tightly between her teeth.

KATE

WE DRESSED and went to Central Park as we planned, walking along the pathways with Sophie in her stroller, which thankfully, Drake thought to put in the back of the car on our way over the previous night. Sophie was wearing her kitten hat and heart sunglasses and looked so cute sitting forward in her stroller, eager to see the world. We passed an old man and woman sitting on a bench. The two of them smiled and waved at Sophie. She smiled and waved back, delighting the old couple. Ahead of us a few paces walked John, who scanned the pathways for any sign of a threat. I wasn't afraid any longer, now that Monroe was in police custody, and Lisa had been put away, but there had been enough publicity about Drake's lifestyle and his face had been plastered enough in the news that someone might recognize him. John didn't think anyone would actually want to harm Drake, but they might harass him.

Drake didn't need it, so John walked ahead of us and one of the other guards from the agency walked behind us.

"Will this ever end? This constant entourage of ours? Will we ever be able to go out again without protection?"

Drake took my hand and squeezed. "It will. I promise you in a year, it will all be forgotten. Some other lucky person will become the press's darling and the tabloids will ruin their lives and forget about ours." He raised my hand up to his lips and kissed my knuckles. "I promise."

I forced a smile I didn't really feel. "I hope so."

We spent about an hour walking through the park, then stopped and watched while Sophie ran through piles of leaves. The vibrant colors reminded me of the year we were married. So much had happened since that day, and my life had changed irrevocably and for the better. As we walked back to the Ritz, I wondered how much our lives would change again in another year, or ten. Where would we be? Would we still be in Manhattan or would we be living elsewhere?

I loved Manhattan, but given recent events, I felt a little sour on it. I hoped Drake was right and it would all change once the trial was forgotten but until Drake got his surgical privileges back, he would be at loose ends.

Of course, then I thought about Southampton and how great the job would be for him. If only the job was here instead, everything would be perfect.

I sighed and pushed the thought out of my mind. Drake seemed happy enough and that was all I cared about.

WE ARRIVED BACK at the hotel and had a nice quiet dinner in the suite, room service providing a delicious prime rib roast and all the trimmings. After dinner, after Sophie had a bath and Drake read half a dozen of her books, we put Sophie down for the night. I felt a little thrill in my belly at the thought that we were finally – *finally* – going to make love. I had no idea what to expect, but Drake said he had plans for me. Whatever plans he had, I knew I'd enjoy them. Already, my flesh was swollen and wet at the thought of the evening to come.

When I came out of the bedroom, Drake was already seated on the sofa, his arm on the armrest, his fingers rubbing his chin. "Come here, Katherine," he said, his voice low and sexy.

I couldn't stop smiling, but then caught myself and forced my expression blank. "Yes, Sir." I stood in front of him, waiting.

"You have far too much clothing on," he said, his gaze moving over my body from my feet to my face and back.

"But it's cold outside, Sir," I said it with a bit too much playfulness in my tone. "If I didn't have clothes on, I'd be very uncomfortable."

He made a mock face of affront. "That's a *very* saucy mouth you have." He stood up abruptly and faced me, his eyes locked with mine. He touched the scar on my bottom lip. "I might have to silence that mouth."

"Sir doesn't like this one's mouth?" I said with a pout.

"I happen to love that mouth, but it would do better for you, Katherine, if you used that mouth for better purposes than to test your Master. Now, about that excess of clothing..."

He quirked one eyebrow expectantly.

"Would Sir like this one to remove her excess clothing?"

He sat back down again. "I just might. But first, climb onto my lap. I'll think of ways to put that mouth to good use, fill it full so you can't be so insolent."

"I hope you wouldn't consider a ball gag," I said and knelt over him one knee on either side of his thighs. I purposely leaned forward so that my breasts were almost touching his face.

"I had something completely different in mind..." He narrowed his eyes and glanced up at me. "And remember your manners..."

"So sorry," I said, fighting my grin. "This one hopes Sir wouldn't consider a ball gag..."

"You should know I only ever think of your pleasure," he said, his face becoming stern once more. "Now, kiss me."

I took his face between my hands and kissing him, my tongue sliding into his mouth and searching for his.

The kiss went on and on, and with each passing moment, my body was even more ready for him, my flesh aching to feel him inside of me.

When I pulled back, panting with desire, he smiled.

"You're quiet now," he said, the corner of his mouth turning up. "On your knees."

I complied, sliding off his lap and kneeling between his thighs.

He stood up. "You know what to do."

I did.

I unfastened his belt and unzipped his jeans. Beneath his boxer briefs, he was hard as rock. He'd been anticipating this as much as I had. When I reached in and pulled down the fabric, his erection sprang out, the tip wet with precum.

I grabbed hold of him and licked the head very carefully and deliberately so he could watch and enjoy the sight, then I glanced up and met his eyes while I placed my lips around the thick head.

"You are a tease, Katherine," he said, his voice a hiss as I sucked, the tip of my tongue running around the rim. "Now, suck. Hard."

The head of his cock was thick and smooth against my tongue and cheeks as I moved on it, one hand circling his shaft. While I stroked him and sucked, I held his testicles in the other hand.

He grabbed my hair, which had fallen over my face and twisted it in his hand, guiding me.

"Deeper," he said. "Deeper."

I complied, but could only manage the first few inches. When he pulled my head down a bit too far, I gagged. He let up, his grip lightening.

"That's so good," he said in encouragement. "Faster."

I moved faster and stroked with both my hands now. In response, his cock hardened under my lips and tongue.

"Stop," he commanded, his voice choked with lust. I stopped my motion, enjoying the way the head felt in my mouth. So hot and smooth. I pulled off and glanced up at him, my hands still gripping the shaft.

He breathed hard, his nostrils flared. "Good *girl*," he said. "I love your mouth. I love your lips."

He took my hand and helped me up. "Now, undress me."

I pulled the sweater up and over his head, revealing his very buff abs and mostly bare chest except for a nice smattering of hair on his pecs. I pulled his jeans down off and helped him step out of them. Finally naked, he was magnificent. His hard cock jutted out, wet from my saliva.

"Now, you undress," Drake said. "Slowly..."

I tried to be as seductive as I could while I removed my clothes. Then, when I was naked, he picked me up and carried me into the bathroom, to the enclosed shower that was big enough for two people.

After he turned on the shower, he leaned me up against the shower wall and I wrapped my legs around his narrow hips, holding on to his shoulders. He kissed me and rubbed his cock over my slit, the water coursing over us from behind. He pulled away, his eyes locked with mine.

"You waxed," he said, a quirk of a grin on his mouth. "Trying to tempt me, are you?"

"We aim to please," I replied, and licked my bottom lip.

He frowned briefly and of course, I remembered my manners.

"This one aims to please her Sir," I said with proper deference, my eyes downcast. Then, I glanced up into his eyes once more, barely suppressing a smile.

"You are incorrigible," he said, shaking his head. "How shall I punish you for being so insolent? Maybe work you up so that you're aching and then deny you an orgasm?"

"Oh, Sir, that would be so mean considering how deprived this one is..."

"Perhaps it would remind you how to properly behave with your master," Drake said. "A submissive should make sure to use the proper form of address and remember how to stay in scene..."

I closed my eyes and bit my bottom lip. "This one is sorry, Sir. She gets too excited at times and forgets."

Then he silenced me with a blistering kiss. When he pulled away, he touched the small scar on my bottom lip. "Perhaps you could merely listen and obey, instead of offering up opinions. More pleasure may be had that way, I assure you."

"Yes, Sir," I replied, trying to sound deferential, but of course, it was all a game now. A game we enjoyed, but a game nonetheless.

He knelt and slid one of my thighs over his shoulder and split my lips with his tongue, one finger and then two entering me, teasing my most sensitive spot. I groaned and watched him, the sight of his mouth of me making me even more aroused.

"I'm so close," I said because despite all the joking between us, I was in need. I knew I'd come fast the first time.

"Relax," he said and glanced up, our eyes meeting. "This is going to last all night, if I have my way."

Then he licked me again, his tongue sliding slowly over my clit, then down again so that I was breathless.

"I need you to fuck me right now," I gasped. "I'm going to come..."

But he merely slid another finger inside of me and that added pressure combined with his lips and tongue now tugging at my clit sent me over. I shuddered, my hands gripping his shoulders, my body clenching around his fingers, hips thrusting towards his mouth. He didn't stop his movements and within moments, I had another shattering orgasm, my legs almost giving out beneath me. I had to grab hold of the support bar on the shower wall to keep from falling, my thighs quivering from the pleasure.

"Two in a row, Ms. Bennet. I believe you were *very* in need."

I gasped, my brain almost shutting down from the intensity of my orgasms.

Drake finally stood, his erection jutting into my belly, his hands against the wall on either side of my shoulders.

"That silenced your saucy mouth," he murmured. "I'll have to do that more often."

I opened my eyes and stared into his. "If you do that, I'll be your slave forever."

He kissed me, smiling. "When you do that, you know it's the other way around." He handed me a bar of soap. "Is your mind recovered enough to wash me?"

I took the soap and smiled. "Almost. Luckily, washing your delicious body doesn't take much brain power."

He grinned and watched while I lathered up, then ran my

hands down from his shoulders and over his abs to his beautiful very thick and hard cock.

He grunted while I slid my hands over his length, palming the head, then cupping his balls. I washed the rest of his body off and he mine, and finally finished, we left the stall and he pulled me to the bed, practically throwing me onto it.

I was glad we had a two-bedroom suite, so I wouldn't have to worry about waking Sophie. We were giggling together as our wet bodies slid against one another.

Finally, Drake reared up over me, his hands on either side of my head.

"And now, *Katherine*, it's time to obey."

I tried to get back into scene at the more formal mention of my name.

He got up from the bed and went to his suitcase, sorting through his clothes, pulling out a long leather rope, and several lambs-wool cuffs. My heart did a little skip when I realized he was going to tie me up, for I knew that meant he was serious. I bit my bottom lip in an effort to stop from smiling too widely.

He caught my grin, his eyebrows raised.

"Katherine, when you see these cuffs and bindings, you're supposed to submit, not tease."

"Sorry, Sir," I said, trying but failing to sound recalcitrant. "It's been a while since you tied me up. I'm a little excited."

"You are insatiable," he said, his blue eyes twinkling from

under a mock-frown. "You just had two orgasms and still want more."

"You made me greedy, Sir."

Then, he returned to the bed and took my hands in his, pulling them over my head, his grip firm to establish dominance.

"You can't distract me with that smile. Now, I want you to focus on what I'm doing here and *now*." Then he kissed me, sending a jolt of desire once more through my body.

"I'm sorry, S*ir*," I said, barely able to whisper. "I'll try to behave."

"There is no try," he said, one side of his mouth quirking up. "Do or do not."

The Yoda reference finally undid me and I laughed out loud. He laughed out loud as well and buried his face in my neck.

We giggled like two children, involved in a caper. When the laughter died out, he became serious, his eyes burning into mine.

"Focus," he said, his voice deep. "Keep your eyes on me, keep yourself focused mentally and emotionally."

I realized I'd been too playful, forgetting that during a scene, even with my loving husband, I had to be submissive. We didn't need this, but we liked it. I enjoyed it – this game of power exchange.

The look in his eyes sent a thrill of desire through my body. I took in a deep breath and let go of any need for control over my mind or my body. I wanted him to have that control and take me where he wanted me – which was always pleasure.

"Good," he said, his hands gripping mine and confining them above my head. He kissed me hungrily and then pulled back, reaching to the bedside table for the cuffs. He fastened them around my wrists and then attached them to the bed frame. I pulled on them, getting a sense of how much I could move.

Next, he fastened the ankle cuffs and likewise fastened them to the bed frame.

I was truly at his mercy, but of course, I never had to worry about his plans. There was never any fear of him – just excitement and wonder.

"You're mine, Katherine."

"I am," I said softly. I was.

He ran his hands over my body, squeezing my breasts and then stroking down my belly to my pussy. He spread my thighs as far as they could go and knelt between them, rubbing the head of his cock over my clit. In this way, he worked me back up again, sliding the head over my lips and pushing into me an inch, then two before pulling out and stroking my clit again.

Soon, I was near my orgasm and gasped. "I'm almost..."

He shoved himself completely inside of me and the sudden pressure of his thick cock sent me over and my orgasm began, the sweetness spreading from my pussy to my groin and then through my body. I spasmed around him as he thrust, harder and faster, and before I was even finished my orgasm, his began, his face straining from his own pleasure, face read, eyes squeezed shut.

It was so fast for us both.

He collapsed on top of me, his hands still gripping mine, and breathed in deeply, his face by mine.

We kissed, deeply, our kiss full of emotion. When he pulled back, our eyes met.

"I love you so damn much," he said, his voice wavering with emotion. "You're all I have left. You and Sophie. Everything else is gone."

I searched his face.

"Drake," I said, my voice soft. "What do you mean?"

He shook his head and didn't answer.

"Tell me," I said, but he merely sat up and unfastened my cuffs, freeing my arms. Next, he moved to my feet, and released them.

I sat up and rubbed my wrists, which had chafed just a bit during sex. Did he really mean that? Was everything else gone?

"Tell me."

"Forget it," he said and smiled softly. "Just feeling sorry for myself."

He grabbed some tissues from the bedside table and proceeded to wipe me off, then cleaned himself. I wasn't sure how much to push on the subject, but it hurt me so much to think that's how he felt.

"Drake, please," I said and reached out to touch his face. "Tell me what you mean, you've lost everything except for Sophie and me. What happened?"

He threw the tissues into the trash can beside the bed and lay on his back, an arm behind his head. He turned to face me, his expression serious.

"I didn't want to burden you with it."

I lay on my side and faced him. "You could never burden me with anything. If it matters to you, it matters to me."

"Earlier today, I got the final papers on the shutting down of the foundation. Donations pretty much dried up and we couldn't afford the new projects we planned. I'm covering the funds we need to finish up the projects we already have started. And I'll keep funding the ongoing projects, but Dave is shutting it down."

"Oh, Drake, I'm so sorry... I knew you were going to wind it down but so quickly?" I reached out and ran my fingers through his hair. "That's too bad. But you still have the corporation."

"Not on the board. They want to buy me out and dissociate the business from me completely."

"Oh, God," I said, my stomach clenching. "That's crazy. You being a large stockholder can't mean anything."

"They want me out. I sold my shares. We're a lot richer because of it, but I'm no longer a major shareholder."

I lay on my back and stared at the ceiling. So much fallout.

"And NYU's off," I said, turning to him.

He shook his head slowly. "Not on the agenda this year. Fred Parker said maybe in a year, but the committee did not look on my involvement in BDSM lifestyle to be a benefit to my candidacy."

I bit my bottom lip. On top of that, Drake no longer had privileges at NYP. He had no patients. They'd hired someone else to take over the robotic surgery rotation at Columbia.

"I'm so sorry," I said, my voice breaking. "This is all so unfair."

"It may be, but it's reality."

We lay there and he pulled me over, wrapping his arms around me.

I knew what this all meant, of course. I knew right away what I had to say.

"You have to accept Michael's offer."

He pulled back and met my eyes. "Are you serious?"

I nodded, and ran my fingers over his cheek. "You have to go. *We* have to go."

"I thought you couldn't leave Ethan."

I sighed. "I don't want to, but I will. You and Sophie are everything to me. I've lived in the same city as my father for my entire life except for Africa and a few months in San Francisco. Besides, I can fly over for a week any time I want, with Sophie. They can fly to Southampton when it gets cold here."

"If you're truly serious, it would mean I could practice medicine again. It's Michael's department and he has full control over hiring and firing. He said he wanted me there to help set up the robotic surgery unit and staff it. I'd be the head. It's an administrative position with surgical privileges. So, I'd be teaching and be involved in the administration of the unit. I'd pick the staff and surgeons. It would be mine, Kate."

I smiled at him. "It sounds so perfect for you. I've been looking at images of Southampton. It looks nice. The weather is good. My father could come and visit whenever he felt like it."

"He could."

"What about Liam?"

Drake lay back. "That's still up in the air. But maybe, if Maureen agrees to joint custody, Liam could live with me during the school year and spend time with Maureen and Chris every holiday and during the summer. I hope she'd be willing to consider it. Besides, Southampton has one of the best children's hospitals in the UK. He'd be in good hands."

He pulled me on top of him, his arms around my waist.

"You're serious about this?"

"I am," I said. "I'm sorry I was so resistant. I'm sorry I made you feel like you had to say no. But if you've lost everything else here, how could I be the one to say no? I can still paint. I can write. I'll still have you and Sophie. And my dad can visit anytime he feels like."

"We'd have to get a really big house there so Ethan and Elaine could come and stay for the winter."

"We would. Somewhere close to the water. Maybe a renovated old house with a huge acreage. I'd love for Sophie to grow up surrounded by nature instead of the streets of Manhattan."

"Seriously? I'd have thought you would want her to grow up in the city the way you did."

I shook my head. "I've soured a bit on Manhattan since all this happened. The way the press treated you. How predatory everyone is -- the tabloids, the paparazzi. The character assassination. I want to live somewhere with a nice rural feel to it, where people are private and polite."

"We could find a place close to the ocean. That would be nice."

We kissed and my heart filled with love for him. He didn't push me to make the decision. He let me come to it myself, giving me the space and time to realize it was the right decision.

"Thank you," he said. "I love you so much."

"I love you so much," I replied and kissed him once more.

We fell asleep that way, lying together, with him spooned behind me.

WE MADE LOVE the next morning but it was plain old vanilla sex.

"I hope you're not disappointed," he said and kissed me, his erection still hard inside me after his orgasm. I had planned on going all Dom on you again after last night's success, but I just wanted to be inside of you as soon as possible."

"Never," I said and pulled him down for a kiss. My body still spasmed from my orgasm, and a thin sheen of moisture from exertion covered me. When the kiss broke, I locked eyes with him. "I told you that you could take control in the bedroom. I know you'll always make me happy and you do."

"Then I'm happy," he said. "Now, let's plan the rest of our lives."

I smiled. For the first time in a long while, I no longer felt that dark cloud hanging over me.

DRAKE

OF COURSE, Michael was overjoyed to hear from me.

"Drake, I am so happy you reconsidered. Seriously. This is positively the best news!"

"I hope you didn't hire someone else," I said and smiled to myself. "If so, it would suck to be that person."

"No," Michael replied. "I spoke with several other surgeons who have experience with robotics, but I didn't commit. You put me in a bad position because none of the other candidates have your level of expertise. This makes me very happy all around."

I cleared my throat. "There'll be no issue with my recent tabloid coverage?"

"No," he said adamantly. "This is my baby and I have complete authority over hiring. I proposed you as my first choice and the administration only considered your experience, your time in Africa and your work in NYP. You were widely approved."

"That's great," I said, a huge sense of relief flooding me. "I don't want to face staff who are unhappy to have me there."

"No need to worry about that. They're eager to learn from you. I can't wait for you and Kate to get here – and that pretty little girl of yours, too."

"Thanks, Michael. This really is the most exciting opportunity I could ever think of. And it comes at the perfect time. Kate will have an adjustment to make, but she's happy that I'll be working, doing what I love."

"She can paint here. There are great nurseries for children Sophie's age. The school system is first rate if Liam comes. Really, I think you'll love it here."

"I'm sure we will."

I hung up after establishing a start date for my position, and then I left my office to find Kate with Sophie. They were on the sofa and were reading a book, with Sophie pointing at each page and saying words.

"Well, it's confirmed. I start January 14th. We'll spend the rest of the month getting everything set up and then start rotations once everything's in place."

I walked over to them and leaned over to kiss Sophie and then gave Kate a warm kiss. I stroked her cheek and held her eyes.

"Thank you so much," I said, emotion filling me. "January can't come soon enough. We should find a house as soon as possible. I've been looking at some online and found one I like."

I sat beside her and pulled my iPad off the coffee table. I

opened a browser to a tab with a beautiful old home. Two story, red brick with black and white trim, it was an eight-bedroom mansion that was more than just a house. It was a real home.

"That's amazing," she said as we scrolled through the pictures of the rooms. "Fit for a prince and princess rather than plain old us."

"Plain old us deserves it, after all we've both been through. It has a pasture, a stable for horses and a huge garden. It's only a block away from the ocean on top of it."

"How far from the hospital would it be? I don't want you driving too far."

"It's no big deal. I want this house, if you think it would do."

"Would it do? My God, Drake. It's a mansion."

"It is, kind of. But it would be big enough for Liam and we could have dad and Elaine come and stay, plus there would be rooms for Heath and Christie and the kids if they did as well."

Kate smiled at me and stroked my cheek. "You have it all figured out."

"I do," I said and kissed her and then kissed Sophie's head. "I keep imagining Sophie and Liam riding horses in the pasture and spending time outdoors instead of on the streets of Manhattan.

Sophie was busy swiping the screen between pictures, stabbing the photos with her pinkie.

"You like the house, Sophie? That's going to be your new home, if I can swing it." I glanced at Kate. "Gotta find something of value to spend all that money from the sale of the corporation. That home is worth it."

"It's beautiful."

We spent the rest of the morning examining the house and then we spoke with a real estate agent and agreed to move forward with the offer. We'd know by the end of the week if the owners accepted it.

"I can't thank you enough for agreeing to this," I said, pulling Kate closer after Sophie climbed down and went over to her toy box to play with her toys. "I feel almost giddy with happiness at starting from ground zero with the robotic surgery unit. I get to plan everything, get all the equipment and staff and then set up the schedule. It's a dream come true."

Kate turned to me, her eyes warm. "You deserve it."

We kissed.

"I love you," I said, emotion filling me. "More than anything."

"I love you more than anything."

"You're not going to be upset leaving Manhattan behind?"

Kate sighed. "At first I was, but since Dad and Elaine are coming for a couple of months to get away from the winter, I know I won't be lonely while we get settled in. So no. I'm not at all upset to be leaving Manhattan behind. I'm actually excited. I can't wait to shop for furniture in Southampton. And I want to use one of the reception rooms as my studio." She rubbed her hands together. "With all that natural light, it'll be fantastic."

"Good," I said and squeezed her.

Together, we turned and watched Sophie play.

For the next two months, we'd have to pack and ship our things to Southampton, and get ready for the move to England. Plus, we had a trip to Nassau in the works at Christmas and had to plan for that.

It would be more than enough to keep us both busy. I knew that in no time at all, the three of us would be in our house in Southampton, starting our new life together there.

I was the luckiest man in the world and I knew it.

In two months, all this would be behind us -- the trial, the threats, the publicity -- all of it in the rearview mirror. I'd be starting my new position and starting the robotic surgery unit from the ground up.

I couldn't be happier and for once, I truly believed that Kate couldn't be happier either.

And that was everything.

EPILOGUE

DRAKE WAS the happiest I had ever seen him.

That made everything worthwhile -- leaving Manhattan, saying goodbye to my father and Elaine for a while, and going somewhere new. After the turmoil of the last few years, with the attack on me and then the murder of Derek Richardson, the trials and the threat to Drake's safety and my own, I was glad to be starting over. I hoped we'd be happy enough in England with Drake doing what he loved best so that we could stay for a few years.

Drake was in his element -- he was back doing surgery and seeing patients, teaching and running the robotic surgery unit. The bad news of the trial was behind us, and seemed more like an extended bad dream from which we had just awoken rather than anything real.

Drake had the chance to start fresh in England with Michael as his mentor and boss and a robotic surgery unit to set up. For the first month, he was hard at work making sure all the proper equipment was on hand for when the unit would become operational.

When he'd accepted the position with Michael, they had started work, purchasing the equipment they'd need for the unit, doing a search for talented surgeons and OR nurses, and setting a grand opening date when they would start accepting patients. By the time we arrived in January after a nice vacation in Nassau, the only thing left to do was get everything in place for the February opening.

Our home in the Southampton area was beyond anything I could imagine. Drake really went all out to purchase a dream home with everything we might need to raise Sophie, Liam when he eventually (and hopefully) came to live with us. It was big enough for my father and Elaine, who planned on staying there with us during the winter. With eight bedrooms and as many bathrooms, and three sitting rooms, there was more than enough space for all of us. I even had to hire a local housekeeper and groundskeeper to come by and keep the place clean. There was no way I could do it myself -- not and raise Sophie and keep up with my art. Besides all the bedrooms and sitting rooms, the house had a great room with a kitchen fit for a chef and a solarium so we could sit out during the sunny days and enjoy the scenery.

While Drake worked at the children's hospital getting the robotic surgery unit set up, I spent the first weeks organizing the house for my father's and Elaine's arrival. Liam had spent the Christmas and New Year's holidays with his mother and was going back to Manhattan for the rest of the school year. Drake's hopes that Maureen would relent and let Liam come live with us instead of his grandmother were crushed, but he wasn't willing to give up just yet. He'd try for joint custody in a year when there was no more publicity around Lisa Monroe.

It was on a sunny February day that I decided to finally go to the hospital to check out the unit. Michael had been pestering me to come by and watch Drake operate, and I had yet to accept. We'd been in Southampton for a full month and so I decided it was time for me to venture out beyond our home and go to the hospital to watch Drake in his OR theatre using his new state-of-the-art surgical suite. Sophia was at her daycare for the afternoon. The woman who ran the small home-based daycare was a former teacher and had dual degrees in psychology and education, so I felt safe leaving Sophie with her. There were three other children under the age of five, so she'd get some socialization.

Until my father and Elaine arrived later in the week, I was alone and free to do what I felt like.

"Come tomorrow," Michael said on the phone. "Drake's teaching a class and you can sit in the audience and watch while he operates. It's the last surgery of the day and so Drake will be finished afterwards."

"I have to pick up Sophie from her daycare but how about you coming over for supper with us?"

"Sounds perfect," Michael said. "Don't let Drake know. It'll be a surprise. I'll pick up some Indian take-away and we can make an evening of it."

"Sounds perfect."

So, I took the second car and drove to the Southampton Children's Hospital and made my way to Michael's office.

From there, he'd take me to the OR theatre and get me set up in the observation room so I could watch with Drake's new students.

Michael hugged me when I arrived, kissing both my cheeks as was his custom.

"There you are, Miss Katherine," he said and ushered me down the hall to the surgical suite. "The surgery is in progress, so I'll sneak you into the observation room. There are a half-dozen students watching."

"Will they mind if I watch?"

"Not at all," Michael replied. "They'll be too busy watching the surgery to care. Besides, when they see me, they'll all be on their best behavior."

We went to a door and inside I saw a bank of seats like you would see in a movie theatre. About seven students were seated in the front two rows, watching through a huge window. Below was the OR suite, with a large robotic arm poised over a reclining patient. Off to the side was a portable CT. Drake in a surgical cap and gown, with special optical glasses on, stood by the patient's head and several of his staff surrounded the surgical gurney. A small boy lay there, tubes and wires attached to his tiny body.

They were watching a screen where the patient's skull and brain were imaged as a thin wire entered and threaded into the interior.

Drake spoke as he did his work, explaining what each action was intended to accomplish. I didn't follow most of it, but I did understand that they were implanting an electrode that would stimulate a particular part of the child's brain and control his epilepsy.

It was something to watch. Drake sounded calm, and in command as he explained the procedure and what each motion did for the patient.

After about fifteen minutes, he was finished and then the resident closed up the wound. Drake thanked everyone and left the OR theatre, and so did Michael and I, returning to Michael's office to wait for Drake to finish his work for the day. He still had to speak with the family and then he would have a quick shower in the staff facilities and go to his office.

Michael had sent him a message asking him to come to Michael's office before he left for the day, not telling him that I was there so it was a surprise.

"What did you think?" Michael asked as we sat in his office waiting.

"He looked like he was perfectly happy. I remember the first time I saw him operate and thought how calm he was. He's had a hard two and a half years since the attack. I'm so happy you offered him the position."

"I'm so happy he accepted," Michael replied. "He said no at first, out of concern for you."

I nodded. "I feel bad that he thought he had to turn you down because of me. Honestly, I didn't really want to leave Manhattan, but it was the only choice, given all the publicity from the trial. Drake lost pretty much everything he had built in Manhattan -- the foundation was closed, he pulled back from the corporation and he lost his privileges at NYP. So he only had us. I couldn't make him turn down your offer. It was his dream come true."

"It is," Michael said with a nod. "He should be busy operating. It's his calling, Kate."

"It is. I'm just happy to be along for the ride."

"You complete him," Michael said. "I know that sounds corny, but it's true. Because he has you and Sophia, and now the unit, he is complete. A very happy man."

Drake stuck his head in the door and saw me, his eyes widening. "Who's a very happy man?"

He smiled and came over to me. "I'm assuming my ears should be burning and that you meant me."

He kissed me, his hands on my shoulders from behind.

"We did," I replied, squeezing one of his hands. "Michael invited me to come watch you do your last surgery of the day. He's going to come by for supper."

"That's great," Drake said. "So this is why you wanted me to stop by before I left."

"It is."

"Well, what are we waiting for? Let's go," Drake said, waving his arm to the door.

And so we did.

LATER, after we had dinner and Michael had said goodbye, Drake and I stood on the patio outside the living room and watched the stars in the night sky. His arms were around me, and he rested his chin on my shoulder so we could watch the sky together. I felt a profound sense of peace at that moment.

Everything seemed to be falling into place.

In the house, Sophie was fast asleep in her room on the second floor, her bedroom next to ours. The western corner of the main floor had been set aside for my father and Elaine. They had a sitting room with patio doors out to a nice space for when they both wanted some fresh air and to watch the ocean. Their bedroom came equipped with a full bathroom with accessible shower and bath. We converted one of the sitting rooms into a bedroom for that purpose and so they would have their own place to retreat when they needed some peace and quiet.

They'd be arriving the following week and I was excited to see them and get them settled in.

"Did you check out the studio space in town?" Drake asked, squeezing me, pulling me closer. "Will it do?"

"It'll do perfectly," I said and smiled, thinking of the small studio in an old building in downtown. "When Sophie goes to her daycare, I can zip into town and spend the afternoon painting."

I turned around and faced him, my arms slipping around his shoulders. "You looked so happy in the OR this afternoon."

"I was so happy," he said and bent down to kiss me softly. "Thank you for agreeing to come to England."

"How could I say no after everything that's happened? You should be working. Michael said it's your calling and he's right. I'd be a selfish bitch to insist on staying in Manhattan given the fallout from the trials. I'm happy here. I'm happy that you're happy."

We kissed again and then I turned around, Drake's arms still around me, squeezing my waist, pulling me against his body. In the distance, the surf roared against the beach and above us, the stars sparkled in the night sky.

They say that home is where the heart is, and it was true. As long as I had Drake and Sophia with me, I would be home, no matter where in the world we were.

THE END

ABOUT THE AUTHOR

S. E. Lund writes erotic, contemporary, new adult and para-normal romance. She lives in a century-old house on a quiet tree-lined street in a small Western Canadian city with her family of humans and animals. She dreams of living in a warm climate where snow is just a word in a dictionary.

S. E. Lund Newsletter

Sign up for S. E. Lund's newsletter and gain access to updates on upcoming releases, sales and freebies! She hates spam and so will never share your email!

S. E. LUND NEWSLETTER SIGN UP

For More Information:
www.selund.com
selund2012@gmail.com

ALSO BY S. E. LUND

THE UNRESTRAINED SERIES

THE AGREEMENT: Book 1

THE COMMITMENT: Book 2

UNRESTRAINED: Book 3

UNBREAKABLE: Book 4

FOREVER AFTER: Book 5

EVERLASTING: Book 6

DRAKE FOREVER: Book 7

THE DRAKE SERIES:

DRAKE RESTRAINED: Book 1

DRAKE UNWOUND: Book 2

DRAKE UNBOUND: Book 3

THE DRAKE SERIES COLLECTION

THE BAD BOY SERIES:

BAD BOY SAINT: Book 1 in the Bad Boy Series

BAD BOY SINNER: Book 2 in the Bad Boy Series

BAD BOY SOLDIER: Book 3 in the Bad Boy Series

BAD BOY SAVIOR: Book 4 in the Bad Boy Series

THE BAD BOY SERIES COLLECTION

∼

THE BRIMSTONE SERIES

IF YOU FALL: A Brimstone Series Novel (standalone)

∼

STANDALONE NOVELS

MR BIG SHOT

MATCHED

Made in the USA
Columbia, SC
31 July 2021

42740015R00181